A Run Up the Coast

Quest for Freedom

Gene Lewis

Colorado Winds Publishing

A Run Up The Coast
Quest for Freedom
Third Edition

Colorado Winds Publishing
Loveland, Colorado

www.arunupthecoast.com
freedom@arunupthecoast.com

Lewis, Gene W.

A Run Up The Coast - Quest for Freedom / Gene W. Lewis

Summary: A futuristic thriller novel about a Vietnam veteran biker in a fight for freedom in a post-technology anarchic world.

1. Freedom 2. Veteran 3. Apocalypse 4. California coast
5. Invisible government 6. Anarchy 7. Motorcycle

ISBN-13: 978-0-9788761-9-7

Printed by United Graphics, Inc.
Mattoon, Illinois - USA

"One great read and WOW what a book! If you're into any type of biker fiction, or just want a good story to read, this is the book. The story line is fantastic. I would recommend this book to anyone in need of a great story. A thrilling adventure filled with exciting characters. Buy it now and let your adventure begin!!"   —*Tom K.*

"As the characters evolved their soul, decisiveness, and mission quickly flushed them out and lured you into their lives and this moment in time."   —*L. Browning*

"Don't miss the Prologue—it will knock your socks off!"
—*Coloradoan Book Review*

"What a great book—you are held captivated throughout the entire story."   —*Janet C.*

"Wow!!! What a story. It was very interesting and entertaining to the end."   —*John H.*

"You've written a real whiz-bang novel!" —*David H.*

"Couldn't put it down until I finished. Good job—and Semper Fi on getting the tone of the Marine in the story. "   —*David L.*

"I think you're right on with the Concern theory—I call it the New World Order."   —*Duffy Z.*

"Haven't read good biker fiction like this in years. Keep up the good work."   —*Weebles*

"One does not have to be a biker to like this book—just appreciate a good story."   —*Coloradoan Book Review*

"Great book and I wonder if there is more truth than fiction."
—*Christina N.*

"Enjoyed your book very much. Makes you think. Was it fiction or a look into the future?"   —*Jack W.*

"This book is Whew! Couldn't put it down once I started—had a few short nights around that..." *—Kali W.*

"This book ROCKS! Makes you think about the true meaning of Freedom..." *—Flash G.*

"I enjoyed the caricatures and storyline. You did a great job and should be pleased with the outcome." *—Aubrey O.*

"What an adventure. This is a book you pick up and don't put down till the last page, and when you close it, the only word is "WOW!" *—Roberta B.*

"This is a must buy for anyone looking for a good biker veteran book or anyone looking for a good adventure story. Pick this one up and you will not be disappointed." *—Jack S.*

"I forgot all about JC's beer can crushing machine and the famous beer can crushing parties...your book brought all those great memories back." *—Duke D.*

"Wow you have a creative mind! The book is clear, cogent, and a page turner. Admire your patriotism." *—Steve B.*

"I can associate with some of the characters from life experiences which makes it even harder to put down and not continue reading." *—Tom K.*

"Just finished reading your book and anxiously awaiting the next. I hope you don't take another 20 years to get the next book out! Thanks for a good read." *—Becky J.*

"I've been reading non-fiction books and this book was a breath of fresh air." *—Mark B.*

"Nobody writes motorcycle fiction anymore. Good book!" *—Ray's Motorcycles*

"To me this could become reality..." *—John L.*

To my very special daughters — Denise & Danielle

"Don't ride faster than your angels can fly!"

The Rise and Fall of the Concern

"Power corrupts - and absolute power corrupts absolutely."

World War II witnessed international devastation and loss of life. It also brought incredible wealth and power to those who controlled the money for the war machinery.

A small group of financiers in America, Britain, and Switzerland acquired significant influence in the world economy during the war. They were smart and ruthless men who did not desire to relinquish this power as the war drew to a close.

These men held a secret meeting in Switzerland before the end of the war in Europe. Their organizer, a prominent American banker, shared his views of history with the attentive group. He suggested the idea that throughout history governments failed because their leaders were visible, and that people dissatisfied with their governments could overthrow the visible leaders.

This charismatic figure suggested to the assembled group that they should create a new form of government invisible to the world. This invisible government would control the real power from behind the scenes with politicians acting as the visible leaders.

The group shared their similar sentiments about creating this new political structure as a way to secretly control the wealth and power of the industrial world. They believed there would always be eager candidates for the visible thrones of leadership who would revel in the attention of the people they appeared to govern. Very few would know where the real power resided so these men believed they could never be challenged for their control. This secret organization named themselves the Concern, and they planted the foundation for their new social order in the midst of the chaos that existed at the end of the world war.

The Concern would operate from Switzerland to help conceal their existence. Switzerland was the world's expert at concealing financial resources, and reveled in their reputation as the bankers to the world. Initially the Concern would plant the roots of their new world order in the United States, Britain, and Switzerland. Their future strategy would be to obtain control over the assets of all the industrial nations of the world. Over time they planned to embed their selected invisible leaders in the true positions of power throughout the economic world.

The Concern needed secret intelligence agencies to collect information, manipulate power, and arrange the elimination of the uncooperative. They established these agencies in the form of the American CIA and the British MI6. These intelligence organizations, by their own secretive nature, could be structured so that departments understood just their specific functions. Only the highest ranking officers of these agencies would know their actual mission as an arm of the Concern. They would be paid well for their silence with the threat of death for any who divulged their secrets. At the conclusion of the Second World War the public was quick to accept the need for international intelligence organizations, and the inherent secret nature of their operations.

The appearance of free elections would be key to the Concern's plan for world dominance. It would be vital to the strategy of the invisible government that the public believed they were electing their own government officials. However, it was the Concern who selected the candidates for the higher offices of state. They would insure these offices were filled by personalities willing to trade public fame for the true power. When elections moved to electronic processes it became even easier for the Concern to manipulate the outcomes. Elections became elaborately staged events which furthered the illusion that citizens had a voice in selecting their leadership. As their ownership of the mainstream media increased over time it allowed the Concern to distort facts and perceptions about any event in the world.

The Concern believed the productivity of the working class could be maintained by catering to their materialistic needs. The United States became the first example of this for the industrialized world. The Concern shared a small portion of the true wealth with citizens as an investment for them to be willing participants in the engine of the global economy. Americans quickly became obsessed with their material needs, and outward appearances of wealth, in exchange for unknowingly giving up their true freedoms.

An international credit card system was created to allow the Concern better management of global financial resources. It minimized the need for paper money and encouraged people to accumulate debt at a growing rate. Debt was an important tool of the Concern to keep the populace dedicated to their jobs while feeding the machinery of consumerism. Stories of the rich and famous would be promoted in the media to create the illusion that anyone could obtain happiness through wealth.

Over time the Concern spread their financial power by selling emerging industrial nations on the concept of capitalism. America and Britain created powerful economies that appeared attractive to other nations as a lure to the banner of materialism.

Communism was the foremost enemy of the Concern as it advocated sharing the wealth among the masses. When the lure of capitalism was resisted at first by Communist countries the Concern supported military enterprises in Korea and Vietnam. To them the soldiers lost or crippled were a small price to pay to spread their capitalist doctrine. These unsuccessful wars taught the Concern the valuable lesson that it was easier to win the hearts and minds of Communist countries through the media and consumerism rather than warfare.

After their failures in Korea and Vietnam the Concern launched a global economic war to attack Communism by offering an alternative world of affluence to the citizens of Communist countries. Materialism became their universal currency which had strong appeal to undeveloped nations. The success of this effort was culminated at the close of the century when Russia and China moved into the realm of the Concern. As their sphere of international financial influence grew the Concern maintained tight vigilance over who was allowed into their inner circle.

The members of the Concern did not believe in a deity. They believed instead that a few were destined to control the many, and that your time on earth was your only existence in the evolution of the universe. They placed little value on life other than their own. They encouraged religion to exist as they believed it an opiate to the masses. They felt religion promoted a work ethic that served to make the economy more productive. The Concern would allow any cause that kept people busy, and superficially content, as long as they continued to feed the economic machinery.

At the close of the century the Concern, and the concept of the invisible government, was in place and working throughout the world. They seemed destined to rule unchallenged for centuries to come. Believing they had created the perfect command and control system of the global economy the Concern maintained a ruthless watch over the clandestine nature of their organization as the secret to their longevity.

As technology rapidly progressed, and sophisticated communication systems evolved, the Concern used these developments as tools to help them better control and conceal their invisible power. Research in some areas such as medicine was shared with the working class to help maintain the integrity of the work force.

The Concern financed the development of the Internet as an extension of their communications networks. They saw the Internet as a source of intelligence which could quickly detect international developments that might threaten their financial empire.

But the explosion of the Internet in the new millennium was too rapid for the members of the Concern to fully understand or control. They did not comprehend at the time that the Internet was evolving without anyone in control. Free, and largely unrestricted, access to international communication became a norm. The Internet became technological anarchy before the Concern understood what was happening. It was moving too quickly for the Concern to manage, and they did not understand the threat it would soon present to their covert organization.

Rumors of the existence of the Concern started to appear in the new millennium but the millions of Internet users took it to be just more chatter among hundreds of popular conspiracy theories. The Internet had become a wasteland of obtuse and irrelevant information with very little taken for face value. The Concern considered shutting down the Internet if it continued to pose a threat, but they had built too many of their communication and banking systems around it. Turning it off would disable an important component of their command and control structure.

The Concern tried to isolate, and eliminate, the source of the rumors about their existence but the Internet was too fluid. It was a growing organism that quickly adapted to environmental threats. The Concern decided to take a different and dramatic tact by creating an international War on Terror to divert the attention of the world from their existence.

They identified various splinter militant groups around the world and offered them anonymous sources of funding to escalate their terrorist operations. The terrorists were not concerned where these money sources came from but only that they could use them to fund their particular causes. They were very willing to take lives, including their own, to gain the attention of the world. These terrorist groups became international zealots with a bank account.

Terrorist activities around the world started to escalate with each one promoting its own ideology. But the world's nations paid only scant attention to these groups if not directly affected by them. As Internet traffic about the Concern continued to grow the Concern decided to intensify the level of diversion they believed necessary to draw attention away from the increasing Internet traffic about themselves.

On September 11, 2001, the world witnessed the culmination of these efforts when a CIA coordinated terrorist group called Al-Qaeda executed the most appalling terrorist attacks ever witnessed. Hijacked passenger planes were flown into the towers of the World Trade Center in New York City and the Pentagon with world wide media coverage of the carnage. The Concern believed this dramatic attack would occupy the minds of the world's citizens, and divert their eyes from the Internet messages about themselves until they could root out and eliminate their sources.

This spectacular event succeeded in getting the world to focus on the Concern's orchestrated War on Terror. Shortly thereafter the United States invaded Afghanistan as the alleged home of this terrorist movement against the United States. In this move the Concern gained control over the lucrative drug trade in Afghanistan which they used to help further sponsor their War on Terror.

After the dramatic 9/11 event the Concern had the Office of Homeland Security created, and the Patriot Act passed, in the US allowing them to better regulate personal freedoms. It also opened the door for implementation of advanced surveillance techniques that could provide detailed scrutiny of the populace and their internet activity. They would follow with similar actions in other Concern nations.

In an attempt to establish a foothold in the midst of the Arab nations who were resistant to the overtures of the Concern they orchestrated an invasion of Iraq by the United States and Britain in 2003. They setup a puppet government of Iraqis with simulated elections in an attempt to appease the world reaction to this bold move. The Concern had already learned that significant profits could be made sponsoring wars irregardless of who was involved.

An unexpected side effect of the invasion on Iraq was increased activity from the underground movement who was working intently to expose the Concern. These individuals persisted even harder to unveil the Concern even though it meant a death sentence if they could find you in cyberspace. The number of vocal Internet dissidents trying to unveil the Concern was increasing.

Despite their considerable efforts the Concern was unsuccessful at establishing a welcome presence in the oil rich Arabic countries. In addition to other issues the Arab nations were growing weary of blame for the Concern's artificial War on Terror. In an attempt to overcome this Arabic resistance the Concern arranged the election of a black Muslim US president in 2008 - but it did little to placate the Arabic opposition to Concern ambitions.

Even with Concern owned media attention continually

focused on the War on Terror the Internet traffic about the Concern still continued to exist. It dramatically escalated in the second decade of the new century climaxing in 2018 when the Internet started carrying stories about the Concern that included names, and sometimes photographs, of Concern members.

Details of the organization and activities of the Concern were being leaked from somewhere inside the secretive group including their backing of international terrorist activities as a means to divert attention from their existence. The anger of the world became intensely focused on the members of the Concern for their willingness to conduct warfare on their own people.

In the Fall of 2018 members of the Concern were sought out and executed in retaliation for the chaos they had instigated on the citizens of the world. The vendetta against the Concern then turned to the visible members of the political machinery who had allowed the Concern to manage the real power. The world exploded into anarchy as people violently attacked the visible seat of the political system. Civil wars quickly spread into international conflagration and started the Regional Wars across the globe.

International communication dissolved during the Regional Wars as the networks had been maintained by the Concern. Power grids started to shut down. Everything built on electric power and technology fell apart. It became a new Dark Ages but with a deadly twist as people in industrialized nations had long since lost the basic skills to survive.

All existing governments disappeared in the Regional Wars and world order violently disintegrated into localized areas of control. As political structures disintegrated around the globe different groups fought to take control of their regions. Whoever was able to seize, and maintain, power in defined geographical territories became the new law. Bloody mayhem was the order of the time.

Billions died from the fighting, starvation, or disease. Regional governments took over control with many instituting cruel totalitarian mastery of the survivors. The modern world disappeared in a few months.

It was an apocalyptic scenario no one had predicted...!

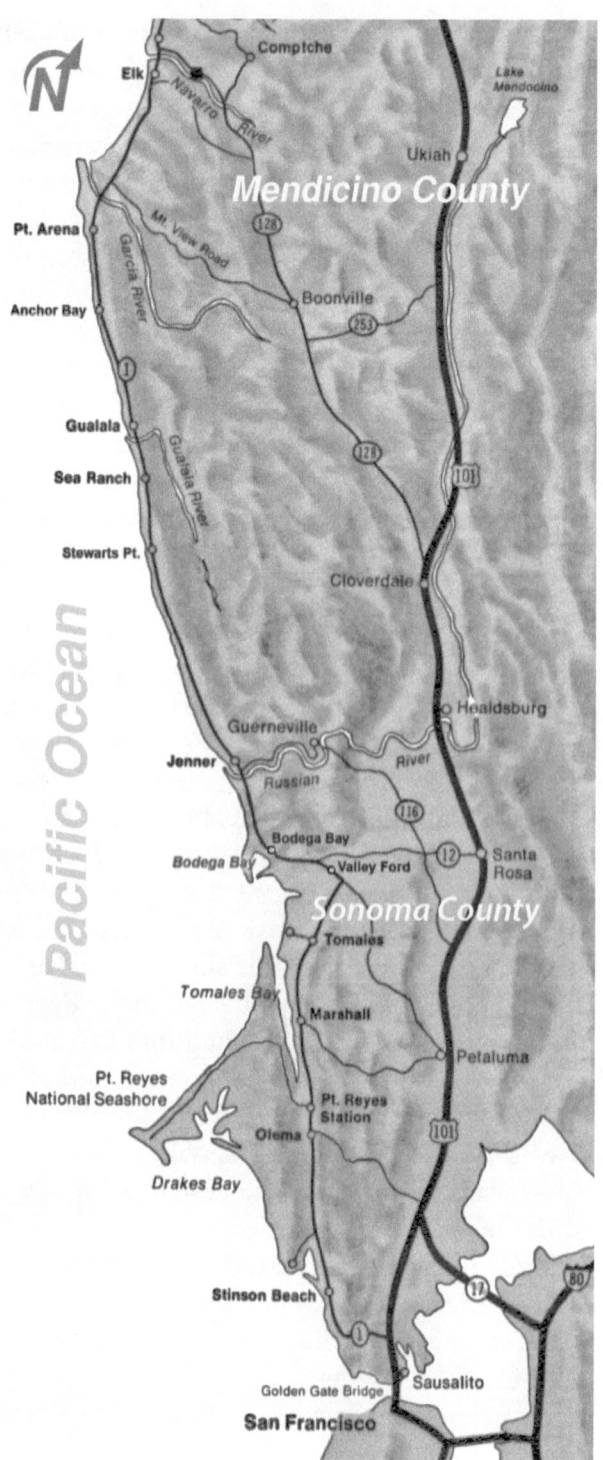

CHAPTER 1

Anger Builds in the Year 2019

It was getting so that a good ole boy couldn't get by anymore! First they took my Harley—and then they took my truck. I was madder than hell I'd lost my freedom and was now a slave. Something had to change—and soon…

The old San Francisco was no more since the Guardians took power during the Regional Wars. It was dark and smelled like death. A smell I once knew in Vietnam. There were dead bodies hung on crosses all over the City. Burnt out buildings and demolished cars were everywhere. It all happened so quickly!

The world plunged into madness during the Regional Wars when civil wars broke out everywhere. The power grids went down and technology shut off. Everything became basic survival very fast. It was a broken world.

Before the Regional Wars the underground media tried telling people that a powerful secret organization called the Concern had been controlling countries since the big war. They claimed they had created an invisible government that was behind all of the industrial governments and controlled most of the world's wealth.

In 2018 accusations on the internet about how the Concern had targeted their own people in the 9/11 attacks became accepted ideas. Identities of the Concern leaders were being leaked by somebody. Armed groups sought out the exposed Concern leaders and assassinated them. But in the anger to eliminate the members of the Concern—and their political agents—no one was thinking about the incredible impact it would have on humanity. This violent action undermined world governments and started the Regional Wars across the globe.

Just before the television and radio went out we heard that millions were dying in the fighting—then it all went silent. Were the stories about the Concern really true? I'd probably never know. For now all that mattered was my survival—and freedom. I had taken my freedom for granted most of my life. Now it had become the most important thing in my changed world.

In the Bay Area the drug lords of the city moved first to seize power when the Regional Wars started. They called themselves the Guardians. They built their army by taking over the prisons in the Bay Area. Inmates were offered the choice to join or die. Very few refused. In a short time they assembled a ruthless army of murderers and rapists. Their penalty for disloyalty was death — on the spot.

There were several military bases in the Bay Area and the Guardians captured plenty of firepower. Some of the street gangs challenged them but were quickly eliminated. It wasn't long before the Guardians had control of the City and the surrounding areas. They had enough food and supplies to hold out for a long time. Anyone who did not serve their purpose was eliminated.

To the north of the City a different group took control. They called themselves the New Society and set up their government in what was once Mendocino county. At night I'd pick up radio broadcasts from them trying to recruit followers to their new order. They talked about the old ideals of family and values. Sanctuary was offered to any who valued freedom and would fight for that cause. In their radio messages they said they were made up of a lot of the military who fled the Bay area. They claimed they were well fortified from the Guardians and planned to defend their new society. It was difficult to believe in anything now — but whatever the truth — they sounded like a better option than the ruthless masters I now served.

The Guardians feared the New Society and worried that once strong enough they would invade the City. So they were taking no chances by maintaining tight security on the routes to the North. The Guardians only kept those alive who provided important work for them. Since I could fix things I was still around. But I was just one of their workers to help keep the machinery running. So I was working on a plan to escape — even though it seemed impossible!

There wasn't much information on the New Society other than the nightly broadcasts. Anyone who tried to get out of the City was never heard from again. Was it just another scam? Like the Concern? There was no way to be certain. I'd have to risk my life to reach the New Society but decided I was willing to take the chance. It wouldn't be easy. The Guardians had well armed security on the roads out of San Francisco. No one was allowed to travel without their permission. If you were still breathing they wanted you to stay and be part of their new empire.

I first came to the City after separating from the Marines in '71. The City was pretty exciting for someone who had grown up in the back hills of West Virginia. I became part of the biker crowd and lived in the biker world. Good times, cheap beer, awesome weed, great rides, fun ladies — what more could one ask for?

Like many in the biker cult I didn't ask much from life and took only what I needed in return. It was easy to make a living in the City as a handyman fixing the common stuff no one could repair anymore. People became obsessed with technology. They forgot how to fix a toilet or rewire an electrical switch. I didn't have much use for technology. It made people lazy and dependent. In my experience it also wasn't very reliable. I liked things that were mechanical or pneumatic. I really enjoyed working on motorcycle — especially if it was a Harley.

Couldn't get a pass out of the City. I wasn't that important. The Guardians took my truck and gave me this old beater station wagon to carry my tools. If I was going to escape I would need different wheels. When they confiscated my '09 Super Glide they weren't too interested in a fairly worn out '75 Super Glide I had sitting in the garage under a tarp. That girl had been my ride for many good years with over a hundred thousand miles on her. I'd done two rebuilds on the motor over the years but the Glide hadn't been out in a long while. She would have to be my wheels again. But could I get her running?

Studying a map of Northern California I decided that Route 1 — the coast road — would be the best chance for my escape route. My military hunch was that it would be the most lightly guarded. Mostly because they wouldn't expect very many to be crazy enough to try it. Probably for good reason. The coast road winds around and runs along the cliffs in many places. It was a slow ride even on a sunny day. I'd ridden that awesome road too many times to remember. But now it would be for the highest stake of all — my life and my freedom!

I had no idea yet how I'd get across the Golden Gate Bridge.

There was no other way to the coast route unless you had a boat. Avoiding the Guardian patrols would be very difficult once I reached the coast—but how to find a way to get there had me stumped. I would start my preparations while I worked on that big problem.

I looked at my map of Route 1 carefully and tried to figure out the most likely places for checkpoints or command posts. I was uncertain how far north I'd have to go to meet up with the New Society. Mendocino County would be a dangerous 120 miles up the coast road. There was little available in the way of military intelligence. My plan was to run at night around their patrols and hide out during the days while I did recon. I'd have to remember the best of my Marine training to survive this run. My age was against me—but my anger would be my strength!

When I returned from the nightmare of Vietnam I swore I'd never take a life again. I'd gone into the Marines a militant—and come out a pacifist. There were too many innocents killed in Nam and I lost a lot of good friends. It all seemed like it had been for nothing now. Many said it was a war the Concern wanted fought to stop their economic enemy—communism. All I know is that I saw too many good men die or disappear. I killed people I didn't really know—or hate—just because we were killing each other. My government told us we were defending the free world. Looking back—I think maybe the Viet Cong were just fighting for their freedom. How ironic now.

Since I lived in the biker world I was offered many chances to become an outlaw. They liked former military who knew their way around a weapon and explosives. But I didn't want to kill or maim again so I never joined. I got into an occasional bar fight over a poker game—or a babe—but I kept that promise to myself. Now I had to think about whether I could take a life again if I had to. I'd hoped I could make it to the north without answering that question but understood I might not get the option.

There was no doubt left I wanted out of this hell with the Guardians. So I was willing to take whatever risks were necessary. We used to have a saying in the Corps—"Once a Marine—always a Marine". I guess I was going to find out if that was true. Even for an old fart biker like me...

Duke the Barbarian

I'd lived in this old house in North Beach for a long time now. It was small and quite the dump but suited my basic needs. The landlord charged me cheap rent because he never had to fix anything on this wreck. I took care of it. Most importantly — it had a small garage with everything I needed to work on bikes — including my beer fridge. But there was no dependable power now to run the fridge and booze of any kind was hard to come by. I got what little I had by trading with the Guardians. I got used to drinking warm beer again. That was too reminiscent of Nam.

There was a large box in the corner of the garage where everyone would throw their empty beer cans. With all the bikers who spent time here tweaking on their machines I was able to throw a party every year with the money from the recycled cans. It became known as "JC's Annual Beer Can Recycling Party." Those were the good ole days that would never be seen again as long as I stayed in the City.

While I thought about my plans I started work on the Super Glide. First I checked the fluids and all the seals. I found some used but low mileage plugs in the garage that would work. Unlike the newer Harleys this ole girl had a kick start. That would be important as I knew the old battery wouldn't have any life in it. It would be too dangerous to try and take it outside to push start. These old glides would kick start even with a weak battery. But it would be better to have a good battery — if possible.

I had a biker babe calendar on the wall I bought myself for Christmas — just before the shit hit the fan here with the Regional Wars. I was marking off the days since then and it was mid April. Over five months in hell now! If I was going to try an escape I wanted to be on the road by sometime in May. That was still in the wet months along the coast so the nights would probably be cool and foggy. The fog could be good or bad news—depending on who was looking for who. I was also tracking the full moons on the calendar as best I could. Patrols were always different in a full moon.

I was working on the bike late at night when I heard someone moving outside the garage. I reached for my shotgun and closely watched the door. If it was the Guardians they were gonna want to know why I was working on the bike. Then I heard a familiar deep voice, "JC—you in there?"

"Who's there?" I asked wanting to be sure.

"Who do you think it is you long haired hippie biker freak—Captain Midnight? Do you want me to slide my decoder ring under the door?" It was Duke. I lowered the shotgun.

"Come on in you smelly old psychotic hunk of scooter trash."

Duke was my closest biker bro but I hadn't seen him in over a week. He'd been a Ranger in Nam in the seventies and was a really big boy. Well over six foot and 300 pounds. In the biker crowd he was known as Duke the Barbarian. He was famous for his short temper and lust for a good fight. I don't think he lost very many unless he was greatly outnumbered. Before I met him he'd been an outlaw but left the club to work on his own. Didn't like taking orders—from anyone.

We were a strange pair to be such good friends. Me being only five ten and about 180 pounds—in better times. We looked like Mutt and Jeff when we rode together. He was known for his rough ways and I preferred to be a lover rather than a fighter. So maybe opposites really do attract?

I first met him at a biker bar in the City called Stinky Dicks. I was playing a friendly game of pool with Big Jim and Nasty Pete—in what Stinky Dick liked to call his Ball Room—when Duke challenged the winner. He smelled like whiskey—matter of fact—he just smelled. I already knew his reputation but had never run into him. So when Jim and Pete quickly threw the game I had no option but to take him on. Even though he dwarfed me I never back down from anyone. Something Dad had taught me from his coal mining days in Morgantown. Maybe a touch of the Marine now to boot.

Dad was a small man but had the reputation for being one

of the toughest fighters in the mines. He told me many times, "When you're the smallest guy everyone will pick on you. But if you fight back they'll eventually leave you alone cause the bullies don't want to get their asses kicked by someone smaller than them. It's bad for their reputation." Mom liked to call me her "bantam rooster" because I never backed away from a fight. But Duke the Barbarian was really big!

So we played our game of eight ball. Everyone thought I would just let him win to avoid the consequences of confronting the Barbarian. But that made me even more determined to whip his butt. When I was a young stud my uncle Zeke owned the little general store back in Mount Pisgah. He had an old pool table in the back room where the local boys met to shoot the shit and sip their moonshine. So I got to play a lot as a kid. Made some good side money in the Marines hustling pool with the newbies.

Duke was drunk and I was determined to beat his sorry ass at the game – even if it meant getting mine kicked. So when I sunk the eight ball the bar went silent. I guess not too many bikers had ever been foolish enough to beat the Duke. He came over and stared at me with his dark eyes that were sunk into a large head of long black hair and scraggly beard. "So the little man is feeling cocky today. Maybe I should just kick your fuckin' ass and teach you a lesson." I grabbed onto my pool stick tightly and prepared for the worst. I wasn't going to start the fight but intended to hold my own as long as I could against this big man.

He just stood there for a while and glared down at me – breathing these long whiskey saturated breaths. I stared back into his dark mysterious eyes. This was a really scary guy who I knew was capable of mayhem without a thought. He studied my vest and saw my faded Marine patch. He leaned over and surprised me when he asked, "You serve in Nam?"

"Yeah – in '69. So what?" I thought he was just playing with me waiting for the right time to throw the first punch.

We stood there for a while locked eye to eye. Everyone was waiting for the fight to start. And then Duke surprised the crowd – and most of all me – when he reached over – grabbed my vest—and said, "Then let's have a drink to remember the boys we served with in Nam!" And he pulled me toward the bar.

To this day I'm not sure why he changed his mind about taking me on. Maybe it was the determination he saw in my eyes? Maybe he was having his once a decade feeling of melancholy? I never asked. But we drank until we couldn't stand up and passed out together in the corner. That was after many toasts to the good men we left behind in the war. I had that hangover for a long day. Damn brown bottle flu. That was when Duke and I became regular riding bros.

"You almost got your head blown off," I teased him.

"You wouldn't shoot anyone—little man—you're too much of a fuckin' paac-i-fist." He kind of spit the words out as he always liked to make fun of my easy going ways. "Workin' on the bike. Good to see that. How's it comin'?"

We moved over to inspect the bike. "She's been sitting for a long time. Not sure yet if I can make it run."

"Hell yes you can! It's a Harley and you're the best damn mechanic I know. And besides—you got me to help you get the ole gal runnin'. Surely two mechanical geniuses like us can figure this out." Duke wasn't the world's greatest mechanic—he preferred wrecking them to fixing them—but he knew his way around a wrench.

"But first I have a present for you," he announced as he pulled out a big joint and a whiskey flask. "I borrowed this from a couple of Guardians. The fuckers didn't want to share so I had to persuade them. Hell—I didn't even break a sweat!" We both laughed because I knew what that meant. Somewhere in town there were a couple of Guardians who wished they hadn't said no to the Barbarian. Hope the Guardians had a good medical plan.

We sat on the floor and mellowed out. The weed smelled like pretty good stuff. Didn't take long before I felt good. It had been a while...

"Did you miss me?" Duke inquired in his deadpan way.

"Hell no—I figured you were dead. How could I miss your sorry ass?" We sat there in silence for a while enjoying the high. Then he got my major interest with what he said next. "Well partner—I been thinkin' about your plan to get out of the City and head north along the coast to the New Society." Duke was the only one I had told about my plans. "Getting across the bridge is your biggest problem to start—so I figured out a way." Now he had my full attention. We sat there quiet as I waited to hear the rest.

"So—are you going to tell me or am I going to have to beat it out of you?" He thought that was funny.

As long as Duke and I had been riding together I'd never known him to care about any woman—except once. Not too long ago he'd fallen for a little biker chick we all called Barbie Doll. She looked just like a little Barbie Doll with big boobs and blonde hair. She was a tiny thing but she captured him completely. Kind of like watching Beauty and the Beast when they were together.

I didn't think he even had a gentle side but he would do anything for Barbie. The crew and I kept trying to figure out what she saw in him. At times it was like watching this really sexy bear trainer with this big hairy beast on a leash. But no one was going to tell Duke he was pussy whipped—at least not to his face.

Shortly after the Guardians took control several of them found Barbie in a biker bar waiting for Duke to show up after a drug run. They tried to rape her but not until she had taken one out with a derringer and kicked another in the nuts. She put up quite the fight but there were too many. They had their way with her and then slit her throat. When Duke found out he went crazy—way beyond anything I'd ever seen him do before!

Duke had fists like steel ingots and a kick like a Missouri mule. Me and several of the boys were at his house when he got the news about Barbie and he went berserk. He punched holes in the walls and took a door off with a kick. I lost track of what all he broke. When we finally cooled him down to a small roar we packed into his van and headed for the bar. It was a mess. Lots of blood. Duke picked up Barbie's small body in his arms and just drove away in the van. We didn't see him again for a while. I never brought up the fact later that I saw him crying as he carried her out.

Duke found out the names of the Guardians at the bar that

day. He started a search to find each of them and take his revenge. He made sure that each died slowly – painfully – and that they knew why this angel of death had sought them out. There was still a few he was looking for but they were hiding out. The Guardians knew of his vendetta but considered it good drama. He knew many of them from his drug running days so they didn't interfere. I even heard they were taking odds on how long it would take him to find all the perpetrators. It became the sole focus of his existence.

"Barbie had a brother you never met," Duke finally continued. "He's a garbage man known as Gladman. He still makes runs for the Guardians taking crap out to the dump at Stinson Beach. He can get you across the bridge in the back of his garbage truck."

I looked at him carefully to see if he was pulling my leg but he was dead serious. "Are you shittin' me? That sounds pretty bizarre – even for you."

"Trust me bro. I know it'll work. I tried it out a few days ago. Both ways. Pretty fuckin' smelly but it worked." He took another drink and told me the story.

"Gladman hates the Guardians for what they did to Barbie so he wants to help. We rigged up a container at the bottom of the load and I went all the way out to Stinson Beach. I stayed there for two days and did some recon for you. Learned a lot about the Guardian patrols and where I think some of their outposts might be. We just hafta make the container bigger to hold the bike." He paused for a moment to let it all sink in. "So what you think about that little man?"

I was stunned. Off all the schemes I'd imagined I never thought about leaving in a garbage truck. I jokingly replied, "Doesn't sound like a very exciting start to my adventure."

"What do you care – if it works?" He was right about that.

"Why didn't you stay once you were across the bridge?" I remembered Duke had talked about heading north also.

"Well – let's just say I have unfinished business here in the City." I saw that familiar anger in his eyes. "When I go I plan on walking to the north and Gladman will be my way across the bridge when that time comes. As long as you two don't get caught." He looked at me intently and I understood. "Besides — what fun would it be to get to the New Society if you weren't there? So you get to go first."

As incredible as it sounded — I now had a hope I could at least get out of the City. "What else did you learn?"

"The Guardians mostly run their coast patrols on bikes. Normally two at a time on some hot lookin' rice grinders — possibly with turbos. They're well armed with M16s but they carry them on their backs so it would take a few seconds before they could get them to the ready. It ain't easy to fire an auto from a bike." That sounded like experience talking.

He continued, "They must not be expectin' too many insane enough to try Route 1 as they only make patrols about every four hours but with no regular schedule. They run them through the night too. Their first checkpoint after the bridge is along the ridge before you drop down to Stinson Beach. Some of them are stayin' at a ranch just on the other side of the hill."

"What about in Stinson Beach?"

"There aren't any there. They can't stand the smell from the dump. So Stinson Beach would be your place to stage once you're off the truck." I couldn't believe he had learned so much. It was pretty good recon info. But then — he'd been a Ranger. I was getting excited about the possibility of my plan working after all. At least the first part…

"How about checkpoints further north?" I asked wanting to know more.

"Nobody seemed to know much about that — just hunches. So we'll check your map and see where we'd put checkpoints if it was us. I have some ideas. Sure you do too. Some of the folks left in Stinson thought it might be as far north as Gualala — or Point Arena — to tie up with the New Society." He turned and stared at me with those black eyes. "You think the old jarhead is up to this?" That was a real good question from a friend.

"Don't think I have many options if I want my freedom again." That was easy to say but it was going to take a lot of determination and will power at my age. But there was no other choice I could see. I had to give it my best Marine try.

"There's one other thing you otta know. The Guardian who

commands the coast road is a real nasty dude called Blackie. He's a killer the Guardians released from prison and he's supposed to be one mean son of a bitch. I saw him with a patrol when I was scoping the road from outside Stinson. He looks like a picture of Rasputin the Mad Monk I saw in a book once. Long black hair and dressed all in black. Rides a black bike. I hear he takes pleasure in catching people trying to get north and torturing them. He'll be a tough cookie if you run into him." These were serious words coming from Duke.

"Well—so much for the good news and the bad news," I responded to his somber advice. "As the Romans used to say before a battle—do you want to live forever?" and I took another swig.

We sat there for a while enjoying the high—and the whiskey—and remembering back on life before the Regional Wars. I knew Duke was thinking about Barbie Doll—though he never said a word.

"So JC—let's take a look at this ole hunk of HD metal and figure out what it's gonna take to make her run like a champ. Once we know what parts we need we can contact Rat if he's still alive. He can find anything. He's the best scrounger in the business and he owes me a favor. Besides—he about shits his pants every time he sees me because he's such a timid little man. Kind of like you—you paac-i-fist!" Duke said laughingly as he put me in a head lock and squeezed. Damn that boy was strong!

After a few seconds he finally let go and said, "Let's get to work little man…"

CHAPTER 3

New Life Into Old Wheels

We looked over the bike for a while making a list of what she'd need to run again. While we worked we recalled some of the old — and told around many a campfire — stories about the rides Duke and I'd shared.

We remembered how Pigpen had swerved to miss a big smelly skunk on a run near Santa Rosa and drove off the road into a large mud hole. It took a long time to dig him out because we were all laughing so hard. I remembered someone asking that considering how bad Pigpen smelled — why was he so concerned about tangling with the skunk? He said it was just professional courtesy.

And there was the time that Slim Jim — after shooting numerous tequilas — decided to impress the crowd at Cold Springs Tavern down in the Santa Inez mountains. He started at the bottom of the hill and did this far out wheelie in front of the Sunday riders — zooming past the bar — and right off the cliff on the other side of the road! It took us a while to get him back up the steep hill and into the van which took him to the hospital. Lucky for him he was too drunk to feel the pain — until later. His old lady took him home from the hospital to find his front door all covered with "Don't Drink and Drive" bumper stickers. Courtesy of some of the crew.

But my favorite story about Duke was when he was leading the pack on a foggy coastal morning in the north. Seeing a dark shape in the road he slowed down a little as he moved to the center line. When he got closer he was blown away as he realized the shape was a big peacock who'd escaped from a nearby ranch. Duke went into a full wheel lock just a few feet from the strutting bird as he was presenting his fine collection of feathers. All we heard Duke yell as he tried to swerve was "Fuck — an — A...!"

When the bird picked up on Duke's screeching tires just a few feet away he jumped straight into the air catching him in the shoulder. Peacocks may not be able to fly—but they certainly can jump! There were peacock feathers floating everywhere. "I still have one of the feathers from that damn bird," Duke cursed. "If he hadn't limped off into the woods I wooda' had him for dinner." It was a good laugh while we worked.

Our list of what we needed to get the bike running wasn't too long. Both tires were dry rotted but the drive chain and rear sprocket looked good enough for the run with a little adjustment and lube. Hadn't checked the primary drive yet. The battery for the Glide I found on the bench was shot. The kick starter would be very important if we couldn't find a better battery. I had the necessary fluids to service the bike. Amazingly—none of the seals were cracked or leaking. I kept my bikes in good shape so that would payoff now. Even though she was old I didn't think she'd need any major engine work. I'd run a compression check on the motor later to get a reading.

The bike was a dark blue metal flake I'd painted it quite a number of years ago. Not a bad paint job—if I say so myself. She had some really nice hand pin striping that was done by Weird Al. We debated about whether to give it a camouflage paint job. But decided to just paint it black so it wouldn't reflect any light—if I could find any paint. That was going to break my heart. Never liked black bikes. We'd either take off the chrome or paint it black also. Stealth would be more important than beauty for this mission.

"We're gonna need some stock mufflers to make it quiet as possible," Duke grumbled as he started to remove my favorite fish tail mufflers. "How many stock mufflers you think we've thrown away over the years—and now we need a pair. That's disgusting..."

"Stock Harley mufflers? I think that's what they call an oxymoron," I joked.

"An oxy what? You usin' them quarter size words on me agin? You scooter trash hillbilly..."

"Never mind." I had to remember at times that Duke had even less schooling than me. I think the Army probably took

14

him because of his size—not his IQ. In the seventies they wanted anyone who could fog a mirror for Vietnam. "Duke—where we gonna find tires and a battery? The Guardians don't exactly have a Harley store on every block."

"I'll find Rat and see what he says. The Guardians keep him busy because he can find things they can't. He'll do it for some weed and the fun of screwing with the Guardians. So little man—what you got for weapons sides that pistol grip 12 gauge I traded for in a drug deal years ago?" Duke knew he was the only one who ever got away with calling me little man. With anyone else that could involve a fight. But with him I was used to it—part of our friendship I guess.

"I have that .32 caliber derringer I won in a poker game years ago which I sometimes carry in my vest. It wouldn't do much good against those Guardian autos but I'll still take it along. Even the shotgun will only be good for short range. Haven't decided yet whether to load pumpkin ball or buckshot?"

"Do like the cops—mix 'em both in," Duke suggested.

I thought for a while before I decided to show Duke a well kept secret of mine. "Let's take a break—I want to show you something in the house." I took Duke into my bedroom and opened up an old military trunk I'd kept around since Vietnam. "Been saving this for a long time. Only fired it a few times but I keep it clean and oiled." I handed Duke a military Colt .45 that took him back in time.

"This is a Nam officer's sidearm. Right? Where'd you get this?" he inquired as he carefully inspected the weapon. "It's in pretty good shape. Were you an officer in a past life and didn't tell me? That would change our friendship you know..."

We sat down on the floor as I told him the story I'd never shared with anyone. "I was down in DaNang doing a supply run for the gunny. He told me to stay for the night and get laid. I was in a really sleazy bar tying one on when I noticed a Navy LT doing the same at the other end of the bar. Looked like a River Rat by his uniform."

Duke handed the weapon back to me and I continued, "I didn't think much about it until these Army grunts came in and started to give him a hard time. They weren't in uniform but I

15

knew they were Army rear echelon trash. Probably supply or cooks. There were six of them—drunk and cocky—and really feelin' their Wheaties."

I went on while Duke listened in silence, "The LT tried to ignore them but they got in his face. Normally I wouldn't give a shit about an officer but we'd been pulled out of a hot spot by some River Rats the month before. They'd taken some serious fire to rescue us. One of them died in the firefight. So I had good things to say about those Navy and Coast Guard guys. That job took some big balls."

Duke nodded and responded, "Yeah—I rode with a crew of them on a rescue mission once up the coast. It got pretty hot when we engaged—but they done their job good that long bloody day. Those boats were fast—but nothin' can outrun a bullet—and we took a shit load of fire. Even mortars. We got our guys out but paid a fuckin' big price for doin' that! Got my purple heart during that patrol." He lifted his shirt to show me the scar on his side. I'd always wondered what that was from. Now I knew. Sounded like he respected them also.

I continued with my story, "When it looked like they weren't gonna leave him alone I moved down the bar and sat next to him. Not knowing if I was joining to join the fight with him— or against him—he gave me one short glance and slugged the closest Army grunt. He was pretty gutsy for an officer. So I jumped into the fray and helped him punch out those boys. I mean—after all—the Marines are part of the Navy even though we never like to admit it." I paused after that rare confession.

"That LT was a tough little country boy and we took those yokels to the cleaners. We finished our drinks and left the bar together. We spent the rest of the night drinking and getting laid. It was the first escape I'd enjoyed from the war in several months and we had a wild time together."

I swigged another shot of whiskey. "The next day we had to get back to our units but I felt as close to this guy as anyone I'd ever met in the war. It was strange. As we were heading back to our units he handed me his sidearm and told me to keep it as a reminder of that night. I took it because I didn't know what to say. Kept it in this foot locker during my time in the war and

16

never showed it to anyone. No one would understand why I spent a night with an officer — or fought with one. I've kept this .45 all these years as one of my few good memories of the war."

"Ever run into him again?"

"No — but I remembered his name — Lee Barr. Remember the year we did the Run to the Wall in DC?"

"For sure! It was a long hot summer ride."

"Well — I found his name on the Wall. He never made it home. I was sad when I learned that after all these years. So I keep this Colt to remember him."

"I never thought I'd offer a toast to an officer — but here's to your friend. Here's to Lee..." Duke offered as we took the last swallow from his flask. I turned around and walked back to the garage so Duke wouldn't see the tear in my eye. I was remembering all of those we'd left behind. I hadn't felt this sad about the war in a long time.

We worked on the bike for a while longer but it was late and the whiskey and weed were catching up. "I'm gonna crash here tonight," Duke informed me. "The Guardians get trigger happy after dark which makes it difficult to get around. I've got one more surprise for you." Duke reached down into his pack and pulled out a sausage and some potatoes. Man — that was a surprise! "I figured you'd know what to do with these in the morning. You always were a better cook than me. Here's a can of beans for the side. I know how you hillbillies like your beans."

"Big talk from Pennsylvania miner trash. Being a better cook than you don't say much. You can't cook for shit."

Duke leaned back against the garage wall lighting up a cigarette. He offered me one and I hesitated, "I'm trying to quit you know."

"Yeah — and my grandmother was a virgin!" and he handed the pack back to me. I took one. Maybe this wasn't the best time to be trying to quit such an old habit.

Duke sat quietly while the smoke drifted slowly in the air. "I been thinkin' little man. While we get your bike ready you need to work out with me on some weights. Build up your upper body strength. Kinda get you ready for the big push. We can review those karate skills I taught you. You might need 'em.

17

And – uh – you're gonna need to learn to shoot with your left hand. We'll mount your holster for the .45 on the right side of your chest so you can reach it with your left hand."

"Why my left hand?"

"If you have to fire while riding you'll need your right hand on the throttle." Have to admit I hadn't thought about that one. "My dad used to tell me how the cops preferred the left hand throttle Indians in the twenties – so they could shoot with their right hand."

"Good idea! Not bad for a high school dropout from Scranton." Duke gave me a short punch to the arm and it really stung.

"You best get a measurement on that battery fore we go shopping." He put his arm around my shoulder as we went back into the house. "Well partner – it's time to kick some fuckin' Guardian ass and get you on the road. I know how you jarheads say – no guts – no glory! Wake me when you're ready to do something with those fixings..." he yelled back at me as he carried his pack into the living room to crash on the couch. It took a big couch to fit Duke.

CHAPTER 4

Duke's Boot Camp

Duke said he was going to put me through "Duke's Boot Camp" and he wasn't fartin' around. He survived in a real hole about two miles from my place. It had a workout room and a backyard big enough to set up a short firing range. When I wasn't working for the Guardians — or working on the bike — he was working on me!

I walked so much in my job over the years that my legs and back were in good shape. So Duke concentrated on my upper body strength. He also had me practicing karate and fighting with a knife. We went over — and over — many of the things I'd learned in the Marines about hand-to-hand combat. I think he was also working on my head to build up my self confidence.

Duke would kid me about the workout by saying things like, "When I get to the north I want you there to greet me with a hot babe and a good joint."

"Maybe the New Society don't believe in getting high and free love?"

"Then we'll just hafta educate 'em on what they're missin'."

"And what if they're a peaceful group? Maybe you won't fit in? After all — you're not the paac-i-fist I am." I was giving him a hard time about his violent nature. Not the first time.

"You think so bro? Well — maybe I can take a class in anger management?" We cracked up over that.

I reminded him about the time he got me in big trouble with one of the local outlaw clubs. I told him when I first started to hang with him not to include me in his fights. No matter how many he took on — he was on his own. I'd rather spend my time hustling the babes. More potential for what I was looking for. Making love beat out a knuckle sandwich any day.

One afternoon a few years back we were headed for a game at the stadium and we took my truck. When I picked him up he threw two big trash bags in the bed I thought was garbage for the dump. He informed me we needed to make a quick stop on the way. With Duke a quick stop could be ten minutes – or a lifetime.

He gave me directions to a house and we pulled in the driveway. He grabbed the bags and signaled me towards the house. "Come on and have a beer," he said. Then I knew this wasn't a garbage run – it was a drug deal. I hadn't been dealing for a while. You know – "don't do the crime if you can't do the time." I didn't want to give up riding for hard time. He must've had about eight pounds of weed in those bags and who knows what else.

I went into the living room behind him. Damn! I knew right away by the colors it was an outlaw hangout. Four of them no less. Duke liked living on the edge! These weren't easy boys to deal with – no matter what the commodity. They offered us a beer and we sat down on their trashed sofa. The house reeked of cigars and stale beer. There was a lot of dough – and a 9mm – sitting on the coffee table. Duke showed his wares and tried to close the deal. He even had a full block of blond hash in the bag. He opened the burlap around the hash and broke me off a small chunk. He knew that was my favorite vice. I stuck it in my inside vest pocket.

During my education from Duke about outlaw clubs he'd told me, "Never shoot or stab an outlaw – cause the whole chapter will come lookin' for you. But you can kick the shit out outta them in a fight and they won't think the lesser of you." I was hoping to never need that sage advice. But those boys had been drinking for a while and they were in a feisty mood.

They started to argue with him over cheating on the weight of the weed. Now – Duke may have been grouchy and mean – and he sure lacked for table manners – but the one thing he stuck to was being honest. It was one of his few virtures. So the words started flying. The level of the negotiation grew until he looked over at me with that disgusted look in his dark eyes and I knew what that meant!

He turned back and punched the biker arguing with him in the face breaking his nose. He went down with blood spurting from his face. The second outlaw dove across the table at Duke but he used his momentum to toss him through the front window of the house. Glass flew like shrapnel.

I saw the outlaw nearest me go for the gun on the table. Now I had no choice but to join in! I carried a small leather billie club inside my jacket. I pulled the club as he reached for the pistol and gave him a solid whack. I heard the bone crack in his forearm. I finished him off with a shot across the head. He went down for the count. Fuck! I'd knocked out an outlaw. That never boded well for one's future in this town.

Duke came over the coffee table and had one hell of a karate fight with the last one. They exchanged quite a few punches and kicks before Duke took him down. The house was majorly torn up. He stepped over the downed outlaw and asked him if he wanted any more. When the biker didn't move Duke went calmly back to the table and counted the money. He took exactly what they owed him and left the rest. He even threw a hundred dollar bill back on the table and told the fallen biker it was to help replace the front window.

Duke left like nothing big had happened. As I followed I was thinking I'd better head for Mexico before those boys got outta of the hospital. But he was right. Nothing more ever came of it — though I was looking over my shoulder for quite a while. It just added to his sordid reputation. He really was a wild and crazy guy with little fear.

Duke got unusually silent after I recalled that story to him. He then made a statement I never thought I'd hear come out of him, "Maybe I'm ready for some peace..."

His remark took me by surprise. I looked at him but he didn't look back — so I left it alone.

I used to be a good shot but hadn't fired a weapon in a while. I didn't have much .45 ammo — and we couldn't afford the noise — so Duke gave me a pellet gun to practice with my left hand. The more I used it the stronger my left hand got and the better my aim.

Then we fixed the holster on my chest to accommodate the left hand pull and I practiced drawing it out. "I suggest you keep a round chambered and the safety off." Duke offered. "If you need it — you'll need it in a hurry. Just pulling back the hammer will take long enough. You takin' the shotgun?"

"No doubt. Think I'll mount a scabbard on the bike for it. You know — like the outlaws do. It won't be much good unless I'm close — but you never know. I'm taking my K-Bar strapped to my leg but hope I never have to use it. Don't like knife fights. Hard to come out ahead."

"Have to agree with that. Don't like a knife fight myself. What else you plannin' on takin' along? Got a set of binoculars?"

"I was digging through my stuff yesterday to find this pair of binoculars my Uncle Cecil used in the Spanish American War. They're heavy but they work. Never thought they'd see action again. I've got my ancient sleeping bag and that little pup tent I used when we went to the biker rallies. It's pretty worn out but goes up quick and should give me some basic protection if it rains. I plan on travelin' at night — working round the patrols — and hidin' out during the day. That's when I'll recon up the road as best I can. Got my GI canteen for carrying water and a boda bag to hold some extra. I'll wear my leathers as it'll be cold riding the coast at night. Just bringing one extra pair of clothes in case I get wet. Don't plan on cooking so I'll eat everything cold. Sure would like some jerky to carry along."

"Yeah — you always could get by on a can of cold baked beans and jerky. Gotta be that hillbilly blood in you. We'll see if we can trade for some extra cigarettes to take along. They'll be good for barter if you need 'em. You don't know who you'll run into and if they'll be friendlies. I'll roll some joints to calm your nerves when you're hiding out but don't be smokin' 'em when you're on the move. Gonna need your wits about you."

"Been collecting canned food but it won't last too long if I have to hang out somewhere — like Jenner. Still have plenty of GI can openers. Wish I could come up with another clip for the .45 and some ammo but that might be impossible. Got almost a box of shotgun shells. You been able to find Rat to see about the tires and battery?"

"Went by his place yesterday but couldn't tell if anyone was living there anymore. Left a note in case he returns. Been askin' around with the few people I trust. I'll check again tomorrow.

If he's not around anymore we'll have to figure out another way to get those tires and battery. Let me take care of that for now. How's the bike comin' along?"

"I finally found that set of points. Almost tore the garage apart looking for them. Getting close to doing a test fire on her. But we're gonna have to be very careful how we do that. Don't want any Guardians hearin' us running the motor at night. Found some really old stock mufflers buried back in my trash pile. They weren't for a Super Glide but I made brackets that should hold 'em. They'll quiet things down a bit. Make it purr like a Honda. So I'm almost ready to see if she'll run."

"Them Guardians are runnin' some fast machinery so I hope you don't hafta' out run 'em. Your best bet is to avoid 'em but that won't be easy. From what I've seen they'll have firepower superiority over you if you come up against them. Your best defense will be surprise—and a good aim."

"At night I'll wait for a patrol to pass before I start my run. My biggest concern is that they'll come up behind me with an unscheduled patrol. I'm gonna wear my old dog tags for good luck."

"They the ones you had on when you got your last purple heart?" He thought for a second. "Sorry JC—I guess that wasn't funny?"

"You're right—that's not funny. And no—these were the ones I had on when we got into that all night firefight trying to get back to the fire base at Con Thien. I didn't think any of us were going to make it back alive. That was when I got my first purple heart. Never liked leaving bodies behind but we had no choice that night..."

"Damn sure I remember that awful feeling. But then there wasn't much about fuckin' Nam we liked—right?" We both shook our heads.

"I'll work out a night to come over this week and help with the test run. We'll recon the neighborhood for several blocks before we try to start the bike. Gladman's been workin' on a way to hide you and the bike in his garbage truck. He's pretty good with wood. Gonna build you a first class hooch in the back with the bike. You'll be stuck there a long time while he fills the truck and makes the slow drive through Muir Woods over to Stinson beach."

Duke continued, "Gladman says there'll be at least one checkpoint before Stinson but the Guardians know him since he makes that run almost every day. He and the truck smell so bad they don't stop him for long. I think you'll make it to the beach okay. But you'll want to travel that night to get past the bay marshes into the woods near Olema. The marshes would be a dangerous spot to run into any Guardians—no place to hide."

"I've been studying the map again and you're right on. I need to get past the ocean and into the woods before I hide out. There might be a checkpoint in Olema so I'll want to find a spot close by where I can camp and recon the next day. At night it'll be hard telling where I'm at. I took out the taillight so no one can see me from behind."

"Hadn't thought about that. Good idea. See—you still got some of that gray matter left you old fart. How 'bout the head-light?"

"I thought about painting it black except for a slot across the middle but I think I want all the light I can get. Put in a switch on top of the headlight in case I need to turn it off and leave the motor running. It'll be dark along the coast if the clouds take my moon and likely foggy. Don't expect to be moving very fast. My distance every night will depend on the Guardian patrols and the guard posts. The Russian River bridge at Jenner is gonna be a serious challenge as they're sure to have an outpost there. I would if I was them. Probably well fortified."

We worked out for a while longer with Duke's weights. I was feeling it. Was amazed how much he could still lift at his age. Glad he was my friend and not my enemy. It was time for me to pack up and head for home.

Duke shook my hand and gave me orders as I left, "I'll be by your place in two days. Be ready—and keep your shotgun handy..."

CHAPTER 5

Search and Procure

Traveling at night around the City was dangerous. The Guardians liked to shoot first and ask questions later. So Duke would try to show up right before dark. I was in the garage wrestling with the front forks I'd just finished putting back together when he came in.

"I got good news!" he announced as he gave me a biker handshake. "Found Rat. He moved from where I'd been lookin'. But he got word to me where he's holed up. He's in some digs down near the Wharf. That's danger close to the Guardian headquarters. But he knows where the Guardians are keepin' their motorcycle supplies. You 'member that hole in the wall cafe over on Taylor Street—Charlie Wongs—where we'd eat all the time 'cause he had cheap American food and he liked bikers? He'd sell us those cheapo knock off Harley t-shirts from China out the back of the store." Duke helped me get the front end back on while we talked.

"Yeah—that Charlie was a character. Supported his wife and eight kids out of that little cafe. Liked to tell us stories about when he was a cook in the Coast Guard. He'd give us a fortune cookie with our steak and eggs and make us read them to everyone. What a laugh it was."

"Well guess what bro? That's where they're stashin' their motorcycle parts now. Rat's sure they'll have some tires and batteries. Mostly for rice grinders but I bet we can find somethin' we can use. Rat was gonna cruise by there today and check out the layout. The place is so small they might have only one or two guards at night. Not much of a demand for bike parts since the fuckin' Guardians are the only ones with bikes now."

"So what's the plan?"

"You'll want to catch a few zzz's as we're goin' out later tonight. I told Rat to look for us around midnight. It's a long risky patrol over there with the Guardians around." Duke was actually excited about seeing some action. To him it was another opportunity to kick some Guardian ass — something he really enjoyed.

He opened up the duffle bag he was carrying, "I brought along my tools for the mission." He pulled out his AK-47 I hadn't seen in a while. "Fat Martha here is a good friend," he said admiringly as he inspected the weapon. "You 'member the VC and NVA givin' us such a hard time with this baby?"

"That's a fact — for damn sure. It had that sound we learned to dread. Sometimes I think it was better than the M16 we carried. Those VC were tough cookies — particularly after dark."

Then Duke pulled out a 9mm sidearm I'd seen many times during our rides. He liked that weapon because it carried a big clip. Took big hands like his to handle it. He checked the chamber — set a round — and put it in his holster.

"You expectin' the Little Big Horn or something?" I was trying to give him a hard time — a dangerous occupation with Duke.

"Hey little man — I believe in the old Boy Scout motto — be prepared! You best be gettin' your .45 and shotgun loaded and cocked for this night. You know Rat. If he's packing at all it'll be some .22 lady's pocket gun. He don't like firearms much."

Duke was busy checking the bike over. "Man — it's really comin' together. You always were hot with a wrench JC. Did you measure the battery?"

"I did. We'll go with whatever we find closest to that size. If it doesn't have acid in it we'll have to see if we can find some. We need a 19" front and a 16" rear tire that will fit these rims."

"Let's get our gear ready and grab some shuteye. Got your night combat uniform ready? Or is that a dumb question to an old Marine? It's gonna be a long night."

"You sure we don't want to take my station wagon?"

"No way bro — a vehicle is too easy to spot at night. We'll take our chances on foot. I know several back ways that aren't patrolled too heavily."

We ate some cold food and tried to catch a nap but it was hard to get my mind to slow down. Duke called me about 10:00. "Time to do our last weapons check and get suited up.

26

When you have your gear on we'll hit the road," he barked like a gunny. My heart was pumping. I hadn't been on a combat mission in a long fuckin' time. Glad I was going with Duke. If anyone could pull this off – it would be him.

Duke pulled a small backpack from the duffel bag and put it on. "What's in there?" I asked.

"You'll find out. Grab your canteen and let's hit it. You carry the binoculars. I might have to move fast if I run into shit on point. As you Marines say – let's get some!" Recon with a Ranger – not the first time...

We left toward the direction of the Wharf. It was spooky to be out this late at night with the city so dark. "Let's try our best to avoid any trouble getting there." He didn't need to be telling me the obvious.

I could tell Duke had done this many times. We quietly made our way through burned out buildings and across streets strewn with junked cars. We occasionally saw Guardians on patrol – always at a distance. So far so good. I was sweating. More from the adrenaline probably than the exertion. Duke would only stop for short breaks while we listened. We saw some other night raiders pass by about a block away but they didn't see us. I hoped no one was watching us.

After over an hour of hiking over the City hills I smelled that we were getting close to the wharf. It was very risky here because many of the Guardians lived in this area. We slowed down and carefully checked every doorway and corner. Finally we slipped into a building and started up some stairs. We came to a door where Duke knocked quietly.

It was a while before we heard any movement inside. The door opened slowly into a dark room. "Come in – quickly." It was Rat's voice. All the shades on the windows were closed and thick cigarette smoke hung in the air. Rat lit a candle and I recognized his lanky body. He was over six foot but only weighed about 140. We used to tell him he looked like Icabod Crane from the Sleepy Hollow cartoon when we were kids.

"JC! Man it's good to see you." He kept shaking my hand like he was really relieved to know it was us. "You guys hungry? I got some seafood from the wharf today. Don't see that much lately but a boat came in today. Here—try some of this."

I hadn't had shrimp and muscles for a long time. We sat on the floor and pigged out. What an unexpected treat. The hike over had given me a serious appetite and Duke was always hungry. It was a strange scene to be sitting on the floor stuffing ourselves with seafood by candlelight right before a mission. Sure beat the rations we suffered with in Nam.

"I even have some wine to wash it down," Rat offered. We were eating like a night out on the town—and we might be dead in an hour. Life sure can take its twists...

"I gotta give it to you Rat. You're the best scrounger I've ever known. So what the hell you been doing?" I asked him while he sipped his wine.

"Oh man—just gettin' by. The Guardians may own the city but there are still things they want only I can find. They like to kick my ass every once in a while to keep me in my place. I'm gonna blow up their headquarters one day just for fun. I'm putting the bomb together now. Gonna set it off by remote. Sure would like to get the hell out of this nightmare but don't think that will happen any time soon."

I looked at what I could see of the room in the candlelight. This was obviously quite the place in it's day but now it was almost empty. There appeared to be blood stains on one of the walls. "This is pretty plush quarters Rat. How'd you find this?"

"I used to scrounge things—real exotic things—for the gay dudes who lived here. When the Guardians took over they disappeared real quick. The Guardians don't like fags much you know. So I been hanging out here. The Guardians took most of the furniture but they leave this place alone for the most part. Could never afford a hangout like this in the old days. So I pretend I'm living big near the wharf." He paused for a moment, "Duke says you might be heading north. That so?"

"I'm gonna try but I need some parts for my old Glide. I hear you might know where to find 'em?"

"You bet ya bro—and not too far from here." Rat said proudly. That café we used to hang out around all the time that was up from the wharf. What was the name—Charlies? This area's crawling with Guardians so we'll have to be very—very—careful." He was looking at Duke and I knew what he was thinking — don't shoot the first thing you see!

"You two eat some more and we'll map out our plan. The parts storage is about six blocks from here. I expect there'll be one or two guards and they have orders to shoot anything that moves. We'll have to take them out — don't think we have a choice." These were big words coming from Rat who preferred to avoid a fight. "We can't make any noise goin' in cause they have radios to call for backup."

"No sweat," Duke replied as he was checking the leg fitting on his Ka-Bar.

We sat around for a while catching up with everything that had happened since the Regional Wars. Rat had his bike taken too and was driving an old Volvo the Guardians had given him. "Damn piece of yuppie shit!" His bike was a real piece of work — a rat bike in more ways than one. "I miss my wheels — and ridin' with the guys. Those fuckin' Concern assholes really screwed the pooch for all of us. I wish they were still alive so I could kill them myself." I'd never known Rat to be this angry about anything.

Duke checked his watch while he finished the last of the wine. "Enough of the good life boys. Let's get on patrol. We'll go down the back entrance through the parking garage. Rat — you stay in the middle and keep me on track to the shop. JC — you get rear."

Rat handed us flashlights. "You'll need these in the store." He put on a pack and handed me a small one for the battery — if we found one. Then he really surprised me when he pulled out what looked like an auto with a silencer.

"Where the fuck did you find that?" I exclaimed in surprise and then I thought for a minute and chuckled. "Never mind — I forgot who I was asking." He smiled then pulled back the action and loaded a round. "I'm loaded for bear." This was definitely not the old Rat I remembered. People change with the times…

"Okay Rat — but don't get trigger happy or we'll have a shit fuckin' load of 'em down on us in a hurry." Interesting words of caution coming from Duke to Rat. "Let's just get the stuff and make a fast track back here."

We slipped out the door and down the stairs to the garage.

Duke went ahead to the street side and signaled us on. It always amazed me how that big man could move so quietly when he wanted. Must have been that jungle patrol experience.

We made our way slowly—block by block—to the parts depot. When we were about a block away we took up a position in a burned out restaurant and checked out the shop through my binoculars. There was one Guardian in a chair at the front door but we couldn't see anyone else moving around. We waited and watched for a while but didn't see any other movement. The Guardian out front looked like he was half asleep.

"There's another entrance around the back I saw when I checked out the joint the other day." Rat added in. "It's probably locked but I can get in." One of Rat's unique abilities was that he could get through any locked door. You could come home and find him sitting in your living room drinking your beer—and know you locked the place when you left. Nobody ever asked how he did it. We just knew he could.

"We'll go in past the back entrance and I'll leave you two there while I sneak up the side to the front. He'll never know what hit him!" That was easy to believe with Duke. He checked the knife he had strapped to his leg. I'm sure it was sharp and ready for action. "The front door should be unlocked so I'll go in there and meet you two at the back."

We slowly made our way around the block to the back of the store. After listening for a few minutes to see if there was any activity Duke used hand signals to tell us he was heading for the front. He had a very serious look on his face and I was glad I wasn't the Guardian at the front door. I watched at the corner—shotgun ready—as Duke's backup while Rat disappeared in the dark toward the back door.

Right after Duke slipped around the front corner I heard a brief scuffle and the muffled sound of a body falling. Without seeing I knew that Duke had slit his throat. I'm sure he then dragged the hapless Guardian in through the front door. Before Duke had a chance to get to the back of the store Rat grabbed my arm. "Come on—I got the door open. Let's go." Rat was off and into the store before I could slow him down. We still didn't know if anyone was inside.

We turned on our flashlights and worked our way slowly through the back storage room. There were motorcycle supplies of all types piled around. I saw tires but no batteries. I was looking for Duke to come the other way but hadn't seen him yet. Rat had stopped to look around the inventory when I saw Duke's hairy head coming in the dark. "I didn't see any batteries up front. How 'bout you guys?" he asked in a low voice.

Rat was still looking around when he stopped and fixed his flashlight on a spot in the corner. "Eureka! I see some batteries." He pointed toward some boxes. "JC—look for what you want. I'll find the tires you need."

I pulled out my measuring tape and Duke and I started going through the boxes. After about twenty we found something that measured close to what we wanted. "Now we need a battery acid kit," Duke said as he started throwing stuff on the floor. We worked our way through a lot of shit before we found a battery starter kit. "Far out! I thought we weren't gonna find one. Where's Rat?" Duke asked as we loaded up the booty.

We could hear Rat in the next room but couldn't see him. "Damn scrounger—I hope he's not taking time to do his Christmas shopping," Duke whispered. We loaded the battery and the kit into my backpack and headed for the back of the store. Duke was in the lead as we groped our way through the dark store. He was about ten feet in front of me when I saw the figure in the shadows...!

There was a dark shape in the corner about fifteen feet to Duke's right and it looked like he was bringing a weapon to bear on Duke's head. I'd laid down the shotgun so I reached for my .45 and was going for a shot. There wasn't time to warn Duke as I took aim and started to pull the trigger. Then I heard a "plock" from the other room. Whoever it was there in the dark—their head exploded before they could take Duke out. I felt warm blood and guts on my face. Rat had wasted him with the silencer!

"What the..." was all I heard Duke say before he was on top of the nearly decapitated Guardian. He just stood there for a while over the body before he started to breathe again. He kicked the body once to vent his anger. "Son of a bitch..." and he paused again. "Mother fucker..." and he kicked him again. Duke was really pissed. I guess he hadn't come that close in a while.

Rat stepped in slowly from the doorway with the smoking gun in his hand. "I've never killed anyone before!" Even in the dark he looked pretty pale.

"Well I'm damn glad you didn't hesitate!" Duke exclaimed as he looked at Rat. "He must of been sleeping in the back. Son-of-a-bitch — that was too fuckin' close." We stopped to listen to see if we heard anyone else in the store or outside. It was dead quiet.

We stood there in amazement for a moment. Duke looked over at me and saw the cocked .45 in my hand. "Did you see him?"

"Yeah — but Rat got him first. What a shot!" I slapped Rat on the arm.

"I can't believe I hit him! Man — I think I'm gonna throw up. Let's get out the hell out of here." He started for the back door. "I found your tires. If you have the battery let's head out." Rat stopped to pick up the tires and then grabbed his pack on the way out.

When we reached the back door Duke stopped us. "Wait — I forgot to take care of somethin'. You two check out the alley and I'll be right back." He took a can from his pack and van-ished back into the store. We peered out into the alley with our weapons ready. I could hear Duke spraying something in the store. "What the hell is he up to?" I whispered to Rat.

Duke reappeared and motioned us out the door. He stepped out and painted a quick swastika on the door as he explained, "I want them to think it was some of the Skin Heads from South San Francisco. That will keep them off our scent for a while." Now it made sense.

"For a bonehead biker you sometimes surprise me," I replied quickly.

Duke didn't respond. He was busy checking our escape route down the block. "Load up. Let's hit it. We're not out of the woods yet. It's a long way back to Rat's with all this gear. When the Guardians find these dead bodies they'll be out lookin' for somebody in a flash. I'll take the lead. Don't get too far behind." I think I had enough adrenaline pumping to climb the Golden Gate Bridge bare handed so keeping up wasn't going to be a problem.

"We're right behind you," I said as I pushed Duke ahead into the street.

We went out the same way we came always listening for sounds of Guardian activity from the direction of the store. Everything stayed quiet. The Guardians weren't going to be happy when they found the bodies and knew there'd been a heist. Though I'm sure they would be wondering why it was motorcycle parts. So Duke's idea about the Skin Heads was a good one. I wouldn't have thought of that cover.

It was a long hike back with all the gear but we made good time. The battery and kit were getting heavy by the time we got to Rat's. We got inside without being seen and flopped down on the floor with our booty. "You got any beer?" Duke asked Rat.

Rat opened a cooler and handed him one. "Not too cold but you're welcome to 'em." He gave me one too. Duke popped the top and drank it down in one long gulp.

"Thanks—I needed that," he said as he let out one long belch. "Got another?"

We sat there in silence for a while thinking about what had happened. Rat still looked like he was in shock. I'd seen that look before—after someone's first kill.

Before anything was said we heard a siren off in the direction of the store and then Guardian vehicles were coming from all directions. We heard shots. Did someone else take the blame for our heist or were they just letting off steam? Probably never know...

Rat finally spoke, "I have sleeping bags in the next room and plenty of grub. You guys stay the night and I'll go check things out in the morning." We leaned back against the wall and listened to the commotion in the distance. We were safe for now. Rat leaned over and opened his pack. He pulled out a couple of Harley Davidson t-shirts he'd some how found the time to take while we were in the store.

He must have seen our looks of surprise. "Fuck-an-A guys— you know what these shirts are worth on the black market around here? Even in the middle of all this mess?" he asked us with this pretend businessman look on his pale face.

Duke threw his empty beer can at him. "See—I told you he was doin' his damn Christmas shopping!" The laugh was good and helped to relieve some of the tension.

We were all pretty keyed up and needed to slow down before we could sleep. Duke lit up three cigarettes. He looked at me as he handed me a cigarette. "Don't be givin' me any of that I'm tryin' to quit shit right now—okay."

He handed the last one to Rat. "You did good Rat. You saved my life." He took a long puff. "What'd you mean when you said you never killed anyone? I thought you were in Nam."

"I was man but I was a Seabee. Drove a fuckin' bulldozer. We got shot at every once in a while but I rarely fired my rifle. I never could shoot worth a shit. I can't believe I hit him on the first shot. My hands are still shaking..."

"If you had to pick a good time to get fuckin' lucky I'm glad it was tonight." Duke looked over at me. "You looked like you were ready to pull the trigger yourself. I told ya you could do it when the time came."

"Yeah—well—maybe! I think it was just instinct. I'm not sure I would of nailed him before he dropped the hammer on you. Good thing we'll never know."

We listened for a while to the noise in the distance and then it all went silent. "I guess we're good for now. I'm gonna try and get some sleep." Duke informed us. "It's been a long fuckin' night!" The floor was hard but we felt safe for now. We'd accomplished the mission and gotten back alive. Not bad for a night's work. Not too happy about the killing but knew it might be part of the job.

I went into the bathroom and tried to wash the blood from my face. The mess was on my clothes too. I was getting too old for this shit...

CHAPTER 6

Beating a Slow Retreat

When I woke up the next morning Rat was already gone. That man never did sleep much. He used to drive us crazy on the overnight runs when we were hung over and he was up and moving. He'd left some coffee in the pot and a note saying he'd be back. Duke was still snoring—sounded like a coal train coming through a tunnel.

I poured myself a coffee and lit a smoke. Somehow those always go together. There was traffic in the streets but the blinds were down so it was dark in the room. I pulled back one of the blinds and could see the bay. Made me remember why I'd stayed in the city so many years ago. This was one of the coolest places I'd ever lived—but that was all gone. It was just a burned out and dangerous place now. Time to get out...

I heard someone moving outside so I pulled my .45 and focused on the door. A key rattled in the lock and Rat came in. "I was hoping that was you. What's going on?"

"Couldn't sleep anymore so I did a drive around the neighborhood. They've got the shop all blocked off and there were two body bags out front. I didn't get too close or ask any questions. When you guys are ready I'll drive you back to your place. My Guardian permit lets me get around during the day. We'll have to hide the stuff in the back of the fuckin' Volvo—under some junk—in case anyone stops us. We'll take the long way round to your place and give them plenty of room. Duke up yet?"

"Nah—but he will be soon. He's usually up and moving by now. We'll give him a few minutes more. Thanks for the coffee and grub bro."

Rat and I sat back down and I asked my regular question these days, "So Rat—why do you think all of this happened? I mean with the Concern and all."

Rat thought for a while before he answered, "If you want my

opinion—I think it was all about people wanting things. The more folk had the more they wanted. That's how I made my living—finding things for customers. Crazy things. Art, drugs, cars—you name it. People didn't seem to care much about each other anymore. Except for trying to impress everyone with what they had. People lost interest in the government as long as they had the toys they wanted. Freedom became an illusion."

He thought for a while and continued, "I believe the Concern traded our freedom for things. And we gave it up easily. We sold out. It was like you weren't normal if you didn't want to collect shit. Now I trade crap to survive. I hate the Guardians. They're just pigs. Life means very little to them. Don't think I'll ever make it out of here so that's why I'm going to blow the bastards up. Maybe I'll wear the bomb myself..."

We sat quiet for a while after that thought. I understood his frustration and anger. I couldn't offer much comfort. His anger was the same reason I was trying to leave. "So why were you willing to risk your life to help me?"

"For sure man—I admire your courage. It'll take guts to do what you're going to try. I've always liked you JC. You treated me like a friend and a fellow biker. A piece of me will go with you now. You're going to do what many of us don't have the courage to try. I want you to make it to the New Society. Maybe they'll know how to live with each other in peace—like it should be—without this obsession with material shit. Maybe something good will come out of all this chaos? You go kick some ass bro!" He reached over and gave me the biker handshake. His words made my day. Maybe what I was going to try wasn't so crazy after all?

Duke started to come to life. He was always a grouch in the morning before his three cups of coffee. He must've had at least a six pack before he conked out last night. But to him that was just a short cocktail. He grumbled at us as he filled the doorway to the kitchen, "Gimme summa that coffee. What's happenin' boys?"

"After you two eat and get changed," Rat answered, "I'll take you back to JC's place with the goods. Give you a new experience in a trash Volvo. Make sure you wear your seat belts. Never know when the wheel will fall off again," he laughed.

Duke looked at his fatigue jacket on the floor and saw the blood on the front. "Fuck! Guess we can't be found with this evidence on us. But I think we made a clean getaway so far. Got the loot we needed thanks to you Rat." He came over and looked out at the bay. "You're right—you got some real nice digs here. This place musta' cost a fortune back in the day. Let's eat and hit the road. I want to help JC get these parts on today. It's time to finish the beast and see if she runs."

"I'm supposed to work on a boiler sometime today for the Guardians but I can make it over later," I responded. "With your help we can get the tires mounted and maybe fire up the engine with the new battery."

We changed out of our bloody clothes and put on some sweatshirts the previous occupants of the apartment had left behind. The only one that even came close to fitting Duke was bright purple. "Fuckin' —don't I look like the biggest fag in the city now?" Rat and I couldn't stop laughing.

"But it goes so well with your complexion!" Rat exclaimed. Duke's eyes flared and I think if Rat hadn't saved his life the night before he would have laid him out.

"Come on," Duke growled, "Let's get movin' fore somebody I know sees me. If any Guardian who knows me spots me in this getup he'll know I've been up to no good."

We packed up and quietly loaded the wagon. We didn't want to be seen loading the tires so we made sure the garage was clear. "Boy you're right—this is an old yuppie piece of shit," Duke muttered as he stuffed his big body in the back seat. He put his AK-47 under a coat on the seat next to him in case we ran into any problems. I had my .45 under my leg and stashed the shotgun under the seat. Rat laid his pistol beneath some rags next to him.

Luckily for us the ride back to my place was long but quiet. Wasn't sure that Volvo was going to make it. What a hulk. Rat had a Guardian pass on his mirror and no one stopped us. Good thing—because we were loaded for action. When we reached my garage nobody was around so we quickly unloaded the stuff into my place.

"I'm gonna head back now. I have some business to conduct

at Guardian headquarters. Bros—it was a pleasure doin' business with you." Rat stuck out his hand but Duke surprised me when he slapped it away.

"Sorry Rat—but you get a big bear hug!" and Duke gave him a hug that lifted him off of his feet. "I'll never forget what you did. If I had a medal I'd give it to you. It took some real huevos to cap that Guardian. You're okay bro…"

Rat didn't know what to say but he had this real shit-eatin' grin on his face. He knew Duke long enough to know he didn't thank people very often. And now the Duke owed him a favor. Rat shook my hand and got back in the car.

Duke leaned over to the driver's window. "We're gonna have a goodbye pardue for JC soon as he's ready to go. I'll let you know." That was the first I'd heard of such plans—but it sounded great to me.

As Rat pulled away Duke turned to the garage. "Let's smoke a joint and get to work on the bike." Even in these hard times Duke always had the best weed.

We worked the rest of the morning on the tires. Changing tires was never an easy job. Breaking the bead wasn't as hard with Duke's strong hands helping out. "These look great. They're even Dunlops. Look like they were made for a Harley. We got lucky," I commented. I was pretty pleased with our work the night before—except for the killing. We mounted both wheels back on the bike.

I'd cleaned and oiled the old chain and it went on easily. The sprockets were worn but not too badly. I aligned the rear end and it was looking good. I'd already gone over the brakes and changed the fluid. Since it wouldn't be a long mileage trip they should handle the distance.

We filled the new battery and hooked it to a charger on the bench. The power grid was usually on during the day so it started to charge. If the grid went out I would start up my generator. The battery should fit into the frame okay.

"I've got some business to take care of—but I'll be back tonight," Duke told me. "We're gettin' close. If the battery takes the charge we'll be ready to test the engine tonight."

"I have that boiler job to get to but I'll meet you here later.

Here—try on this Harley sweatshirt for size. Sure beats that lavender model you're sporting."

Duke grabbed the sweatshirt and put it on. "It's a little tight but it'll do. We'll load in some gas tonight and see if we can fire her up."

The old Super Glide was looking like a running machine again. I couldn't wait to be riding her. Didn't think I would ever get this chance again. It was exciting and scary at the same time. "I'll catch you later my man—be safe," I offered to Duke as he headed out. With the Guardians safety was always a touch and go situation...

CHAPTER 7

Test Fire

It was late before Duke showed up at the house. I'd been back long enough from my boiler job to catch a short nap before starting to work on the bike. Found at my age the naps helped my body renew. Sure wished I had some beer.

"Okay Duke – the battery should have a charge now so let's see how it fits." I explained as we went to the garage.

Duke pulled out four beers from his pack. Fuckin' mind reader! "Not much – but better than nothing," he offered as he handed me one.

We struggled with the battery for a while – it was a tight fit. I taped some frayed spots on the cables and the battery was in and mounted. Finally – the last step – I filled the gas tank and opened the petcock. Nothing was leaking as the carb filled. "She's got good plugs and points. Just hope the alternator is working. It liked to give me a hard time when I was on long runs. Always waited until I was at least a hundred miles from home before it crapped out. I seem to remember replacing it at least twice."

We stood there looking at her for a while admiring our work. The old girl was showing her age but I think she was ready to fire up.

"We'll need to check out the neighborhood to see if anyone is around," Duke said as he prepared his AK-47. "I'll sweep the blocks to the left and you go right. Meet you at the other end."

I grabbed the shotgun and we split up and made our way down the blocks. There weren't many neighbors left in this area and everything was quiet. After a walk down several blocks I headed for the other side. I saw Duke's big form waiting on the dark corner. "The coast is clear. Let's give it a kick," I said with excitement.

We hustled back and ducked in the garage while Duke

closed the door. Just have to live with the fumes for a few minutes—if she started. I climbed on top and opened the choke. The battery might not have much of a charge so I gave it several slow kicks. The engine was stiff with the new oil and it took some effort to work it through. Then I jumped hard on the kick starter several times but it never fired. "Damn!"

After a few minutes more of trying the kick starter I was winded. This wasn't a good sign. "Here little man—let me give it a try." Duke straddled the bike—twisted the throttle—and gave it all of his weight. I heard one cylinder fire! It didn't start—but it had fired. Without saying a word he put his full weight into it again. We got another fire. "C'mon baby—talk to me," he urged the old girl.

He jumped on it again and it started to fire then died. Black smoke came out the exhaust. "We're gettin' close," he mumbled before he gave it another jump. The engine started to turn—slowly and roughly. Duke babied the throttle and all of a sudden the engine caught and started to run. The room quickly filled with smoke but she was finally running. We looked at each other in excitement—like we had just landed a man on the moon.

"Open the door," Duke ordered, "I'm gonna make a short run." The engine was warming up and running smoother. It had that familiar Harley sound we hadn't heard in a while—even with the quiet mufflers. It was dangerous to take it out but we were too fired up to care. Duke took off into the darkness and I could hear him going down the block. Kept my fingers crossed there weren't any Guardians cruising by.

In a few minutes he came back and the bike was running good. Duke had a big smile on his face like he'd just gotten laid by three uptown hookers. "Man oh Man! That was totally fuckin' awesome. You take it for a spin."

"I was wondering if you were going to give me a turn. Never did like sloppy seconds..." I couldn't wait to step on and open her up. As I sped down the block it brought back such great memories I wanted to just keep riding. I was so thrilled I took it down a block further than we had checked out. Wanted to just keep on going. But I had to get her back to safety. It felt so good to be in the wind again—if only for a brief moment. I turned her around and headed back to the garage.

I rode into the garage—quickly adjusted the idle—and then shut off the engine. Duke closed the doors. He grabbed his weapon and motioned me to follow him outside. "We need to hang out for a while to see if anyone heard us. Let's burn one."

We climbed up on the porch of the empty house next door and sat down on a worn out glider listening for cars. "You do good work man," he whispered to me. "Always said you were the best damn Harley mechanic I ever knew. Have a shot," and he handed me his worn out flask.

We sat there in the silence enjoying his whiskey. I was getting worked up. My wheels were running. Now I could finish my preparations.

After a while Duke asked, "Can you be ready in four days? You been saying it'll be a full moon comin' soon and that would be good for your night ridin'."

"I'll be ready. Just have a few things to work out about what I'm taking. I want to go over the bike one last time. Sure wish I could ride her some more but it's too much of a risk. At least we know the ole gal runs. She'll do better when I get some miles on her."

"I want to throw a goin' away party for you. We haven't had a pardue in a while. I know where a few of the old crew are and Rat wants to come along. He earned it. Besides—you never know what that old scrounger might bring along. I might have a big surprise for you too."

"Yeah—what would that be?"

"If I told you it wouldn't be a surprise would it? I'm just gonna keep you guessin'. I'll see if I can get some folks together for two nights from now. We'll have it at my place so the bike won't be there if the Guardians come nosing around. We'll start before dark. I'll chill down some beer and dig up some weed. Might have to twist a few Guardian arms for that. All anyone needs to know is that you're gonna do a breakout. Don't need to know the details."

"No offense man—but your place is a bit of a pig sty."

"Yeah—for fuckin' sure. But I promise to get the dead bodies outta the corners before anyone gets there. Besides—we can trash my place all we want. I won't be staying there much longer. I'll open the windows and burn some incense. Might help to get the smell out — well maybe a little."

"Here — let's enjoy my last," he said as he reached inside his jacket and pulled out a joint. "We earned it tonight."

We fired up and relaxed in the glider. Our weapons close in case we heard anything in the neighborhood. We talked about our bikes and some of the rides we'd shared. Sometimes — when you're enjoying yourself — you wonder if it will be the last time...

I asked Duke a question I'd been pondering for a while, "You think I really got a chance of pulling this off? I mean — like — am I crazy to try this? I ain't no young stud any more."

Duke answered in a quiet voice — the one he used in those rare moments when he was lost in thought, "You 'member what it was like fore you went out on a patrol? All the crazy thoughts that went through your mind 'bout whether you'd come back or not. Or maybe you'd make it but one of your buddies was going to wind up in a body bag? Or laying in the jungle with their guts shot out and you couldn't get to 'em? Or worst yet — taken prisoner."

"Yeah — I remember that horrible feeling. It got worse the closer you got to rotation home."

"I think any dangerous adventure starts with doubt about whether you'll make it through. I'll bet ya every great explorer — you know like Admiral Byrd or Edmund Hillary — laid in bed the night fore he left thinkin' he had to be crazy to be leavin' his home and family to travel to some far off place in search of who knows what. It's easier to just stay and accept things as they are than take the risk to do the journey. That's what separates the men from the boys. Takin' the risk..."

Duke continued, "That summer you wanted to do the Run to the Wall in DC and I kept puttin' you off. Didn't want the hassle of travelin' round the country in a hot summer sleepin' on the ground. I was bein' lazy. So kept makin' excuses to you. But you wouldn't let up on me. I never told you this but the week before we left leave I had a dream. I was talking to the men I left behind in Nam. Saw their faces real well. It was a sign

44

I had to make the trip to the Wall. So I shut up and went along."

"Yeah—you were being a real grouch about it. More than usual."

"Well—you got your way and it was one of the greatest road trips of my life. Got to ride with all those Nam veteran bros from California to DC. Member them babes in Colorado?" I was nodding my head. Couldn't ever forget them. That was quite the night. "We had a great time that summer. The Wall was a trip—not easy to do. Then we went up to see my folks in Pennsylvania. Dad and Mom were real happy to see us. They liked your southern charm. Then we went down to that back woods town you were from in West Virginia. You showed me the family cemetery with all those generations of your folk there. 'Member how we took our time coming back to California. Doin' whatever we wanted. Fuckin' awesome summer." He paused for a moment. "You and my dream were right about seeing the Wall. Made me realize how lucky I was to come home in one piece."

Duke didn't usually ramble on but he was on a roll so I didn't interrupt. "I think you got a good plan worked out and I know your strength. Age is just in the mind. You have the heart—and that's what counts in the long run. Traveled a lot of miles with you JC. Courage is something you don't lack for little man. I wouldn't be helping you if I thought you didn't have a chance. Wouldn't send you to no death sentence. You been a good friend in this crazy world and I intend on doin' some more rides with you down the road. The biggest problem you face on this journey is how to get 'cross the river at Jenner. That could be a tough nut to crack. You might have to abandon the bike and swim across. Then just hike it to the New Society. Nobodies got more faith in you than me bro," and with that he slapped my leg. That was the most connected set of words I'd heard him speak in a long time—except when he was telling a story. Duke wasn't much at talk most of the time.

"Thanks for the words of encouragement bro. This won't be easy. Some good luck along the way wouldn't hurt either."

"Sometimes you just hafta' play the cards that come along—good luck or no." He sat silent for another minute.

"Enough of this touchy feely stuff—okay? Might make me want to get all slobbery and such," he said as he pulled out his pocket hanky and pretended to sob in it. Occasionally Duke had a sense of humor—occasionally. He never did like saying his feelings much—mostly kept it all inside. But it was good advice from a friend who understood war. Worrying about things didn't feed the bulldog.

"You making your plans to get out?" I asked him.

"Have been for a while. I'll go out with Gladman then I plan on hikin' it across land to the north. Lot of mountains off the coast so it won't be an easy hike for over a hundred miles. Expect there will be folk hidin' out in the hills I could run into. Won't know if they're friendly—or looking to collect a bounty from the Guardians. Hope to maybe trade some cigarettes for food along the way. Also plan to live off the land when needed." Duke was someone I knew who could do that.

"When will you leave?"

"Still have a piece of business to take care of." I knew what that meant. "In 'bout two or three weeks I guess. So this will by my pardue too—in a way."

Duke was right—it was time for a pardue. There hadn't been much celebrating since the wars and we weren't sure how many of the brothers were still alive. Duke was determined to have a bash even if it was a small one.

"I've been tryin' to find some of the old crew. You know—Big Jim, Stinky Pete, Injun Joe. Rat is lookin' for some of the guys too. He gets around easier than me with his Guardian pass. He said he'd round up some booze. Rat always finds premium stuff."

"Yeah—and what about my surprise?" I thought I was being sneaky bringing it back up. Maybe he'd found some hash?

"No can tell—don't know if I can make it happen yet. Just have to wait bro. You'll see…"

"Then I'll shoot for two nights from now and be ready to leave two days after that. You make the plans with Gladman. Will he be at the pardue? I haven't met him yet and I'll be trusting my life to him."

"He'll be there for sure. But not to worry—Gladman's a righteous dude. He may be short and round but I believe he can hold his own if things got sticky." Big words of praise from Duke. "He's ready for you. We just have to say the word. I'll let everyone know you're lookin' for canned food or jerky donations. Things you can eat cold."

"I've been stockpiling some canned food but still looking for jerky. I just wanna see folks before I leave—that's plenty of a going away present."

"I'll put the word out tomorrow. I'm lookin' forward to a really good drunk." A good drunk with Duke was always an experience...

CHAPTER 8

Pardue...

It was time for our pardue and I headed over to Duke's with my sleeping bag. I was carrying the .45 with me everywhere but inside my jacket for now. I'd been practicing the left hand draw and was getting it down. Scored a little weed from one of the Guardians I worked for so I was ready. Sure hoped Rat had the beer — but knowing Rat — that was a stupid thought.

I got there about an hour before dark and parked around the block so we wouldn't draw too much unwanted attention. Duke was in the kitchen when I came through the back door. Rat and Duke had a head start on the beer. Shoulda' guessed. "Hey partner!" he yelled out. "Good to see the guest of honor is here. Have a beer." It was even half chilled. A true luxury these days. "I want you to meet someone before the rest of the crew shows up." Duke motioned me into the living room. There was a short — but very round — man sitting in the worn out recliner in the corner. "JC — meet the Gladman."

Gladman looked pretty relaxed in that old chair and already mellowed out. I shook his hand. "Good to meet you at last," I offered. "I understand we'll be taking an adventure together soon. You sure you wanna be taking this big risk?"

"I'm ready for you JC. I like fuckin' with them Guardians. Don't you have no concerns. I understand the risk but I'm more than willin' to help someone get to the north. If Duke says you're the man — that's good enough for me. Wish I could go with you. But I can help more here by getting folk across the bridge. Duke says you'll be ready in two days. I'll come by the night before so we can load up the bike before dawn. I'm building a nice box for you and the bike. Piece of cake dude..."

"Well — all I can say is thanks for the chance. Looking forward to seeing the coast. Enjoy the party," I offered as I shook his hand again. He went back to hitting the water pipe. He didn't say much but I was comfortable with him taking care of things. Just like Duke said.

Over the next hour people started to show up. Man it was good to see some of the old gang. Big Jim actually looked like he'd lost some weight. "Yeah — them damn Guardians are trying to starve me to death bro. One of these days I might just have to cook one of 'em up and see how they taste." That cracked us all up.

Nobody had seen Nasty Pete in a long time. Probably dead. Had a quick temper and he likely snapped at the wrong time. But Panhead Tim showed up with his round girlfriend Becky the Boobs. Slim Jim showed up smelling like cheap wine — that was his trademark.

We lit up and started swapping stories trying to catch up with each other. The two things we all agreed on was we hated the Guardians — and really missed riding. About an hour after dark Injun Joe slipped through the back door. "I heard you white men were having a pardue," he yelled out. Everybody gave him a big Indian whoop in return!

"Didn't think you were still around," I said as I gave him a big hug.

"You white guys are always trying to kill off us Injuns but I'm too tough to give up. And I have some powerful medicine for this pow-wow!" he proclaimed as he handed me a small bag of mushrooms. "Let's all transcend together bros!"

We were checking out the bag when the Enforcer showed up. He was an ex-cop we'd partied with back in the day. He wasn't very tall but built like a fire hydrant. Had someone with him I'd never seen. She was tall with a hooded sweatshirt on that made it hard to see her face. "You're all busted!" he yelled. "The patty wagon will be here soon to take you away. Damn biker degenerates."

Everyone threw their empty beer cans at him. Things were getting rowdy. I really missed these good times. Rat had put some tunes on the box and it was songs from the '60s. We were rocking now...

Duke took the girl by the arm and introduced me. "JC — here's my pardue surprise for you. Meet Rhonda the Magnificent!"

I just stood there stunned. She dropped the hood and there was this angel with a nasty scar across her face. She took off the sweatshirt and wow! Right in front of me was standing this exceptional babe. She took off her baggy sweat pants and she had on short hot pants. Legs to infinity and back. Long blond hair and blue eyes. Yeah—this was a real surprise! Whatever the reason she was here—it didn't matter. She was a beauty just to look at. And a scar among bikers was a sign of courage.

She gave me a long and close hug. Her hair smelled like flowers. Then she pushed me back and looked me straight in the eyes with those bright blue eyes. "Pleased to meet you JC. I've heard a lot about you. May I join the party?"

I kept trying to think of something to say—but nothing was coming out of my mouth.

After an awkward silence Duke jumped in, "He's not always this shy but you kinda took his breath away. I've never seen you speechless before JC," and he gave me a sharp elbow to the ribs. Ouch…!

I finally found some words, "You want something to drink?"

"Got any bourbon? Maybe with some ice?'" she asked with a quiet voice. This was some lady. How she wound up here with all this biker trash was a mystery. But I wasn't going to ask her to leave. All the guys were just standing around staring at her—as mesmerized as me.

"Come on boys—let's get back to the party. Who's got a joint?" she asked. Rat came up with one first and about four lighters showed up. "Did I hear something about mushrooms?"

It was going to be quite a night…

We kicked back and shared the mushrooms. In a while every-one was laughing and having a great time telling their favorite biker stories. Duke was entertaining everyone with how Rat had taken this Guardian's head half off with just one shot. Rat was beaming from ear to ear like he was the baddest dude of them all. Big talk and big stories—it was fun being back in time.

I was really flying—but couldn't take my eyes off Rhonda. She was spectacular—even with the scar. While we were out-side taking a piss break Duke briefly told me her story. She'd been a good friend of Barbie Doll. A professional call girl—very expensive in her time. I could see why. But the Guardians messed her up when she wasn't friendly enough to them. She still looked pretty hot to me.

Later on Jake the Snake showed up with his gal Tweeter. That was probably as much of the old crowd that was still around. It was turning out to be one hell of a party. And Injun Joe was right—we were transcending thanks to the mushrooms. For a while everyone forgot about the wars and the Guardians. Tonight it was just about bikers and good times.

It was a big shocker when Crusher and Masochist made their appearance. Hadn't seen them since the shit hit the fan back in January. They were brothers who'd been professional wrestlers back in the day. Had muscles in places I didn't know you could have muscles. They brought some 'shine with them but I passed. I was already flying...

The next tune on the box was "War". Everyone remembered this one and we formed a circle while we sang the lyrics together. "War! What is it good for? ABSOLUTELY NOTHING!! Say it again..." We hollered out as we rocked to the song.

The Animal's song "We've Gotta Get Out of This Place" came on. "We gotta get out of this place—if it's the last thing we ever do." We sang and danced like there was no tomorrow. I remembered this one from Nam. Only this time it was about the Guardians—not the Cong.

After some time Duke waved at everyone and announced, "Listen up you scooter trash. Time to give JC your gonna away tokens." We sat in a circle while everyone rummaged through their bags. Rat passed around another joint. He said there was hash mixed in it. Rhonda came and sat by my side. I was feeling like a sheik of Arabi. Packs of cigarettes and canned fruit were being tossed into the middle. Crusher and Masochist threw in some nice looking beef jerky—I'd been looking for that. Protein in a small package. Felt like a little boy at Christmas.

Tweeter pulled a pair of long johns out of a bag. "Here JC— you'll need these to stay warm on your run. They're an old pair of Jake's—but I patched them for you and washed out most of the stains." Everyone got a big laugh at that.

Rat handed me a small box. I opened it to find a spare clip

for the .45. Rat was always good for a surprise. "Duke said you might need this. It wasn't easy to find — but that just made it all the more challenging." With Rat that was true. "I also found a new box of ammo to go with it. Make sure you deposit it in the right place." I gave him a high five.

Slim Jim pulled out a metal flask. "I've been saving this for you — it's brandy. You don't know how hard it was not to drink it myself." Knowing Jim that was really saying something. "It'll warm you up on a cold night. Put it away so we don't break into it tonight."

Jake the Snake threw in a packet of Trojans, "Never know when you might run into some of them feisty northern California sheep!" he offered. Sounded like Jake.

Gladman made a donation of trash bags. "These can be used for many things. Keep your spare clothes dry. Take them along," he suggested.

While we were sharing the gifts Rhonda leaned over and whispered in my ear. "I have a really special present for you — but it's for later." I could only imagine what that meant!

Duke handed me a small box. "I know how you hate to wear a watch but you'll need one on this journey. This was my dad's but I want you to have it. It's very special to me and it'll bring you good luck on your journey." He was sporting a big grin behind that almost combed beard as he handed it to me. I opened the box to find an old engineers pocket watch. I was really stunned — and touched. Didn't know what to say. I placed it in my inside vest pocket and shook his hand. "Nice — very nice," was all that came to me.

Duke raised his mug. "Here's a toast to JC. All of our best courage goes with you. We know you can make it. Take a piece of each of us along on your journey. You show them New Society folks what bikers are all about." This was pretty deep stuff for Duke.

"Here! Here!" Everyone shouted as we downed our drinks and shared sloppy hugs all around. I was really going to miss my old friends who I'd shared so many miles with.

I raised my drink and made a toast back, "Here's hoping I will see all of you someday in the north — for sure!" I was dumbstruck for more words. It was a serious wish—but for now it was just about the friendship. So we partied into the night...

Many hours later people were laying out their sleeping bags to hang for the night. It was going to be a biker slumber party—like we'd shared so many times before. The only problem with a good party is they slow down sooner or later. Rhonda had disappeared for a while and I wasn't sure where she'd gone.

Then Rhonda came out of Duke's bedroom and motioned me her way. I didn't argue—I was really cooking with those 'shrooms. Duke was crashed out in the living room and he leaned up on one arm while I crossed the room. "Good luck man—hope you come back alive. Remember your training..." and he fell back to the floor.

As I entered the room I was amazed. She'd picked up the room—quite the task with Duke's room—and lit candles all around. Even the bed had clean sheets—sure didn't find those in Duke's place. "Now it's time for us," she said in a soft voice as she closed the door.

I was really high and couldn't fully believe what was happening. It'd been a long time since I'd been with a woman. And definitely not one anywhere as classy as Rhonda. She unbuttoned the top buttons on her blouse and was showing some serious cleavage. It was easy to see why she'd been such an expensive hooker. She had the body of a centerfold. Maybe in her 40's and still looking real tight.

"I want to give the hero a proper sendoff," she whispered in my ear as she drew me near.

"I'm not a hero—just an old guy tryin' to do the right thing," was all I could think to say.

"Well—for tonight—you're my hero," she said as she placed my hand on her breast. My heart—along with other parts—was racing at full throttle!

We started to kiss while she undressed me. I just followed along and did what came naturally. I wanted her to feel like the million dollar babe she was. She started to turn me every which way but loose.

"I have a bath ready for you. I want to bathe you and wash

your long blond hair," she told me as she pulled me to the bathroom where she had incense burning. I'm sure I needed the bath – but to have such a sensuous lady giving it to me was an incredible fantasy. I wonder if the gladiators ever had it this good before the big game?

She bathed me slowly – and all over. Since I was tripping I wondered if I was going to explode. I think at least my ears were going to pop – if not something else that was really throbbing. Rhonda washed my hair last. "You have such long pretty hair. Not even too much gray yet – still plenty of blond. Makes you look like some Viking warrior with your blue eyes. You just need a helmet with horns on it." She laughed quietly and reached over and gave me one long very hot kiss.

"I was thinking about cutting it off for the run. You know – like back in the Marines." I said.

"Don't you dare JC! Remember how long hair gave Samson his strength? So you just let it go the way it is."

What an incredible woman. After she put my hair in a braid we climbed into bed and I finished undressing her. I lay there for a while admiring her incredible body and stroking her gently. When I couldn't stand it any longer I started kissing her – slowly working my way down her body. Her breasts were awesome with great nipples. When I reached what I was looking for I tasted her goodness. God – she was sweet! She tasted like strawberries – how do women do that? I couldn't get enough while she responded with her whole body.

We made love for a long time – in many positions – until we both ran out of steam. I only hope I did her justice. This was one of the most unforgettable nights of my life. Old fart bikers like me didn't deserve this kind of luck – or lady. We slept in each others arms until the first sun. What a night…!

When I awoke – still not believing what had happened with Rhonda – I crept out to the kitchen and found some warm coffee somebody had made. Probably Rat. Most everyone was still passed out on the floor but he was outside having a smoke. I filled a cup for Rhonda and went back to the bedroom.

Rhonda was half asleep but thanked me for the coffee. Just looking at her naked on the bed was one hell of a treat. She spoke softly and still half asleep, " JC—it was nice having a man make love to me for me. Not just doing it for the money," she murmured. "I wish I'd met someone like you a long time ago."

"Yeah—uh—really?"

"You ever been married JC?"

I thought about that for a moment. "A long time ago it seems now. Dianne had an accident on her bike in '95. Killed by a drunk driver. We were seriously in love. Went all over the country together in a VW bus. She was as comfortable in a tent as a luxury hotel. She didn't care about material things—just being together was all that was ever important to her. Had some affairs after that but was never really in love again. Guess I never gave anyone a chance to get into my heart after that. I think I was lucky to know that kind of love at least once."

"You were—you really were." She rolled over and was looking at me with those bright blue eyes. She had really nice buns to go with that blond hair.

"How 'bout you?"

"I came close but never tied the knot. Never sure if they were in love with me or just my body. So much of our society was built around beauty. You know—the Playboy Syndrome. It was all around us—the media—everywhere you looked it was about being the perfect woman. I didn't want to be just somebody's trophy wife. Made a lot of money selling my skills but it hardened my heart. After a while I didn't feel like I could be ordinary anymore. I became too obsessed with beauty—my own. Learned not to trust men also—isn't that sad?"

"I never thought about it that way but I think I understand. Men thought they had to look for that totally awesome looking woman. That's why Dianne surprised me. She was pretty—but never showed it off. She didn't want attention for her looks. The guys all liked her because she was cool and could out drink most of them. She was a fun party girl. But I never worried about her because I knew she only wanted to be with me."

"Then she really was a gift. A lot smarter than me. Maybe the New Society won't think that beauty is so important?" she offered with a sigh. "Do you think that such a place could exist?"

"It would be nice to believe so..."

I reached over to my worn out leather jacket and opened it up. I'd pinned my two purple hearts and bronze star inside for good luck on the trip. I took out one of the purple hearts and handed it to Rhonda.

"What's this for?" she asked.

"It's a purple heart. You know – for being wounded in battle. I think you've earned it," I said as I was looking at her scar.

Her eyes lit up like I'd just handed her the Hope Diamond. "Wow! That's really special. Really – really – special! I won't forget you JC," she remarked as she gave me a big hug and a long kiss.

We sat there for a while sharing a cigarette. I wasn't thinking about quitting the habit at this moment. This was one far out lady. She started to stroke the inside of my leg which immediately got my attention. "You think you got one more round in you? One for the road – so to speak." She didn't have to ask twice...

We woke up a while later when everyone was getting up and looking for the coffee. Rat had made a few pots and it went quickly. I dressed and came out to the kitchen to see everyone.

We said our sad goodbyes. There were plenty of tears around the group. We didn't think we'd ever see each other again – but nobody wanted to say that. So we just left it at "...til' we meet again..."

Duke was going to make sure Rhonda made it back safely to her place. What a babe! I knew I'd never forget her and the special gift she'd given me. Was at a loss of words for how to tell her just how special the night with her had been. All I could think to say was, "Thanks Rhonda – I'll never forget you." Didn't seem like enough to say. We gave each other one last big embrace. It was hard to let go. It might be the last time I'd ever get to hold a woman. The thought overwhelmed me...

"Come on you two. It's time to go," Duke said. "Glad to see you enjoyed my surprise JC." Rhonda stepped softly out the door.

I slapped Duke on the back as I exclaimed, "What can I say man but – INCREDIBLE! She is really something. Wish I could take her with me. Get her home safe. And thanks for the pardue—it was great bro. Just great."

"I'll be over in two nights to help get everything ready. Gladman knows the plan. He really enjoys the idea of stickin' it to the Guardians. See you then." Duke slipped out the back and disappeared up the street with Rhonda.

I sat there for a while trying to believe what a great pardue it had been. Now that everyone had said their goodbyes and given me their gifts there'd be no backing out. But that wasn't an option anyways. I was even more determined to make this happen. Seeing my friends had clinched the deal.

I kept thinking about how I was going to make one of the most important—and dangerous—journeys of my life alone. I guess that's just how it has to be sometimes...

CHAPTER 9

The Adventure Begins

W e got up before the sun to run the final pre-mission check of my equipment. I didn't sleep much thinking about all the possibilities to come. I was excited – and scared. Nothing about this was going to be easy – or safe. Thought by my age I'd be sitting on the front porch in a rocker looking over the hills of West Virginia yelling at the grandkids to leave the chickens alone. Who could have predicted I'd be leaving on a mission to find my freedom – or die in the attempt? Life can take some strange twists...

I closed my eyes and said a prayer I was up to the journey. I asked God for the strength to endure. Hadn't tried to talk with God in a long time but I hoped he was listening. After all that had happened in the world – wasn't sure anymore there was a God.

Gladman arrived early with his garbage truck ready for the trip across the Golden Gate Bridge to Route 1 and Stinson Beach. He'd built a decent compartment out of wood for the bike and a smaller one next to it for me to sit. Duke gave me a long look with his dark eyes. "Well – this is the point of no return bro. You ready to do this gunnie?"

"Come too far to go back now. I'm gonna make it. And I'll be waiting for your sorry ass. When you leaving?"

"In two weeks. Just tyin' up some loose ends before I split. Found out where the last Guardian I'm lookin' for is hidin' out. I'll have to get through a few of his bodyguards to get 'im. But his days are numbered. He knows I'm comin' so I'm lettin' him sweat it out for a while. I hear the head Guardians are bettin' the odds with me. Then I'm leavin' if Gladman is still in the transport business. Got my topo maps of Marin County and been plannin' my escape route. Crossin' the rivers will be a trick but I don't expect too many patrols where I'm goin'. You'll see me again little man – count on it!"

We loaded the bike first using the lid of the box as our ramp. Tied her down good. Then we closed it on the top. Gladman was going to make his regular run during the day to fill in garbage around the compartment.

"I had an idea after running Duke out and back," Gladman explained. "I hooked up an oxygen mask for you cause of the smell. The hospital is one of my pickups so I find an occasional canister. Also hooked up a simple connection for me to talk with you and let you know where we are. But it's only one way. Sure hope you're not claustrophobic cause you won't be able to get out easily once I fill up. Here's a crowbar to knock on the box to let me know you hear my messages. There's a water bottle and some jerky inside. I'd advise a good whiz before we leave—here's a bottle in case," he laughed. "This will take a while. You ready...?"

I turned to shake Duke's hand but he shook his head and said, "Not enough little man!" and he gave me one of his massive bear hugs. "You can do this—jarhead. Remember what I taught you and keep that .45 handy. You're smarter than them Guardian dudes and they don't know you're comin'. If you run into Blackie put a round in 'em for me. He's probably just some retarded draft evader who belonged in prison." We chuckled at that.

"I'll be thinking of you Duke We've had some great rides together. We'll get some more down the road. I know it - for sure. See you soon big man..." I just stood there for a while not knowing what more to say. It's hard to leave friends you may not see again.

After a good piss I crawled into the box and Gladman closed the lid. Took out my .45 and laid it and the shotgun next to me. I heard Gladman slam the door on the truck and then he tested out his mike. I could hear him fine so I wrapped the bar on the box. He started the truck and it was time to go. It was going to be a long day inside this small and smelly hooch.

Gladman began his rounds and started to fill the truck. He had to make sure the bike and me were covered completely. He also didn't want to show up too early at the checkpoints on the way to Stinson Beach. Fortunately — it was a cool day in the city as this would be even worse if it was hot or rainy. When the truck was full we started across the bridge. I thought it sadly ironic that on my last trip across the bridge I couldn't see it or the bay. But that wasn't important right now.

After the bridge we turned off the freeway onto Route 1 and started the long windy climb through Muir Woods. Even though I couldn't see anything I'd made the ride so many times I remembered most of it in my mind. Gladman would check in every once in a while to see if I was okay and give me a status update. He told me the Guardians kept a checkpoint at the top of the hill where the road flattens out. We wound our way through Muir Woods for a long while in that slow and noisy truck.

It was mid-afternoon when we reached the checkpoint on top. I could hear a little of the conversation between Gladman and the Guardians when we stopped. It seemed like they all knew him and didn't stop to chat for long. Apparently – the last thing they suspected was an armed biker in the back waiting to open fire if anything went wrong. Gladman's message came over, "Everything is clear. Starting the downhill to Stinson. There might be other trucks when we arrive so I have to be careful. I'll pull way over to the back of the dump and get you out first. Usually there aren't any Guardians hanging around but I'll have to be sure." My bladder sure hoped he was right. The truck was too bumpy to use the bottle.

I felt us level off and turn toward the ocean. The dump was where the old state beach used to be. Soon I could tell we were off the paved road as it bounced me around pretty good. Gladman finally shut off the engine and got on the mike. "We're lucky – it looks clear. I'll start to dig you out. I can't dump the truck because it might hurt you and the bike."

I could hear him digging around for what seemed like an eternity but he was getting closer. Finally – the box opened – and none too soon. I jumped clear of the truck – took a quick look around – then took the longest whiz I can ever remember. What a feeling of relief. Old men and their prostates.

We sat down on the ocean side of the truck and Gladman offered me a cigarette. "I'm trying to quit you know," I responded to his gesture.

"This may not be the time or place for that ambition," he

replied as he lit one for me. Oh well—when in Rome...

If felt so good to breathe the ocean air and listen to the waves and seagulls. Gladman handed me a flask and said, "Take a short belt and relax. We're gonna be here for a while. We can't get the bike off until dark. Here—I have some pb and j sandwiches. I washed my hands 'fore I made them in case you're wondering." He got me to laugh at that.

I sat there in awe of the view. I was finally out of the city—with it's darkness and death smell. This was my first taste of freedom since the Regional Wars. It was exhilarating! The ocean and beach was just plain fantastic.

There was another dump truck pulling in to unload. "I'll put the hood up on the truck like I'm cooling off the engine," Gladman said. "I'll go over and talk with the other driver to keep him away from here. The Guardians offer a reward for anyone who turns in someone trying to escape. So let's not give them any temptation. Stay close to your shotgun. Kick back for a while. We'll unload the bike later when everyone is gone. Then I'll help you get started. I'll keep an ear out for their patrols. It's easy to hear those Guardian bikes when they pass through town."

"Won't the Guardians be expecting you back today?"

"Nuh. They know I sometimes spend the night so that won't be a problem. I have some friends here in town. I'll visit them later to see what they know and if there are any Guardians around. Guardians don't normally stay in town cause the dump smells so bad. But we want to be sure before we fire your bike up. I'll be back..." and he strolled off with his double barrel shotgun over his shoulder.

I sat there leaned up against the truck not believing I'd actually made it this far. Seeing the ocean was a good omen I might get to do this adventure. It was late in the afternoon and would be a few hours before dark. Finished the sandwiches while I just enjoyed the view. After a while I crawled under the truck where I could keep an eye on the dump and take a quick nap. It was going to be a long night but I was ready for whatever was to come. Was hoping I'd see sunrise the next day. I needed to get up the coast a ways tonight—past the marsh lands into the woods before I hid out. One step at a time…

It was getting close to dark when Gladman finally came back to the truck. I was beginning to worry about him but should have known better. "Let's get the rest of the garbage off the truck so we can unload the bike," he said. "Here's some gloves to use." It took a while to unload the truck — a dirty job. But we got it done as the sun disappeared. We uncovered the bike and backed it slowly down the ramp.

Gladman suggested, "Let's push it to the corner of the dump and get you ready. There don't seem to be any Guardians around town. You probably heard that patrol a while ago heading south so we should wait until they come back through town again. How 'bout you check out your equipment and give the hog a test run around the dump so we know it will start."

I checked everything over — made sure the .45 had a round in the chamber and the thumb safety off. I tried starting the bike several times with the electric but the battery was getting low. So I tried to kick start her. She fired up on the third kick and I let it idle for a while. It sounded great to hear the Super Glide running again — even with stock mufflers it was still music to my ears. I took a short test run around the dump to check out the gears. Didn't get past third since I couldn't see much in the dark but she was running fine. I was excited and anxious to get on the road.

"Let's push it closer to the main road and behind one of the empty stores," Gladman recommended. "Then we'll wait for the next patrol. The clouds are drifting in and out but it's close to a full moon so you'll have some visibility. How far you gonna try for tonight?"

"It turns inland and gets pretty wooded once you pass the marsh lands. But that's about five miles or so of open riding on the water. There might be a guard post in Olema so I want to get into the woods before town. I'll recon during the day. Getting past the bay and the marshes will be dangerous cause it's exposed — nowhere to go if I run into anyone. Everything looks different at night so I'm trusting my memory I'll know when I'm close to Olema."

We got the bike close to Route 1 and parked behind an old

store. "Now we just sit and wait..." Gladman whispered.

Gladman offered me another cigarette while we talked in the dark. He was keeping his shotgun handy. I asked him why he thought all this stuff with the Concern had happened. He thought for some time before he answered, "You know JC — we became this disposable society. People would rather throw things away than fix 'em. Sure kept me in business all these years. People threw away good stuff that still worked. You know — TVs — stereos — appliances — everything. The dumps were always busy. Didn't have to buy anything major in the last decade 'cause I could find it all in the dump. Used to give a lot away to friends. Been driving garbage truck for over thirty years now — what a job huh? Don't think that's a job that will ever go away — and you can't send it overseas." He had a point.

He took a long drag on his smoke and continued, "I guess we became too interested in stuff — instead of each other. Maybe that was their plan from the beginning? Keep us busy working trying to buy more stuff. Didn't follow politics much. Hadn't voted in a long time but guess that didn't matter much now if it was all rigged by the Concern — like they said. I don't think anyone as unimportant as me coulda' made a difference anyways. I was just doin' my job gettin' rid of everyone's garbage and trying to survive. You think that's what it's all about JC — just trying to survive?"

"Would like to think there was more to it than that but I was doing the same. Just getting by one day at a time. Nothing came to mean much anymore except riding with the boys and getting high. Getting laid was nice when it happened but nothing ever lasted long - except for my wife Dianne. You ever get married?"

"Once — a long time ago. She left me for someone who did-n't smell so bad. Never had any kids. My younger sister Barbie was my only family. That's why I'm helping you — to get back at them for what they did to her. Duke will settle that score for me but it won't replace her. She was an angel. I really miss her." He took a long drink of water. "So why you takin' all this risk if you don't believe in anything?"

"That's a good question Gladman. Sure been thinking 'bout it a lot. After Nam I didn't believe in much except my biker buddies and some would let me down at times. Usually over drugs or a woman. I guess that's why Duke is such a good friend. Even with his rough ways I could trust him. Turns out I was right about him all this time."

I thought about it some more. "I guess I want to find out if I missed something important along the way. Maybe freedom does mean something and is worth dying for? I figured this was a better way to go than being a slave for the Guardians. Expect I'll find out soon enough. Maybe this is just the way old Marines should die—in a blaze of glory. I don't plan on going peacefully."

We sat there talking into the night. I was getting anxious to get moving but Gladman kept telling me to wait. We finally heard the next patrol coming up from the south. He was right—you could hear 'em coming from a ways off. Those turbos have their own crazy sound. There were two of them and they were cruising right along. We waited until they passed and then got the bike ready to go. "Let's give them at least twenty minutes in case they decide to stop for a smoke break," I said as I bummed one last butt from Gladman. I was going to need the nicotine to stay alert—or so I told myself.

It seemed like an eternity before we started the bike but I was timing the patrol with my new pocket watch. The bike was stubborn again but finally fired. I let her warm up. My heart was racing. Gladman gave me a big shake with his stubby hands. "My best to you JC. If there's a God I hope he travels with you. I'll tell Duke you got off okay."

"Thanks for everything. Couldn't have gotten this far without you. Take care Gladman…" You know—I never did find out his real name.

I turned onto the coast road and started north. The partial moon passed in and out between the clouds. It was cool along the ocean but it woke up my senses. Good thing I had my good luck long underwear on from Tweeter—even with the stains. I had that queasy feeling that always came over me when we started on patrol in Nam but I knew it would pass as I focused on the mission. The bike was running good and went through the gears without problem. I briefly tested the brakes and everything seemed okay. Quickly reached the ocean and knew

I'd be following it for several miles. My eyes searched into the darkness. I saw nothing except the road outlined between the ocean and the bushes on the right.

I watched the mileage closely as it seemed like the marshes would never end. After some time I estimated I should be getting close to where the road turns into the woods. Just then I saw a reflection of light on the bay coming the other way. Just a quick glimmer. "What the fuck!" I exclaimed out loud.

It only took a second to register—someone was coming the other way! I couldn't wait to find out who or what. Started looking for a place to ditch on the right side of the road. I couldn't see too far in the haze. When I scoped what looked like some bushes off the shoulder I slowed down long enough to head for the dirt. I was going too fast as I hit the berm and the bike started to slide in the sand. There seemed to be a small open spot behind some bushes so I headed there in a skid and tried to tuck in behind them. I killed the motor while putting the kickstand down and pulled out the .45. Was this journey going to end so soon?

Waited for a few seconds and then I heard their bikes. Had the Guardians seen my light and turned around? Or was it an unscheduled patrol? No matter—it was all going to happen very quickly if I had to fight it out. My .45 against their autos. Duke was right—first shot counts. I was off the bike and kneeling to bring aim. I drew a bead on the lead Guardian as they came out of the mist. Figured if I hit him the other might run into him.

They were moving fast like maybe they hadn't seen me. Hopefully the dust cloud from where I slid off the road was lost in the haze. Kept them in my sights as they approached. When they passed by without looking my way I started breathing again. I waited in silence to see if they were going to turn around. Maybe they were too busy following the road and never saw me? I listened carefully as their motors echoed off into the distance. Damn—that was way too fuckin' close for my first hour out...!

As I stood there in the dark waiting in case they returned I recognized an old familiar taste in my mouth. It was something

I'd experienced in combat — like sucking on nickels. Someone told me once it was the adrenaline pumping in your body. Mine was definitely working full bore. When I figured they weren't coming back I took a quick piss and headed for the woods and Olema. It was time to find shelter for the night.

In a few miles I left the ocean and was in the woods. There were large Eucalyptus trees that were easy to smell. I was nearing Olema now and needed a place to get off the road and hide out. There used to be ranches in this area so I was searching for a dirt road I could take into the woods. The road suddenly left the big trees and I knew I was getting real close to Olema — too close if there was a guard post.

Before I knew it there was the sign for town. Shit! This was far too close to Olema for comfort. I did a quick stop — a U-turn — and headed back down the road. Sure hoped no one heard me. I would know soon enough...

In about half a mile I saw a turnout on the left with an old broken gate and slowed down to check it out. The dirt road headed up into the woods so I took it. I'd had enough of the Guardians for this day.

I followed the worn road into the trees and went far enough to be out of sight from the coast road. Tomorrow would be the time to figure out my next move — right now I just wanted shelter. Found a flat spot and pulled under some trees where I killed the bike. Grabbed the shotgun and listened for some time in the dark to see if anyone had followed me back from town. Lucky for me — silence.

This would have to do for the night. It didn't feel like rain and I was exhausted so I just laid out the tent and threw my sleeping bag on top. Had a shot of brandy from the flask and then crawled into the bag. I laid there for a while watching the stars come and go between the clouds. The cool ocean air felt great. It'd been a really long day but I was still alive — and on the road again...

CHAPTER 10

Jake and his Shotgun

My sleep was broken by a dream about a shootout with the Guardians but I woke before it ended. Sure wanted to know how that came out. I lay there in the mist for a while trying to remember where I was. It was very quiet in the woods. Eventually — I went back to sleep.

I slept until dawn but awoke when I had the uncomfortable feeling I wasn't alone. I rolled over in my bag as I reached for the .45. Then I heard a growl that made my breath stick in my throat. "Better sit still or I'll let the dog rearrange your face!"

I slowly turned to see a nasty looking black German Shepard just inches away with a set of fangs that meant serious business. Behind him was an old man with a double barrel pointed right at me. Even if he was half blind he wasn't going to miss at this range. I wouldn't even have time to get the gun out of the holster. Shit — this wasn't a good start to the day!

"What's up old man?" My heart was racing but I was trying to appear calm. Hoping I was a good actor as I didn't have many options at this point.

The old man studied me for a while as the dog kept his attack position. "You don't look like one of them Guardians. Particularly on an old hog like that. What you doin' on my property?"

I thought he'd never ask. I figured this was no time for bullshitting so I told him straight out. "I'm on my way up the coast to join the New Society." I was hoping he wasn't looking to collect a bounty for turning me into the Guardians.

He checked me out closely as I sat up in the bag and then he told the dog to back off. That was a good sign. "Get out of the bag — slowly," he ordered. I stood up with my hands in the air so he wouldn't think I was going for the .45. He gave me a long once over.

"I see by your emblem you were in the Marines. That the

case?"

"Yup—'68 to '71. Third Marines."

"See any action?" he asked as he kept the shotgun pointed at my gut.

"Vietnam—eleven months."

"Didn't make the full tour huh? Purple heart or dishonorable discharge?" The old coot knew his shit about the war. I pulled open my jacket and showed him the medals that were fastened to the inside. He stared for a time and then lowered the gun. "I'm Jake. I was with the First Marines at Chosin Reservoir."

Any Marine worth his salt knew about the Frozen Chosen in Korea. Not very many Marines walked out of that one—and here was one standing in front of me. He had to be in his late 70's at least. "It's a privilege," I said as I extended my hand. He shook my hand. For an old timer he still had a hell of a handshake. "My name's JC."

"The dog must have heard you come in last night as he's been wanting to get out all morning. You're lucky I came with him."

"Yeah—no shit!"

Jake gave a quick look around and then motioned toward the bike. "Let's get you up to the house. I haven't heard any Guardians in a while so fire it up and follow me through the woods. I have an ATV just over the hill." With that remark he slung the shotgun over his shoulder and headed into the woods. I started the bike and followed. When we reached the ATV he fired it up and we continued farther into the woods. It was pretty cross country for the Harley but I stayed with him.

After the woods opened into a valley I saw an old ranch house in a grove of trees next to a pond. Some cows and pigs were in a corral next to a small barn with a few chickens running around. After we reached the house Jake directed me to park the bike in the barn. Jake explained, "I blocked off the main road in here after the Guardians took over and filled it full of potholes. I was trying to make it hard for them to get back here with their bikes. So far they haven't tried—that I know. But I'm always on the lookout. The dog's got good ears—not like mine."

"It wasn't easy following you through the woods. The old

girl wasn't meant to be an off roader," I kidded with him.

"A good Marine can overcome any obstacle," he quickly responded back. He pointed around the homestead as he continued, "I bought this place after the war and been ranchin' here all these years. Not much left now but enough to get by. My wife died about four years ago. Glad she isn't around to see all this change and devastation. She was a gentle woman who liked the quiet life here on the ranch."

"How far we from Olema Jake?"

"'Bout one mile—as the crow flies. You're lucky you stopped when you did or you might've had a big surprise. The Guardians use the old campground in Olema for a junkyard and sometimes they hang out there. No one is left in town but there are some survivors still living on the ranches around here. The Guardians took most of the cattle and killed anyone who resisted. I'm not sure they even know I have a place back here. Like to keep it that way." I wasn't going to tell him I'd almost run right into town last night by mistake. Not a confession I wanted to make to the old Marine.

As we walked toward the house he stopped and yelled out, "It's okay Amber—we have a guest." The door to the house opened and a teenage girl stepped out with a rifle at the ready. "This here's JC and he's going to bunk with us tonight." The girl checked me out before she reached out and shook my hand.

"If Grandpa says you're okay—I trust his judgment. We don't see many strangers around here since the wars. Surprised old Fang didn't chew you up the way he was carrying on this morning. He likes fresh meat."

Jake and Amber laughed as we stepped onto the porch. Guess they both had a good sense of humor in spite of everything. It was good to be with such friendly company on my first day out. We sat down on the porch to get to know each other.

"You got any store bought cigarettes on you?" Jake asked. "It's sure been a while. I'll trade for a snort of my homemade shine. It's not too bad if I do say so myself."

"Sounds like a deal to me." I didn't mention I was trying to quit as I gave him one of my cigarettes. I took a snort from his jug and he was right—it was as good as anything I'd ever tasted back in the hills. "Wow — that's some special shine. You sure know your way 'round a still gunny." He gave me a big smile like he hadn't been called that in a long time. He enjoyed the cigarette as though it was a ten dollar cigar.

We kicked back on the porch while he told me their story. "My son and daughter-in-law tried to make one last trip into the City after the Regional Wars started to bring out some friends. They never returned. I still don't know if they're alive or not. I keep praying but I'm losing hope of ever seeing them again. Amber stayed here with me so it's just been the two of us since then. She's a great kid. Keeps a close watch on her grandpa." He gazed at Amber and smiled.

"I taught her how to shoot and we get by with what animals and canned goods we have left. Have a small garden out back. I worry about the Guardians finding us here." I saw a tear form in his eye as he looked away from the girl. We sat quiet for a bit enjoying the buzz from the hooch before he started again.

"There were some supplies left in the hotel and restaurants in Olema that we raided before the Guardians took them all. Now we just get by with what we have. Not much of a future for the girl. I've had my life but hers has a long way to go. I thought about trying to get to the north but don't think we could make it. Too many places where they could catch us — like Jenner. Don't know how we would cross the river either. It all seems pretty desperate at times." He looked over at me as he handed me the jug again. "So — what's your story JC? I have to tell you how good it is to see a friendly face in these hard times."

I told him what things were like in the city with all the death and destruction. Both of them thought it was pretty funny how I'd gotten across the bridge in a garbage truck. "So there's not much hope it will change anytime soon?" he asked.

"No — not in the City anyways. I think the whole world went crazy from what we heard before the TV and everything went out. I've been listening to radio broadcasts from the New Society which is why I decided to make this journey. Don't know what they'll be like but it couldn't be no worse than the Guardians. I figured I'd make the attempt even if it meant my life. I'm beginning to understand what freedom really means now."

"I only heard a little about the New Society before it all went dead," Jake responded, "But I think you're right. It has to be better than the Guardians. Maybe they still believe in family and the old values. All those things we lost way back. Everyone seemed to lose touch with the importance of family in the fast pace of life. That's why Magdalene and I stayed here on the ranch—where we could love each other and remain connected to the land. But I couldn't get my son and his family to give up the bright lights of the city. It seemed like they worked hard to buy more possessions but just kept getting further in debt. I guess that's what the Concern wanted all along. You think the stories about the Concern were true?"

"They might be," I answered. "It all happened so fast. Hard to believe such a powerful organization could have existed without people knowing. But then—if everyone was like me—we didn't care as long as we took care of ourselves. After Nam I was really burnt out and just thought about myself and my pleasures. That's why the biker lifestyle worked for me. I never felt like I really had any say in what the government did anyways so I just stopped paying attention. Maybe we all did."

"Yup," Jake nodded his head. "We felt like nothing we could do would ever make a difference in how the country was being run. So we just worked the ranch and watched it all pass by. I was disillusioned after Korea so I know how you felt. Some say it was one of the first wars the Concern backed to stop Communism but for economic reasons. Telling us we were fighting for democracy was how they got us to offer up our lives to their cause. They didn't seem to care much about us once we returned. Veterans have always been expendable!" I recognized that familiar anger of his.

I was feeling mellow from Jake's shine and enjoyed sitting on the porch listening to the wind in the trees. The smell of the ranch animals was one I hadn't experienced in some time. I was feeling alive again. "What can I do for you while I'm here?" I inquired.

"We'll talk more about that later. You're welcome to stay here and help us work the ranch you know. I could use the help." But I knew what he really meant as he looked over at Amber sitting on the steps playing with Fang.

"That's quite the offer for somebody you just met but I have to finish this journey now that I've started. I could use any recon intelligence you have about the Guardians and how I can get around Olema."

"I have some info about that to share with you but you must be hungry. How 'bout you help me in the barn while Amber fixes some breakfast. When was the last time you had ham and eggs with biscuits?" He must have seen my eyes light up at that.

"I have some canned peaches in my pack – a small payment for the hospitality." We got up and started toward the barn while Amber went into the house. It was going to be a good day with my new friends.

After we were in the barn Jake looked back to make sure Amber was still in the house. "I didn't want Amber to hear us. You're going to need help to get around Olema and I know how to do it but I want your help in return."

"What do you need?"

"This isn't any kind of life for the girl and I don't know how long my health will hold out. I want to get her out of here. I'll help you if you take her with you." He had a very sad and concerned look in his eyes.

I thought a while before answering. "Jake – I wish I could help. But my chances of making it are just fifty-fifty – if that. The Guardians have me out manned and out gunned. And I don't know where they are – I'm just guessing. The only thing I've got going for me is that they don't know I'm here yet." That sure was a hard thing to tell him. "Do you understand?"

He sat on a hay bale and looked at the ground. He was thinking hard. "I know you're right," then he paused. "But will you make me a promise? If you make it to the north and the New Society will you try to figure out a way to come back and rescue her?"

"If I get there in one piece – and there's a way back – I'll come back. Make you that promise." I reached out and shook his hand. It was a contract between Marines.

"My friend Duke is gonna try and hike to the north soon. Maybe together we can figure out a way back. Then you best keep your fingers crossed for me to make it."

"I'll pray for you JC. Real hard…" I hadn't had anyone offer to pray for me in a long time. Not something people typically did for a crusty old biker.

Jake showed me around the ranch and then we headed for the house. I could smell the biscuits cooking as we stepped onto the porch. And wow — real eggs! This was going to be better than crab on the wharf.

As we ate the wonderful breakfast Amber had cooked Jake talked about our plans for the day. "Before we get started on chores I have a big favor to ask but it will dangerous," he told me. "I'm low on gas around the ranch and there's some in those old cars in the junkyard. They don't normally have a checkpoint in town but sometimes hang out around the campground. Can you help me get down there and siphon some fuel?" He was right — that would be dangerous if the Guardians liked to hang out there.

"What's your plan?" I asked. "You know the area."

"Been thinkin' about it. We'll take the ATV a couple of hours before sunset to an overlook where we can observe the town. If that's clear we'll move further north across a paved side road from Olema to where we can see a little of the junkyard. We'll reconnoiter from the woods a bit before we go down into the junkyard to find the gas. I'm real low on fuel to run my machines but I haven't been anxious to try it on my own. Don't want to run into those automatics with just my shotgun."

It was a brave plan. The Guardians could be back inside the junkyard and hear us coming. But I wanted to help out this old Marine and his granddaughter. They were being pretty generous to me — someone they had just met. I felt I could take the time — and the risk — to help them out. "Okay Jake. You can count me in. But if it don't look safe we can't go in," I cautioned. He shook my hand and nodded to Amber. By the look on her face she didn't seem to happy about her granddad going on such a risky mission. But she didn't say anything. Guess she had learned that once he set his mind on something he didn't change it easily. I liked his spunk.

"Between me and a young Marine like you — we can pull off this mission." I didn't know about the young Marine part but the old man definitely had the necessary courage. We would set his plan in motion.

It was a great meal and we had some laughs telling stories about the Corp. Jake had a lot to be proud of in his life and I told him that. The girl was a real teenage charmer with a quick wit — probably from hanging out with the ole man. It was obvious she was close to her granddad and I understood why he wanted her out of this mess. Sure wished I could take her with me but I had to stay focused on getting to the New Society myself first. Hopefully in one piece.

"Do you plan on leaving after we raid the junkyard or waiting until tomorrow night?" Jake asked.

"I already thought about that. If it's okay with you I'll stick around another day and help out with chores. Then I'll take off tomorrow night. Right after the first patrol goes through. I want to use this full moon while it lasts." I looked over at the girl. "After all — how could I pass up such great cooking?" She grinned back at me. We were enjoying each others company. Made me feel good I was able to bring a little sunshine into these good folk's dangerous lives.

"Hey Grandpa — let's have some beans and ham tonight — maybe some cornbread. How's that sound JC?" Amber chimed in.

"Like back home in the hills on a Saturday night," I answered.

"Then help me cut some wood for the oven," Jake suggested. "I rigged up this old wood burner stove cause the propane is so precious. Maybe you can also help me fix some things around the farm I been puttin' off. Then we'll get some rest before supper." Jake sounded pretty excited to have a new friend in town to help with his ranch.

"I'm pretty good at mechanical things if you have anything that needs attending," I offered.

"You bet I do!" He put his arm around my shoulder as we went outside — just like my dad used to do when I was a kid. I was starting to feel what I had missed by not staying back home after the war. It would be fun helping Jake and Amber by putting my fix-it talents to work. And I sure couldn't complain about the cooking.

Jake threw me an axe and we started for the woodpile. As I swung the axe it was like being back in the hills and breaking a good sweat. Working around a farm brought back fond memories of my youth. Tried to forget for a while we had a dangerous mission ahead this night. It would be very important I get Jake back home safely to Amber. She would be counting on me...

CHAPTER 11

Valley Recon

After supper we caught forty winks and then got ready for our patrol. Jake had his combat face paint on. He must have been one tough jarhead in his day. Had his shotgun all ready for the mission. "Can't see much past close range after dark so the shotgun works best for me. Good thing I got a young whipper snapper like you to work point. You ready?"

"Let's get some!" I responded as I put on the last of my leathers and ABATE ball cap to keep my head warm. Started up the ATV and let it warm up for a minute. Seemed like Jake kept it in pretty good shape and it was a good size unit. We'd strapped a siphon pump setup to the back along with his jerry cans.

Jake told me to take the controls of the ATV as he crawled on the back. "Take it slow," he asked over the idle. "These bones don't like this much anymore. Head back up the road to the fork and then go right." Fang came along and kept up front — like he knew where we were going.

I kept it slow as we headed out of the valley. Jake leaned against me for protection from the chill. We didn't talk much — just concentrated on the road. When we reached our first observation point there was about an hour of daylight left — according to my sturdy watch.

"We can look over the town from the ridge over yonder. Bring your binoculars — we'll hike it to the top." Jake said as he was off and moving. We made the short way up a grassy knoll and sat down where we could see some of the town and Route 1. "Let's check for activity on the road. The hotel you can see was burned out shortly after the wars started. I cleaned out the general store real good 'fore it got too dangerous to go out. We can't see the campground yet. We'll need to go to a spot much closer to town when we leave here to observe it."

We took turns studying the town through the binocs.

Everything looked quiet. In about half an hour Fang got restless — then we heard a patrol coming in from the north. We laid down and waited for them to come through town. They slowed down and stopped at the general store. We laid still and watched. They were stopping for a smoke break. I studied their bikes as best I could through the binocs. Some kind of flashy rice grinders. Looked fast. And definitely automatics — seemed like M16s just as Duke had reported. The boys were looking a wee bit scroungy for soldiers. But then I wasn't exactly sporting my combat fatigues either.

"Good news that they stopped there for their break," Jake whispered.

"Why's that?"

"They didn't stop at the old campground where the junkyard is. That probably means nobody is there or they would have stopped there." Jake was a smart cookie.

As soon as they took off south we headed back to the ATV to make for the next destination. "We have to cross the paved road that runs east from Olema to get across from the junkyard. Our chances look good now. Put the pedal to the metal JC," he barked as he got on behind and grabbed on tight to me. Fang took off up the road and I followed him. It was good to have his keen ears along on this patrol.

We came out of the woods and headed through a clearing to get across the paved road. We crossed the pavement and started uphill over a meadow for the woods. Before long we were back in the woods on an old foot trail. Not too far north of the town we turned west and went down a hillside. "Stop at the edge of the woods before you head for Route 1. We'll watch the junkyard until it gets dark," Jake ordered.

When I reached the next clearing on the downhill side I stopped just short. We shut off the engine — got off — and observed the dump for a while. "Man," I said. "I remember that campground. We stayed there once on a run up north and got thrown out for being so rowdy. We had to pack up in the middle of the night and head north in the fog. It took a while to find a spot to crash where we could spend the night. We were all soaked, drunk, and grouchy. Those SOBs..."

"Yeah—it was a strange couple who ran that campground for years. Didn't like you biker folk none!" Jake chuckled quietly to himself. "Maybe you guys were the reason why...?"

"Probably didn't help their attitude about bikers any," I replied.

Everything was quiet except for the crickets that were starting to sing. "Let's go now," Jake spoke quietly as he got his shotgun ready. "Keep a close watch out. There could still be some Guardians at the dump. We'll park at the main building first and take a short walk around." He was pointing where he wanted me to go.

We got back on and fired it up. Then we made a beeline across the open field for the other side of Route 1 and parked on the backside of the first building. At the campground after killing the engine we dismounted and peered into the darkness. Luckily there was little cloud or fog yet and the moon was glowing strong. We circled the building to the front where we could see most of the dump. Quite a collection of junk cars and trucks.

Jake backed up to the building. "You walk the first ring of cars and see if you smell anyone. I'll keep watch here on the entrance."

"Roger."

My eyes adjusted to the darkness as I slowly walked the first campground road. It appeared quiet. When I came back to Jake I told him to wait while I brought the ATV around with the siphoning equipment. He'd brought three cans we wanted to try and fill. "Let's head to the back of the dump. Might be a better chance of still finding some gas," he told me.

We jumped on the ATV and headed for the back end of the campground. When we got off Jake pointed to some cars. "You try those while I look around to see if there're any propane tanks." He lit up his flashlight—handed me one—then went off into the darkness. After checking several cars I found an old Chevy that had some promise. I inserted the hose and started to work the hand pump. Jake's siphon setup worked real slick. I heard gas running into the jerry can. Didn't know if it was good gas—but it was gas. Eureka!

I was busy on the second jerry when Jake came back down the

road. "I hit pay dirt," he said. "Found a pile of propane tanks and a couple of 'em might have some gas left. Got tired before I could lift too many. Let's hit it on the way out. How you comin'?"

"It's slow but I got the second can almost filled. I'll have to try another car for the third one."

Jake checked his watch. "We can't dally too long. Been almost two hours since that last patrol. I'll go lookin' for another car," he spoke back to me as he disappeared down the row.

"Don't light a match to check the level," I told him thinking I was being clever.

"Up yours—you fuckin' gyrene," Jake muttered in the dark. In a few minutes he returned. "I think I might of found a donor."

"Good—this car's about done. Two cans so far."

I moved the ATV and worked on the next car Jake had found. It had some gas and we slowly finished up the third can. "Show me those propane tanks and then we'll hit it." I made sure the cans were secure and we moved out.

We wound around the campground until Jake put his flashlight on the pile. We only had room for two so I checked several to feel their weight. We loaded up the two best and strapped them on.

We were just ready to mount up when Jake saw a flash next to one of the old bathhouses! We froze in our tracks and turned out our lights. Fang started to growl but Jake silenced him. "Quiet mutt..." The dog went quiet and glared intently into the dark.

In a few seconds we saw someone moving around the bathhouse. I heard Jake cock the shotgun—both barrels. We hadn't heard any bikes so we just kept watching. The figure started our way. I don't think he saw us. I had my shotgun following him as he came closer. It looked like he had a handgun—I couldn't tell in the dark. As he got closer Jake reached out and put his hand on my arm. He wanted me to back off. I trusted him.

"Isaac—is that you?" Jake called out. The figure froze. He shown his light our way and stared into the darkness. He saw two figures with shotguns pointed in his direction but he didn't raise his gun.

"Jake? Jake?" he answered back as he studied us with his flashlight.

We slowly approached until the two old timers recognized each other. Jake lowered his shotgun and the two embraced with plenty of back slapping. "JC—this is a good friend of mine—Isaac. He lives on top of the mountain in an old cabin."

"What you mean old cabin? It's my palace," he kidded back.

"Yeah—so you say. What the hell you doin' down here? We almost cut you in two."

"I'm after some gas for my generator. I'm about out."

"How'd you get here? We never heard you come in," Jake asked.

"I have that old electric golf cart I salvaged years ago. Used my solar panel to charge the battery. I'm parked over behind one of the bathhouses." He pointed his light back to the north edge of the campground. "I just got this one jerry can. Can we fill it quick?"

"Well—I don't know about quick but we'll help you out. What you think JC?"

"Whatever you say gunny but we need to hurry. We been here a while now," I answered checking my watch again. "You bring the ATV and I'll look for another car that might have some gas. Get your cart over here Isaac."

We headed back for the cars and started looking for another tank of gas. I went through several before I found a possible candidate. Isaac was back with his cart and I started the siphon. The moon was coming and going between the clouds that were moving in. It was getting chilly. Jake had to be feeling it in his bones but he never let on. He was determined to finish the mission. Sturdy ole coot...

While I pumped the two of them were catching up on old times. Guess they hadn't seen each other in a while. Sounded like two old chums swapping school yard tales. I finally finished filling his can. It was time to scoot. We strapped it on his cart and got ready to exit. Jake told Isaac to follow us back up the hill once we crossed the road. That old cart didn't move too fast as we made our way out of the dump.

As we were almost out of the campground we heard that horrible sound—a Guardian patrol coming from the south was running early. Damn—this wasn't good! "Let's duck behind the front building until they pass," I ordered. "Take Fang with you and keep him quiet."

We made a path for the building and parked as close we could while killing the engine. I moved to one corner and Jake and Isaac headed for the other. We waited and listened. The patrol was slowing down as they pulled off the road in front of the campground. I hoped this wasn't going to be the gunfight at the OK Corral. We had the drop on 'em but then there'd be the question of two missing Guardians in the area where Jake lived. Might not be the best for them when the Guardians came looking. I'd promised Amber to get her grandpa back in one piece and I intended to keep my word.

They only pulled in a little way but close enough to hear them talking. They were within shotgun range and I had a bead on 'em. If they figured out we were here it would be a question of who got the first shots in. I knew Jake was ready. My finger was on the trigger as I waited and listened.

"I can't believe you have to piss again," one of the Guardians complained. "Told you not to have those brews before we left. If Blackie ever catches you drinking on patrol he'll cut off your nuts with a rusty blade."

"Fuck you. I've seen him take a few shots himself before patrol." I was close enough to hear him pissing — like a cow on a flat rock.

"But that's Blackie — not you. I don't like having you half soused when we're out. What if we ran into trouble. What good would you be?"

"Up yours — you pussy. We run these patrols every night in the cold and never see anyone. It's gettin' old."

So I guess job satisfaction is a problem anywhere you go...

"Keep this up and I'll ask for someone else to run with. I'm real tired of your shit." Neither one of them had any idea how close they were to this being their last piss. I was ready to blast them if I needed but had to think about Jake. So I stayed frozen with the shotgun ready.

"Come on — let's get movin'. I wanna get to Jenner so we can have a shot and sack out." I guess that answered my question. There was a command post at Jenner just like we thought.

Sounded like a major hangout for the Guardians.

They finally saddled up and headed out. That was too fuckin' close!

"I thought I was gonna have to separate them in the middle for a while there," Jake boasted as he came around the building and un-cocked his hammers.

"Sorry gunny—but it wasn't part of the mission. Let's head out."

We mounted up again and darted across the road back for the woods. The golf cart had a hard time with the hill and I thought Isaac might not make it. I knew Jake was getting tired because he was hanging on as best he could. When we hit the spot where Isaac was going to head up the mountain we stopped for a minute.

"Why don't you come back to the ranch for the night and share some company?" Jake offered to Isaac.

"I could really use that. Haven't seen anyone in a while. How 'bout I leave the cart here in the woods and ride back with you two. Might make better time."

We hid the cart and our fuel in the woods. Somehow we found a spot on top of the ATV for Isaac to hang onto and we headed for the ranch. What a sight we must have been. It seemed like forever on that bumpy road in the dark but we finally reached the ridge and made our way down to the house. Amber was outside waiting with her rifle. Fang started barking when he saw her like he too was glad to be back from the patrol.

"Grandpa! Grandpa! I was so worried about you," Amber yelled out.

Jake was pretty stiff and tired so we helped him into the house. The fatigue was showing on his face. "Let's get him warm. Where's the shine? He could use a short shot," I told Amber.

We covered him up with a blanket while Amber poured shots for all of us. "You think I could bother you for one of those cigarettes JC?" Jake requested. We lit up and sat there in the kitchen enjoying the fact we were back home safe. Isaac seemed to be very content to have some people around. In the light I saw he wasn't no spring chicken either.

"You did real good Jake. Just like a Marine. I was proud of you.

I'd go on patrol with you anytime." I patted him on the back.

"You too JC. What a Godsend to have you here."

Godsend? Hadn't ever been called a Godsend before! A lot of things—never a Godsend. These were really good country folk. The down home kind I hadn't been with in a long time. In just this short time I felt very close to these people. Wished I could do more for them but knew I'd have to be leaving tomorrow. A difficult choice either way.

"Amber—get your grandpa off to bed. He was quite the warrior tonight. See if you can find a spot for Isaac too. They're both pretty pooped. I'll make do on the sofa."

I went out on the porch while Amber got Jake and Isaac off to bed. Sat down on the swing and watched the stars come and go through the clouds. Hadn't felt this good about helping someone in a long time. Maybe this is what I'd missed all these years by never returning to the hills. Guess I'd never know. But it felt rewarding to help these kindhearted people.

After some time to unwind I went back into the house and got the sofa ready. Amber had left me several blankets and a pillow. She crept quietly out of her room and gave me a big hug. "Thank you so much for helping grandpa today and bringing him home safe to me. I worry about him all the time. He's not feeling too good but he tries not to show it. I know he wants you to stay but you have to do your journey. Maybe it's your destiny? We will pray for you. Grandpa and Isaac will be good for each other. We'll get by for now." She stood up on her toes and whispered in my ear, "I'll fix a good breakfast for everyone in the morning. You really liked those fresh eggs. I'll cook you three tomorrow." Then she gave me a short kiss on the cheek before heading back to her room. That girl definitely deserved a better shot at life than what she was facing now.

Destiny? What a big thought for a tired biker who still had a long ways to go. As I stretched out on the comfortable sofa I thought sleep would come easily tonight...

CHAPTER 12

A Day from the Past

I woke up to the smell of biscuits cooking in the kitchen. Amber was starting breakfast for the crew. I'd heard Jake get up earlier and head out to the barn. He was already up and going after such a night. Just like sturdy hill folk.

I lounged a while longer on the sofa but when I smelt fresh coffee brewing I couldn't pass it up. "Grandpa wanted you to have a good ole fashioned country breakfast with coffee. Sorry if I woke you," Amber told me.

"I don't mind waking up to this delicious smell. What's Jake up to?"

"He's off doing chores. Isaac is out giving him a hand. He told me to tell you to hang out and enjoy the coffee until they were back." Didn't have to be asked twice.

"Mind if I take a cup out on the porch?"

"You can smoke in the house." She read my mind.

"That's okay. I want to enjoy the country air and just feeling alive." I sat on the front swing and savored having a smoke with some really good coffee. Somehow those two always go together. I could almost forget about all the craziness and what I still had to face up the road. It was tempting to take Jake's offer to stay but we'd always be worried about the Guardians. I had to go the distance and see what the New Society was all about—if I could make it there alive.

Jake and Isaac were coming back from the barn with a basket of eggs and still chattering like long lost cousins. "I see you're enjoying a cup of jo. Amber knows her way around a kitchen for sure," Jake spoke over to me. "Isaac has been giving me a hand with the morning chores. Sure nice to have someone close to my age around."

"I can see that," I commented. "So you old timers been plotting the overthrow of the regime—or figuring out a way to create your own New Society?"

"I sure would have some opinions on that subject," Isaac quickly replied.

Amber poured the boys coffee and refilled mine. I handed Jake a cigarette and offered one to Isaac. "No thanks son. I prefer my own homegrown." And with that comment he pulled out a fat hand rolled number that sure looked like a joint.

"Is that what I think it is?" I asked somewhat surprised.

"I'm sure it is. Started using it several years ago for my glaucoma. Grow my own now up on the mountain. You want some?"

I looked over at Jake first who said, "I know what your generation likes—so help yourself. My son used to grow some back in the woods. Tried it myself on occasion but never could get into it. Prefer a hand rolled Cuban myself."

Isaac passed me the joint and I have to say it was pretty good stuff. What a mellow start to the day. We sat and chatted for a while before Amber called us to breakfast. It was biscuits and gravy with eggs on the top. The kind of breakfast that really sticks to the ribs. She made plenty and I had two helpings.

The breakfast conversation was like a day back on the farm. We talked about the weather—planting crops—what chores we had to do that day.

After a while Jake pushed himself back from the table and smiled. "I have an announcement to make. Isaac and I've been talking and I've convinced him he should come live with us and share some family. We could use each other's company. Is that okay with you Amber?"

"Of course grandpa. I agree—we would love having Isaac stay with us," and she gave Jake and Isaac each a big hug. Everyone seemed pretty happy about the announcement.

It seemed like a good idea to me too. "You could use an extra gun around the homestead," I offered.

Jake got a real laugh at that one. "You kiddin' me! I used to take Isaac hunting. He can't hit the broadside of a barn. And anytime he's lucky enough to actually shoot something he gets all sad about what a beautiful creature he just killed." Isaac was nodding his head in agreement.

"Can't say I enjoy hunting much anymore myself," I replied,

"but it was a way of life back in the hills when I was younger. I guess it was hunting men in Nam that turned me off." I'm not sure why I said that but it just slipped out. "Sorry—I didn't mean to change the mood."

"I understand JC. Hunting men is no fun and not something anyone should ever have to do. I had my fill of killing and dying in Korea. But I'll still fight to protect my own," Jake proclaimed with his head high.

"I believe you will. And in my short stay here I know why." The old family values were coming back to me. Jake was a good example of what it was all about.

"What about you Isaac? You ever serve?" I asked.

"Nope—can't say I did. Did a stint in the Peace Corps back in the day when it first started. Went to Africa and tried to help some poor natives just get by. It sure opened my eyes to what real poverty is all about. It disgusted me when I got back to the States and saw what a greedy society we'd become. We had enough wealth to feed the world but we only made a token effort to help those in real need."

He paused for a moment to pour another cup of coffee. "When I got back I changed my plans to climb the corporate ladder and went to work for the Salvation Army—trying to help others. I spent most of my adult life with them. Traveled quite a bit and led a pretty humble life. Got married and had three kids. But I could never get my kids to want to share my kind of life. They wanted the material things our society had to offer. I still don't understand how I failed them."

"We didn't fail them!" Jake shouted. "The temptations of the outside world they saw every day on TV and in the movies took them away from us. Living on the land didn't have any appeal next to the fancy cars and fast lifestyle. If that is what the Concern was selling—they did a good job. Our kids lost sight of the value of family."

"I have to agree," Isaac replied. "After years of trying to teach my kids otherwise I finally gave up when I knew I'd never reach them. They were always willing to go into debt for the new toys—you know—the latest and greatest. They were swept up in the race to always have more. It never ended. After my wife died of cancer I packed up my goods and came to the mountain. Haven't had much to do with society since then."

"Well—we're certainly glad to have you join our family," Jake replied. "Let's go sit on the porch for a while 'fore we get back to chores."

I asked Jake what he needed me to get done that day since I wanted to help out as much as I could before I left. "We'll get to it here in a bit. I have some jobs that need a young man like you." Glad to know that someone thought I was young. "Don't worry—you'll get to work for your supper today." I'm sure the gunny wasn't kidding about that any.

"I'm ready to help out too," Isaac piped in. "JC and I will have another hit and be ready to go." Then he lit up what was left of that fat joint.

"I thought that stuff made you lazy?" Jake asked.

"Naw—it gets me all fired up and ready to work," Isaac answered. "But then I really crash when the work is done. Take nice long naps. You agree JC?"

"Sure do. It gets you wired for a while. Just the thing for chopping wood," and with that comment we headed off to take on the day.

Jake gave me some work gloves and we jumped in. Chopped wood—fixed some roof—moved some hay—shoveled some manure—good ole fashion farm chores. The three of us were having a good day and breaking a sweat in the sun. I could see why the old man was in such good shape for his age. Isaac wasn't any slouch either. It'd been a long time since I felt like I was really helping someone. It felt good.

After a busy morning we took a break for lunch. These old men were giving me a run for my money. They weren't afraid of hard work. Amber had fixed up another great meal and we talked away about life before the Regional Wars. That kid didn't have much future right now but maybe I might have the chance to change that later. It gave me even more reason to get to the north in one piece so I could try and return for her. I took my promise to Jake very seriously.

After lunch we lounged on the porch and Isaac lit another of his jumbo joints. He shared some of his stories about the many places he'd traveled. This was a man who'd spent most of his life taking care of others. I was learning a lesson from him about the giving of your time and not just for yourself. Maybe it was an idea I might get to practice with the New Society. But who knew what lay down the road for me…

We worked hard all day on the ranch and we got a lot done. I was feeling it in my body. Good thing I'd been working out with Duke before this journey. We slowed down when it got toward what Jake called his cocktail hour.

"I think we need to call it a day if you're going out tonight. You'll need some rest after we eat. Let's sit on the porch for a bit and have a shot of the shine," Jake offered.

"I could sure use that about now." I was starting to think about what I could be facing this night.

"I've been pondering the road from here," Jake commented. "If you want to get to Jenner you'll have a lot of miles to cover—about forty or so. And there are several towns. I got the county map out to look over what lies ahead." He spread it out on the table and we hunched over it while we studied Route 1.

"Here's where we are in Olema," Jake started. "If they have a command post in Jenner—like we think—it'll be across the river where they can see people coming from the south. It's wide open over there with clear visibility of the bridge and river."

"I think we know for sure that's where they are," I agreed. "Probably well fortified."

"If that's where they have their troops campin' out then the question is would they have another checkpoint between here and there. If they do—the most likely place is Bodega Bay—just north of where the Santa Rosa road comes in. Or maybe even north of town where the road runs along the coast," Jake commented while we studied the route on the map for a while longer.

"I'm going to guess they don't have a checkpoint in Bodega Bay but I'll be very careful when I get there," I responded. "Point Reye's Station is a possibility also. I'm gonna try and stay on the side streets in those towns but the towns aren't that big. Sooner or later I'll have to get back to Route 1."

"What time you wanna get off tonight?" Jake inquired.

"Before dark I want to go back to that knoll where we looked over town and watch for a patrol. After they pass I'll head to the road which leads to town and then turn north on the coast road. I've got to try and make the distance to Jenner before the next patrol. Done the coast a lot but it all looks different at night. The roads turns a lot in places and I won't be makin' good time. Just hope the clouds or fog don't take all my moon."

"So JC — how about you catch some zzz's and then take a hot shower to relax your sore muscles. I'll turn on the water heater now so it'll be ready for you. We'll have a good meal and Isaac and me will go with you to the overlook before dark." Jake paused for a moment. "Sure wish you could stay longer."

"Believe me Jake - so do I. Amber's cookin' is a real treat. But I need to get movin' while I have some moon left. Don't know how long I'm gonna sit at Jenner before I figure out a way over. I'll be way too close to them Guardians for comfort," I remarked thinking about the night's mission. "I'm glad I was able to help you out with the gas and propane. It's good to know that Isaac is staying with you two. You could use each others company right now."

We all shook hands on the porch and I went into the back bedroom to grab a nap. It promised to be a long night. The hooch and my fatigue helped knock me out for a while. I had crazy dreams about being chased by the Guardians and my bike getting slower and slower. What lay ahead was a mystery. It seemed safer to just stay on the ranch but I had to keep focused on my goal of reaching the north. It wouldn't be easy leaving these nice folk who were so much in harm's way.

I took that long hot shower Jake promised me and it felt real good. Took some of the aches from my body. I stayed until the hot water ran out. What a luxury something as simple as a hot shower could be. I still believed the hot shower was one of the greatest inventions of the twentieth century — screw all the technology and computers.

Once again Amber had fixed a good hearty meal of ham and beans with homemade bread. We all joked about the extra mileage I'd get that night from the beans. Guess they weren't familiar with hillbillies and beans?

As I watched Amber work in the kitchen I admired what a

strong person she was for her young age. I wasn't sure who was protecting who. I made a silent promise to myself that if there was anyway I could return—I would. I even asked God to give me a hand if he saw fit. Pretty big request from an old biker who'd long since forgotten about God.

We sat around the table swapping stories about better times. Isaac had some good yarns to tell about adventures with the Salvation Army that amused us. He was a good man with a generous heart. He and Jake were a real pair—true companions. Good thing we didn't shoot him at the campground...

CHAPTER 13

Back to the Mission

While everyone cleaned up in the kitchen I started to load the bike and get ready again for the mission. Made sure the shotgun had one in the chamber and the .45 was ready for action. Packed the binoculars on top as we would need them on the knoll. I started the bike and let it warm up for a while. She was running good. Jake and Isaac came outside to make our plans for the evening.

"Sure like the sound of a Harley—nothin' like it," Jake commented over the idle. "Always wanted one after the war but had to put what little money I had into the ranch. It took a long time but we finally paid it all off back in ninety eight. I buried Magdalene out in a clearing in the trees and I'll be put to rest next to her. God willing…"

I shut the bike off and we tried to figure out what to say to each other. To make such good friends and then have to leave them—didn't make much sense.

"Here JC," Jake finally said, "I want you to have a flask of my hooch to keep you warm. Enjoy it when you're safe for the night. It's also good for snakebite." I took the flask and put it in a pocket of my pack.

"Here," I offered back, "I want you to have a pack of cigarettes. It's a small price to pay for your hospitality. I know how much you'll enjoy them."

Jake pushed them away. "You might need them for barter down the road. Maybe I can get used to Isaac's homegrown." We both knew he was kidding about that.

"My friends took good care of me when I left so I have several packs." I reached over and put them in his pocket. "And besides—I'm trying to quit." They got a good laugh at that.

Isaac handed me two joints. "This is all I have on me but I want you to have them. I've got more at the cabin. Take it easy

95

with these — they're strong stuff. Good luck son — hope you find what you're looking for. Kick some Guardian butt for me."

I put the joints in my cigarette pack and shook his hand. "Glad you're movin' in with Jake and Amber. You'll be good company for each other."

"Isaac and I will go with you to the overlook," Jake informed me. "After you leave we'll retrieve his cart and the gas cans. Tomorrow we'll head to his cabin and pick up some of his belongings. He's got a dog we could use around the ranch. Fang is getting old and could use a friend too. Never hurt to have another set of good ears around."

I went back into the house and gave Amber a big hug. Told her what a great young lady she was. "I'll see you again if I can make it happen." I wondered if I should have said anything.

"I understand that grandpa wants me to be safe," she answered, "but right now we need to protect each other. One day the Guardians might come back this way and it could get tough. So we take it one day at a time. I hope you make your destination safely. We'll pray for you." She hugged me again as tears came to her eyes. She was one really smart kid.

I went outside and started the bike up again. Jake and Isaac were ready on the ATV. Isaac was driving and Jake was riding shotgun. Good thing — he was the better shot. I put on my leathers and we headed out. Took the lead and watched the dirt road carefully for holes. We slowly wound our way out of the valley and through the woods back to the grassy knoll. Fang ran along side Jake on the ATV. When we got in sight of the knoll I parked the bike and we hiked to the top. Fang laid down next to us and perked his ears up. That mutt had some sharp hearing for an old timer.

We were there for quite a while before we heard a patrol. It was just turning dark. They were coming from the south. This time they just kept going and didn't stop. We listened carefully and they didn't stop at the campground either. The sound of their engines faded to the north. "Let's have a smoke and then I'm headin' out." I passed my pack around. Even Isaac took one.

"You do remember when you hit Goathead Rock that the road will take a sharp downhill turn to the right to the bridge at Jenner?" Jake asked—trying to remember any other last minute advice.

"Yep—that'll be the sign that I'm close. I'll probably stop on the downhill to observe the bridge. I remember there's a restaurant on this side of the bridge so that is where I'll hide briefly until I find a better place to hole up."

We finished our smoke and headed back for the bike. I fired it up and got ready to make the short descent to the paved road that led to Route 1. We shook hands one last time. "Wish me luck!"

"God sent you to us JC and God will travel along with you," Jake offered. I'm not sure how much of that I believed but I appreciated the thought.

"I agree," Isaac chimed in. "God speed..."

I put her in gear and headed slowly for the paved road. It was dark now but fortunately it was only a short way down to the pavement. When I reached it I turned left for the downhill to Olema. My heart was racing. At the bottom I stopped for a moment to see if I could see any movement either way and then I turned north. I went slowly by the campground but didn't see any lights. That was a good sign. I opened it up to about thirty miles per hour and headed into the chilly night.

It was only a short distance until I reached Tomales Bay. The moon was full and passed between the clouds. There was a little fog drifting but visibility was good. The next Guardian patrol should be coming from the north but I was planning on a couple of hours before they would be heading this way. That should be enough time to reach Jenner depending on what I encountered in Bodega Bay. I sped up a little but that was about as fast as I could go in the dark and fog.

It wasn't long before I reached the town of Point Reyes Station. I remembered that Route 1 would make a ninety degree to the left into town and then another ninety back to the right after the main street. Stopped on the edge of town to check if I saw any lights but everything I could see was dark. I drove slowly into town keeping my eyes peeled for any movement. Took some back streets to stay off the main drag. Everything was quiet. In just a few minutes I was on the way out of town and heading back for the woods. Hadn't seen any activity. I think I'd forgotten to breath the whole way through town.

Then I was back along the bay again. It was cold along the water and if anyone showed up my only place to hide would be on the right side of the road. There wasn't much cover so I was hoping that wouldn't be necessary. Put that thought aside and kept moving.

I passed signs for the Marconi Conference Center so I knew I was getting close to where the road would turn inland. All of the houses along the water looked deserted. Many were burned out. There appeared to still be some boats in the bay but most were half sunk. Hard to see too far in the dark. The moon was reflecting off the water. Would have been a pretty night on the ocean but I was too focused on the road to appreciate it much.

The road eventually turned inland from the ocean and started to climb into the woods. I could smell the eucalyptus trees again. It was almost twenty miles since I left Olema so I was about half way to Jenner. Still making good time. The bike was running good and the old girl sounded mellow in the quiet. Guess there was something to be said for stock pipes — though not much.

I reached the intersection where the road hits a T and the right turn goes to Petaluma. It was in the open and I could see a ways in the moonlight. There weren't any lights anywhere so I took the left and headed up the hill for the little town of Valley Ford. I slowed down when I reached the edge of town but Valley Ford is only a few blocks long and I was through it in a minute. I did see a few lights way off in the distance at one of the farms but figured it didn't concern me so I pressed on. The road was fairly open here and I had my speed up to about forty. I was watching the horizon as closely as I could for the signs of a patrol coming south. I was out in the open here with nowhere to hide.

At about thirty miles I saw signs for the Bodega Highway which led back to Santa Rosa. This meant I was just outside of town. I was still trying to decide whether to blast through town and hope for the best — or take one of the side roads a few blocks east that paralleled Route 1. As I got close to town I opted for discretion and turned at the first road to the right knowing it led up to a firehouse at the top.

One of the guys we rode with years ago — Rowdy Ryan —

had a brother who worked at the firehouse so we used to stop and say hello. Sometimes his brother would let us camp in his backyard if there were just a couple of us riding together. None of the houses in this old part of Bodega Bay were very big.

I pulled up next to the firehouse and shut off the bike. Decided to walk through town a ways and see if there was any activity. I knew it would take valuable time but this was a good spot for a checkpoint so I wanted to be safe. Didn't want to overrun some Guardians stopped for a smoke break either. I grabbed the shotgun and headed into town.

There wasn't any activity or lights down near the water for several blocks so I was starting to think it might be safe. I stayed parallel to Route 1 until just short of the point where it turns uphill and starts out of town. Everything seemed quiet so I turned back to get the bike. It'd taken a while to walk to the other end of town and I was eating up valuable time. I'd only gone a block back when I saw a light flicker off toward the water. I listened for a while but couldn't hear much. Then I heard some voices — way off toward the wharf. The main road is a little lower than where I was so I made my way back to where I could see some of Route 1 near the ocean. Then I saw 'em...

The patrol had stopped near the docks and were hanging out there having a smoke. Boy — did I call that one!

They must have been far enough through town they didn't hear me come in. I crouched down and watched them but couldn't make out anything they were saying at this distance. They stretched their legs and had another light. Wished I could have one but couldn't take the chance. It was probably around twenty minutes before they started their bikes. They revved the engines for a while in the dark — sounded like they had some serious machinery in those rocket ships. As soon as they headed north I made a beeline for the bike but it was a ways back through town. I was feeling the fast hike and breathing heavy.

By the time I reached the bike I figured they had a short lead on me but not much. Hoped they wouldn't be stopping again before Jenner and I wanted to get there before the next patrol south. So I took a quick potty break and started the bike through town toward Route 1. I remembered there were some tight turns at the very end of Bodega Bay before the road opened up on a ridge above the ocean.

When I reached the ridge outside of town I looked carefully to see if I could see the patrol's lights in the distance. The road was flat here and ran along a cliff over the ocean. I could see the surf in the moonlight but no lights ahead. So I carefully made my way. This part of the coast goes through a small village and it wasn't long before I was passing along the houses. My visibility would go from close to far between the houses so I kept looking for flashes of light on the sky. It was about another six miles to the downhill turn at Goathead Rock.

I was keeping it at about thirty as I figured the Guardians were moving a little faster. The fog was rolling in slowly here along the water. I was moving in and out of it and starting to lose my visibility. Trusting to luck now. I asked God to keep an eye out for me—maybe some of Jake had rubbed off?

I knew I was getting close to Goathead Rock and finally the sign appeared out of the fog. I slowed way down as the road made a sharp turn to the right and headed downhill to the bridge. The road parallels the river here as it goes down through the woods. I was looking for a spot about half way down where I remembered there was a break in the trees and you could see over the river. The fog opened up as I got lower and I spotted the overlook. I turned off my lights and killed the engine while I coasted off the road into the berm. Came to a stop where I could see the river. My binocs were on top of the pack and I grabbed them.

There it was—exactly what I'd expected. A full command post across the river with bunkers and tents. There were lights and activity. The other patrol had just come in and Guardians were moving around. I studied the closest bunker and saw what looked like a machine gun behind some sand bags. It was pointed south across the river.

I watched for a while and then tried to see the bottom of the hill where the road turns onto the bridge at a ninety-degree angle. There was an old restaurant on the opposite corner of where it turns but it looked like the top half of the building was gone. Couldn't tell very well in the dark. There didn't appear to be Guardians on this side of the bridge – didn't need to. They had good command of the bridge from where they where.

As I studied them I saw one dude who seemed to be in charge. He was pretty big with a lot of hair and dressed in black. He appeared to be giving someone a hard time but I couldn't hear anything this far away. I wondered if that was Blackie? I only got to watch briefly when I saw several of them heading toward their bikes – including the big one.

Before I understood what they were doing they started their bikes. Oh my God – they were taking out a patrol and it might be this way. I was exposed here so I needed to get moving – and quickly!

I tossed the binocs over the pack and fired the old girl up. I was hoping their bikes would cover the noise of mine starting. I left the headlight off as I hit the pavement and headed down the hill. Luckily the moon was out just enough to see the outline of the road. I was moving toward the old restaurant and praying I made it there before they started across the bridge – or they would surely see me. They'd have me cold with far superior fire power. It would be a short battle.

As I approached the bridge I pulled in the clutch and killed the engine. I could see some lights moving off to my left toward the bridge on the other side. They were starting to leave. I was going way too fast when I passed behind the restaurant and into the darkness in the back. I slammed on the brakes as best I could and went into a slide. It was pavement and I wouldn't leave a dust cloud – I hoped – but I was going way too fast. I saw a large black object coming close and I locked up the brakes. The bike and I were in a sideways skid and almost stopped when the black shape loomed up on my right. Damn – it was a dumpster – and I was gonna run into it!

I hit the dumpster hard with the right side of my body as the bike stopped. My head whacked it and I saw stars. The bike was leaning on me with its weight against my body and the trash bin. But I had to sit tight until the patrol made it across the bridge and started up the hill. I tried pushing the bike back so I could take a stand but it had me pinned. Son-of-a-bitch – this was an awkward spot with well armed Guardians so close by!

I could hear their bikes coming across the bridge while my head tried to clear. I made one last push and my adrenaline must of made the difference because the bike moved back upright. I was weak in the knees from the collision and didn't have time to find the kickstand so I had to let the girl go down on her left side while I stepped off. I drew my .45 and cocked the hammer as I stepped behind the dumpster for cover. If there wasn't a dust trail from my skid they might not see me back here. I peered into the dark and waited.

In a few seconds their bikes rounded the turn and started the uphill climb. They were working their motors for the hill and made quite a racket as they disappeared into the fog. I couldn't see them from next to the dumpster but the sound told me they didn't know I was here. Man that was way — WAY — too fuckin' close!

My head was still ringing and my shoulder hurt. I grabbed the shotgun and binocs and made for the corner of the restaurant. I could only see directly across the bridge from here but I didn't hear any other bikes. I slowly made my way down to the north corner of the building where I could see across the river. There was activity in the camp but things seemed settled in for a while.

I moved back around the building to the downed bike and fumbled for my pack of cigarettes and the shine flask. I took a long swig to try and dull some of the pain. Tried to lift the bike but wasn't having any luck so I shut off the petcock to slow any leaks. Didn't realize how bad my hands were shaking until I tried to light the cigarette. I was getting too old for this shit! Damn them Guardians...

Sitting there as the fog started to come in my heart gradually slowed down to a small roar. I listened carefully but couldn't hear anyone across the river. The command post was set back a ways. I needed to get the bike up and figure out where I could hide out for the night. This spot was way too close to the road. If I could raise the bike maybe I could find a spot to hide us both out in one of the abandoned houses on the river. It would mean a dry camp close to the Guardians but right now all I wanted was shelter.

There was a steep hillside off to the right. Hopefully there might be a spot up there where I could set up an observation post tomorrow. But that would have to wait until daylight. I was still trying to get my legs back when I heard some movement in the bushes down the road. It might just be an animal but I pulled the .45 as I listened. The bushes moved again and I took aim. The sound of a shot would tip off the Guardians I was here. What the hell was it...?

After a few long moments a voice came from the bushes. "You okay man? I heard something hit the dumpster. Was that you?" I just watched and kept my gun pointed toward the voice in the darkness. "Can I come out?" he asked.

"Sure—but slowly. Put your hands in the air." I could only see a short ways in the mist as the figure moved closer with his hands over his head. He could've shot first so I was taking the chance he might be a friendly. I didn't see a gun in his hand but it looked like there might be one in a holster. "Come closer where I can see you..." I ordered him.

He approached within twenty feet with his hands still high. "I won't pull my gun," he said. "I want to help you. You probably figured out by now I'm not a Guardian. My names Dick. Some call me Tricky Dick—you know—like Nixon."

He went on to explain. "I was down at the river getting some water for my camp when I heard you come skidding in. Sounded like you hit pretty hard. Sure scared the shit out of me. I almost fell in the river. Couldn't figure out what the hell it was. You need help?"

I watched him for a while but he seemed for real so I lowered my weapon—though not all the way. "I'm pretty sore from kissing that dumpster. What are you doin' here?"

The stranger came closer and answered me, "I'm on my way to the north. Walking along the top. My camp is on the other side of this hill where they can't see my fire. I been watching for days trying to figure out a way across. They got this bridge pretty well covered. I was going to go up the river a ways to find a spot to cross. I don't swim that well and I have a big pack. Seems like you sure figured out an interesting way to head for the north. Is that a Harley?"

"It was the only transportation I had since the Guardians

took everything. I'm trying to work my way up the coast at night around their patrols. I expected this command post here at Jenner. This could be a tough nut to crack."

We spent a few moments sizing each other up. He extended his hand. "Maybe we can work together. I need to figure out a way over also." I put my sidearm back in the holster and shook his hand.

"I'm JC. Good to meet you. Maybe we can help each other out as you say. Right now I'm really sore from smacking that dumpster. Where's your camp?" I asked as we walked back to the bike.

"It's a hike from here. Especially in the dark. We can hide your bike in one of the abandoned houses here along the river. Should be safe from view. I'm sure they cleaned these places out a long time ago. I'll help with your pack. Sure you feel good enough to make the climb?"

"Don't have much choice do I? Help me get the bike up and find a place to hide her." We both took hold of the bike but she was a handful to get back upright. Tricky seemed pretty strong for his small size. We tried several times and finally got the old girl back on her wheels. After I caught my breath I coasted the bike down the road to one of the small houses along the river that had a garage. Seemed as good as anything for now. We opened the door and pushed her inside. Tricky turned on a small flashlight while I unloaded my pack. I pulled out some canned goods from the saddlebag and threw them in the pack along with Jake's hooch.

Tricky didn't seem too old — maybe in his forties. "I'll carry that," he offered as he grabbed my pack and sleeping bag. I didn't have much time to check over the bike before we closed the door and headed out. I grabbed the shotgun and followed along quietly in the dark. Just wanted to lie down and get warm but if he had a safe campsite I had to make the hike — no matter how far.

As we slowly made our way up the hill and over the top he didn't have much to say. Sure appreciated his carrying my gear. I followed along trying not to trip in the dark. Already had enough injuries for the night. Took over half an hour before we cleared the top and started down the other side. As we left the woods I spotted his tent in a small clearing.

"Here we are," he pointed. "Ain't much but it's home for now. You get your tent up and I'll start a fire. It's pretty chili tonight with the fog." He already had the wood ready and it didn't take long before there was a small fire. I got real close to the warmth after setting up my tent. My shoulder was still hurting like hell.

I opened the flask of brandy that Rat had given me and took a long shot. "Care for some brandy?" I asked as I offered him a swig. Wasn't ready to share Jake's hooch just yet. I found my pack of cigarettes and lit one from a stick in the fire.

"I've got something that might help your shoulder a little," he said as he crawled inside his tent. He came back out with a bottle he handed to me. "It's just aspirin—but take a handful. Don't have anything good like codeine."

We sat around the fire not saying much at first. I decided we had a mutual interest in getting across the river so I would have to trust him for now. Offered him a cigarette and he hesitated for a moment. "I've been off the nicotine for a while now."

"You don't know how long you're gonna live these days—so you might as well enjoy your time." That was a pretty philosophical statement for me. I guess this trip was making me think about everything in a different light. I pulled out one of Isaac's joints. "Care to share some of this instead?"

"Didn't give that up though—so you bet."

We lit up and sat there in the silence and misty fog while I enjoyed the fire. I wasn't in the mood for much talk and he didn't press me. Guess we both figured we'd get to know each other more in the morning. We had a tough obstacle ahead and I'd have to figure out if he was up to the challenge. Time for that later.

After some time the fire started to die out. "Look—I'm pretty stiff from that encounter with the dumpster and I need to sack out. I think the brandy and aspirin are helpin' out a bit. I'll see you in the morning." With that I made my way into the tent and tried to get warm in my bag. Dick stayed out by the fire as I fell into a restless sleep. I would've greatly preferred the couch at Jake's right about now...

CHAPTER 14

Tricky Dick

I didn't sleep well—waking up every time I turned on my sore shoulder. Took a shot of Jake's shine in the middle of the night. Don't know about snakebite but it was a good pain killer.

Not long after the sun came up I heard Tricky Dick working outside. I was curious to get the story behind that name. He'd started a fire and I could smell something cooking on a spit. It smelled familiar but I wasn't quite sure.

I laid there half awake for a while. The early sun on the tent felt good after the chilly night. I crawled out of my tent to catch some rays. As I approached the fire I recognized what was cooking—a rabbit.

"Damn—thought I recognized that smell. Haven't smelt a rabbit cooking since the mountains. They're pretty good eating. How'd you catch it?"

"I grew up in Lincoln Nebraska but my family sent me to my Uncle Gill's in Waco every year for part of the summer. He had some nice ponds and woods on his acres and he taught me how to hunt. He also instructed me on how to clean and cook game. My favorite is pheasant." He looked into the air for a moment. "Nothing like a pheasant with Uncle Gill's cream corn and a good wine. He bartended at the Flying V Ranch and always had a good liquor closet." He turned the spit some more. "He also showed me how to snare a rabbit. Thought it might not be good firing a gun this close to the Guardians."

"Good thought. I have some canned fruit to go with the rabbit." I reached into the tent for my pack. "And by the way—thanks for the help with the gear last night. It was a long climb up here."

He saw me rubbing my shoulder. "I bet you're sore. You really whacked that dumpster last night. Good thing they were on those loud bikes or they might have heard you. Are you black and blue?"

I pulled off my several layers of clothes and yeah—I was bruised. "Had worse in a bar fight—but it's been a while. My head still hurts too. Another inch and I would've cracked it good. I got lucky—even with the dumpster. Would've come up short in a shoot out. They're carrying some serious hardware." I sat down near the fire to get warm and savor the smell of the rabbit.

"The Guardians are pretty well equipped," Tricky responded. "Looks like military M16s. They have three .50 caliber machine guns and what looks like 81mm mortars in the pits. I don't think there's any mines around the camp but that's only a guess. They've got a good command of the road south, north, and east to Guernville." Now I was wondering how this farm boy from Nebraska knew so much about armament.

"You been in the military?" I asked with curiousity.

"Well—not really." He looked around like he was trying to see if anyone was listening out here in the woods. He sat there quiet for a while and then looked me straight in the eyes. "I guess I can tell you. No harm now. I was CIA."

I was stunned. "Really?" was all I could think to say. "Met a few of you boys in Nam. Strange bunch..."

"That's a fact. We are. Got even crazier over the years. My Dad was CIA in Vietnam. I never knew that until they recruited me after law school. He kept it a secret all those years. Didn't seem like he was too proud of it."

"You went to law school and then the CIA? What a weird mix."

"I didn't want to sit in some vine covered law firm waiting to make partner. I wanted excitement. So when the CIA came to campus to do some recruiting I went to see them out of curiosity. Didn't think I'd be signing up. That's when my dad told me about his experience with the CIA. He tried to talk me out of it. But you know how you never listen to your folks at that age."

"For sure. I signed up for the Marines at seventeen before I even finished high school. Lied about my age. Nobody kept good records back in the hills. And the Marines weren't asking questions in '68. My dad tried to talk me out of it too. Said it wasn't a just war and people were dying needlessly. Boy—was he ever right. It was a fuckin' mess. The CIA was no help either—just made things worse with the locals."

"I'm sure they did. That was all Concern business." He took the rabbit off the fire and set it aside to cool down. I was working on getting a can of fruit open when I heard him say "Concern business".

I stopped working on the can to make sure I heard what he said correctly. "What do you mean Concern business?" I asked him.

"Vietnam was a Concern project to slow the spread of Communism because they wouldn't get on the capitalist bandwagon. China wasn't interested in materialism—at that time - which was an issue with the Concern. Capitalism was the commodity the Concern used to increase their sphere of influence. The CIA was a direct operation of the Concern to gather intelligence—spread their doctrine—and commit assassinations. Kept us all very employed and well paid for our services."

"You mean to tell me the Concern was real—like the underground media was saying before the Regional Wars?" I'd never met anyone who knew this for sure. Not a lot of secret agents hanging out with the biker crowd in the City.

"Big time. I was on the executive staff for the Director of the CIA. Somebody—and it sure as hell wasn't the President—was running the show. We went to Switzerland for a lot for meetings. The President and Congress were just a front for the Concern. Popular amusement—as they used to call it. You didn't ask too many questions or you might disappear. After all—that was part of our business. Making people disappear."

I was amazed. Here I was sitting with someone who had worked for the Concern—or so he said. I wanted to try and figure out if he was telling the truth while we were camped out on this mountain but for now I was hungry. "That rabbit looks ready. Let's give it a try." I suggested.

"I have another surprise. I have a little salt. Adds that little touch of civilization don't you think? This coffee is my last—so don't spill any," he said as he handed me a cup.

I took a piece of the meat and salted it. It sure tasted good. And the coffee was right on. Tricky Dick may have been a crazy CIA man but he sure knew how to cook a rabbit. It was quite the breakfast. And my fruit topped it all off.

After the meal I reached over and shook his hand. "Thanks for the fine chow. How 'bout a joint to start the day?"

"You bet. Don't have to ask twice."

I was starting to get comfortable with Tricky. He seemed for real so far and as interested as I was in crossing the river. Maybe together we could figure out a way. I took a few slow hits and passed him the joint. That Isaac knew how to grow some good shit. We sat there next to the fire getting mellow and enjoying the sun as it warmed up the day. It felt good to be alive and outside — no matter what lay ahead.

We laid back for a while before we decided it was time to start our recon. "I have a good spot on the ridge where we can see the command post and all the area around," Tricky informed me. "Let's take some water and head up there." We took care of our toilet duties and headed for the ridge. Sure glad I had those two rolls of TP I'd packed at the last minute. Felt like I was back in Nam — squatting in the woods and all.

It didn't take long to reach the lookout spot. Tricky had a powerful set of binoculars so we took turns at surveying the command post through his. I could almost make out some of the Guardians. They were a scruffy bunch but well armed. Didn't see anyone that looked like Blackie.

"They run patrols up and down the coast about every two hours during the day and every four hours at night," Tricky explained as he gave me his intelligence of the Guardian activities. "At times there's as many as twelve of them at the command post but sometimes only six or so when they're out on patrols. There's two tents for sleeping and the covered area is the command tent and mess. By the antenna I'd say they got a radio in there. They have good command of the road and bridge to the south. They can also see a good distance to the east up the Russian River. They must have reinforcements to the east – maybe in Guerneville. I saw a supply truck come in from that direction yesterday. There's a small tanker truck for gassing up the bikes. They have their armament set to cover any direction."

"I guess they don't seem too concerned about people coming from the south across the bridge." I added in. "Probably more interested in a possible attack from the New Society coming from the north or even the east. It would take a well armed force to take them on across the bridge. And I don't think such a threat exists from what I've seen so far on this trip."

"You might be right but I think the New Society is too far north to be a threat to this command post. My guess is that the Guardians have their forces concentrated on Route 101 and just keep a token number out here on the coast. Just for the occasional crazies like us who are trying to get north."

"This is going to be a tough outpost to get around. Got any ideas?" I asked.

"Not yet—still working on a plan. Been thinking about swimming the river at night farther east and then heading back into the woods. It would be a job for me to get across with all my gear in that cold water which is why I haven't tried yet. And I sure don't want to have to swim it twice. If you want to get your bike across we'll have to use the bridge. No choice."

"You're welcome to try your plan and swim." I was testing the waters with him.

"Well—I'd rather think about some other options. Maybe we can figure out a way we can both use the bridge. But it might mean someone swimming across to help neutralize the command post." We looked at each other over that comment—with the unanswered question as to who that "someone" would be.

"So JC—you served in the Marines during Vietnam? That was a long time ago." I took that as a comment about my age. Now he was checking me out.

"Yeah—in another life. Vietnam in '69. Came home with two purple hearts. Don't have much good to say about the experience."

"Where did you see action?" Tricky inquired further.

"All over—but mostly up north near the DMZ. The firebase at Con Thien was a regular hangout. I was also near the Ashau Valley and there was always something going on there. Took a round through the calf during that mess." I rolled up my pants and showed him the wound. "Still bothers me at times. How 'bout you—seen any real action?" Now it was my turn.

"I was trained as a sniper in the beginning. Got damn good at it over time. Been involved in a number of assassination teams. It was a right of passage in the CIA to be one of the boys. I was in the field during the Persian Gulf War and again in Afghanistan."

"Ever pull the trigger yourself?" I asked looking for a specific answer.

He glared back at me before he answered, "Yeah — I've done the deed several times. It got easier each time."

"But you ain't never done it eye to eye — you know — like up close and personal?" I could tell by his look he was getting my message.

"No — not like you have I'm sure. You got me there." So I made my point. It was one thing to kill an enemy long distance through a scope but another to fight him hand to hand when you look in his eyes and see the hate. It brought back memories I hadn't thought about in a while. We were both killers but I didn't want to do it anymore. We fell silent for some time as we went back to observing the command post.

Then we saw a patrol come in from the south. "When you see three bikes like that," Tricky told me, "it usually means their leader is with them." I took the binocs and studied the Guardians closely.

"Looks like Blackie alright," I said as I observed the patrol pull in to the command post. "He sure is a big mother fucker!"

"Blackie? You know this guy somehow?" Tricky became very interested.

"Just by reputation. Hear he's the meanest of the bunch. Likes to capture folk headin' north and torture 'em. We'll want to stay the hell away from him if we can."

I watched Blackie ordering people around. He looked a little like Duke. Long black hair and beard with all black riding gear. Made me wonder how the two of them would fare in a one on one fight. My money would be on Duke. I'd seen him reek some serious mayhem with some pretty big dudes since I'd known him.

They disappeared into the mess tent and we couldn't see them anymore. I'd seen what I needed to know for now. This wasn't going to be easy at all. "Let's go back down the hill where we can have a smoke," I suggested.

We made our way down from the ridge and I pulled out my pack of cigarettes. "Sure you don't want one?" I offered as I held out the pack.

"I quit after Afghanistan. Cigarettes were a major money maker for the Concern. People couldn't quit and it made them millions. They exported the habit to a lot of third world countries." He thought for a moment. "Oh — what the hell — give me one. You can't live forever."

We lit up as we enjoyed walking in the sun. "Got any ideas about something to eat for lunch?" I asked.

"I want to check my traps again. Maybe we can have another rabbit for supper with any luck. If I could safely get to the river we'd have some fish but that's just far too risky."

"I agree. I have some canned chili. Got anything to warm it up in or do we just eat it cold?"

"I've got a pot. Let's get back to camp and see what we have in the larder. I also got some jerky we can share."

"Sounds like a plan to me." We got back to camp and took stock of what food we could share while we talked about further plans. We agreed if there was anyway across this river we'd have to work together. So — for now — we'd have to trust each other. That was a hard concept with a CIA assassin but maybe that would work to my advantage. I'd just have to see...

CHAPTER 15

The Concern

After a lunch of chili and jerky we sat back and talked. I wanted to learn more about the Concern so I offered to share another joint with Tricky. Figured it might limber him up a bit and get him talking. I waited until we were done and then asked the big question.

"So — Dick — tell me about the Concern. Were they for real?"

Tricky thought for some time before he answered. "The Concern was all about money and power. They created themselves at the end of the big war. It was conceived by some of the major money citizens from the United States along with Britain and Switzerland. They needed Switzerland to process the money. They built an invisible government that was the true power behind what they called the visible governments. It was a clever concept because they could create a secret organization that held the real power while the others — the politicians — appeared to be the actual government. So when anything went wrong it was always blamed on the visible government. They didn't have any problems finding people who wanted to hold the visible offices. They made them feel like royalty with all the trappings of public office. But they were simply figureheads — you know — puppets."

"But how could they keep all of that secret for so long?"

"Easy — money can buy you anything. They had the money and the power to make almost anything they wanted to happen — well — happen. And they were ruthless. Life was cheap to the Concern. If you crossed them you disappeared. The best example of that was John Kennedy. He had enough money to run for office without the Concern and they weren't too good at that time with fixing elections. He truly intended to change the social fabric of this country which was a significant issue to the Concern. So when he won — and he wouldn't go along with their agenda — they had him assassinated. Did the same to his brother before he ever got into the White House. After Kennedy the Concern had complete control over who was crowned president of the US. It was who they wanted and who would allow them to run the show from behind the scenes without revealing they were the real control behind the throne. The same thing was happening in Britain and Switzerland."

"How did they get control over so much of the world before the Regional Wars?"

"They sold capitalism to the world. Counted on greed as the motivating force to bring other nations into their fold. The Communists were a real hard sell through the fifties and sixties. They actually believed their communal system would work. That's what Korea and Vietnam were all about. Trying to further their sphere of influence. When the Concern realized the Communists were too powerful to defeat militarily they just bought them out over time. After Mao the Chinese gradually put in leaders who wanted to work with the Concern. Their reward was incredible wealth from creating one of the largest manufacturing markets the world had ever seen in the twenty first century. Gave them Hong Kong as a gift for joining the Concern. How much stuff did you buy in the last decade that was built in China?"

I thought about that for a minute. "A hell of a lot. It seemed like everything was coming from there. Cheap shit too — not very dependable."

"See — that's what I mean. And when the American workers became too high priced or complained they moved their jobs overseas. It was a way to keep spoiled Americans on their toes by making them worry about their jobs and maintaining their materialistic lifestyles. The Concern needed a lot of the technology that came from America so that was an important part of our economy. If they could keep you in debt up to your eyeballs they could keep you working and not asking questions. Americans were naïve enough to believe they controlled their own fate by electing their own leaders but it was all superficial. The Concern liked to call elections the Super Bowl of politics as it was one of their favorite forms of entertainment. Once the elections went mostly electronic it was very easy to fix the outcome. Plus it was another way to keep the masses preoccupied and spending their money."

Tricky lit up one of my cigarettes and kept talking. "Did you ever notice how anytime we took over a country—like Afghanistan—the first thing we did was implement what they called free elections? It was all part of the show. No one has been really free for many decades now. Freedom was an elaborately created illusion."

"You accepted all of this?" I asked trying to keep him talking to learn more about whether I could trust him.

"After several years I was in so deep there was no way out. You kept shut or disappeared. As long as I had my fast cars—and easy women—I didn't care any more. Just became part of the machinery. Assassinating people became a game after a while. Not much different than a video game. Kind of sad to think about that now. Sure wasn't the way I was raised in the church and all."

So I guessed this was a good time to ask, "Where'd you get your nickname?"

"Tricky Dick? Oh—that was a reference to Nixon and Watergate—which was before my time. Everybody in the field with the CIA had nicknames and the guys tagged me with that one. I was part of the political dirty tricks team in the beginning—the rigged elections and all. I was quite good at making politicians look bad by planting dirt on them. The Bill Clinton and Monica Lewinsky scandal was my favorite media coup. If a president—or senator—whoever—got to feeling too cocky we would set them up in some type of scandal. Just a reminder to them who was really in charge. It was always fun and the public ate it up. People were so desperate for someone else to point their fingers at and the media would do anything to sell coverage. Some of those media people were really low lifes now that I look back on it all."

I guess I was thinking slow today as what he had said about Vietnam just sunk in. "So the Concern was behind the war in Vietnam? It had nothing to do with trying to keep the people free from Communism?"

"Well—yeah—it was about stopping Communism. But not some great political ideology like you were told. It was about the Communists not cooperating with the Concern and the concept of capitalism. The Concern used the military as an international police force. Whenever something wasn't going their way they figured out a political excuse to send in the military. Just like the war in Iraq. The Arabs had all that oil money but they weren't playing ball with the Concern. So the Concern decided to set a capitalistic wedge in the midst of the Arab nations. They used the excuse of weapons of mass destruction to invade Iraq. It wasn't hard to get the world to hate Saddam. He was quite the tyrant to his own people."

"So all the talk about vets fighting for freedom was just Concern propaganda?" I asked with a little anger in my voice.

"You might say that. The Concern needed a well equipped and on call military. The U.S.—in it's arrogance—was always willing to play the role of the so called peacemaker. They recruited young people to serve with promises of glory, education, travel—whatever it took. You vets were a major victim of the whole scheme because once you came home you were forgotten about. To the Concern you were an expendable commodity and an expense they didn't want around once you'd served your purpose. In my opinion the last real war for freedom was World War II and the people who came out on top of that in the long run were the Concern." He paused for a while to think.

He continued, "I've thought about this a lot. The idea about what it means to fight for freedom that is. I often wondered what I was fighting for as an assassin for the Concern. For a while I thought I was killing undesirables for a good cause. You know—freedom and the American Way and all that crap. But then I reflected about the history of warfare back through time. Whenever a nation like the Romans invaded a country to expand their control their soldiers were fighting for conquest and economics. So that actually made them mercenaries—not freedom fighters. After a while I came to the conclusion that I was a mercenary for the CIA. With the Concern it was all about profit and power. But soldiers have to be told they're there for the freedom of the people to get you to make the ultimate sacrifice. Just like Iraq and Afghanistan. It's all part of the nasty game."

"So according to you there are no freedom fighters?"

"No—not exactly. People who fight to protect their families and homes are the true freedom fighters. If you fought the Romans to keep them out of your piece of the woods then you were fighting for your freedom and that of your people. So yes—there are freedom fighters. How would it upset your view of your time in Vietnam to think that maybe the Viet Cong were the freedom fighters? When a vet comes home mangled from Vietnam or Iraq—wherever—could you look him in the eye and tell him his missing legs were a sacrifice for the Concern?" He looked at me with that statement and saw my questioning look. "Of course you can't—so you tell him he did it for freedom. What else can you say? And that's how we keep the insane wheel of international politics turning. Those Concern bastards sacrificed a lot of soldiers over the years to keep their agenda moving along."

"I hafta' admit when I first arrived in Vietnam with the Marines I was gung-ho all the way and believed we were there to save the country from the terrors of Communism. But after a while I started to question what the hell we were doing there. The mission never seemed clear. The VC did atrocities to us and anyone who cooperated with us but we weren't much better at times. It was a lot of an eye for an eye. Once you were there you just tried to survive and make it home. At the time it made me really angry how the war protestors treated us who'd served. How strange now to think they might have been right if it was a war fought for the Concern—like you say."

I was running all these crazy thoughts through my head. "Guess if I had to think about their side of things it'd be like asking how we'd react to an enemy who invaded West Virginia. Just how hard and nasty those old hillbillies would fight to stay free. Maybe I can see your idea about who the real freedom fighters are. And yeah—I still know Nam vets you couldn't tell we were there for any reason other than freedom. I couldn't tell someone in a wheelchair for the rest of his life that it was all for nothing."

Now Tricky had me on a roll so I shared some of my feelings about the Iraq war, "I never accepted the Iraq war either as it seemed like another Vietnam—just in the desert rather than jungle. But it seemed so impossible to stop the government from doing anything they wanted to do. I remember some younger vets we rode with who joined the Vets Against the War after Iraq but they never seemed to get much attention to their messages. Hafta' give' em credit though for trying to tell folk we shouldn't have been there either."

I took a long swig from my canteen and finished my thoughts. "It always bothered me to hear some speaker at a vets rally thank us for our sacrifices for freedom when I was never sure that's why we were there. Still gets me angry and sad to think about all those friends I lost in Nam. Sometimes I still see their faces in my dreams. Never completely got over the nightmares I had after that horror show. Now they call it PTSD. Hell—all we wanted to do was be back home cruisin' the hamburger stand and makin' out with our gal. Not fightin' in some nasty fuckin' war half way 'round the world."

"Yeah—it's a tough pill to swallow isn't it? If you look back at that time most people never knew what happened to Vietnam several years after the war. Companies like General Motors and Coca Cola built plants there. Did you know that? That certainly wasn't Communism at work. It was the Concern. After their hatred of the U.S. subsided Vietnam sold out for the golden apple just like everyone else. Now they're just another spoke in the Concern wheel."

Just for fun I decided to ask Tricky, "So who's the freedom fighters here—us or the Guardians?"

He laughed briefly. "That's easy man. It's us. They're some fucking out of control bizarre collection of misfits terrorizing people for control and their personal pleasure. Probably deserved to all be killed by what I've seen of their terror on the way up here. You and I are trying to find freedom—if it even exists. None of us know too much about this New Society. They could be just another scam like all the rest. But I'm going to give it one hell of a try to reach them. Maybe just for once I'd get to fight on the right side."

"I'm still not looking forward to pulling the trigger on any of them," I commented more to myself.

"Don't think we'll have that choice if we want to get across this river in one piece. They're sure not going to just let us walk across and then head on our merry way to the north. We either shoot our way across or head upriver and try to find a place to swim. You'll be on foot the rest of the way if that happens. Figured you preferred to stay on your wheels."

I nodded my head to that while I lit up another joint and passed it over. Wanted to keep him talking to finish his story about the Concern. Even though this was very frustrating information I somehow believed him. It all seemed to fit together and explained a lot.

After smoking the joint I opened with another question that had my curiosity as it was on my mind about myself. "What about religion? Did the Concern believe in a God?" I was trying hard to put the whole picture together of what he was telling me.

"Yeah—they believed in a God and it was them. They thought they were chosen to rule all mankind and that their divine ordination gave them the right to make decisions for the world. Traditional churches—and faith—were supported because they gave the masses something to believe in to keep them sedated and working. Religion taught people to accept their humble lives and unpleasant circumstances as part of God's will. Remember—it was Jesus who said 'Give unto Caesar what is Caesar's.' The Concern didn't believe in an afterlife so they wanted all they could have in this life. And they took a lot."

"More than money and power?"

"Yes—more than that. Their favorite vice was sex. From some of the stories I heard they couldn't get enough of that drug. They kept fancy villas around the world that were well equipped with the most beautiful women and men—basically sex slaves. They believed sex was the single greatest pleasure available on earth and wanted as much of it as possible. The drugs they used were there to heighten the pleasure of the sex. Where do you think Viagra came from? I even heard rumors they were spending billions on medical research to prolong life so they could enjoy those pleasures as long as possible. It was all pretty decadent."

"How did you accept the whole God thing?" This talk was getting pretty deep for me.

"You know JC—that's a good question. I was raised in the church back in Nebraska. But you know them Midwest Lutherans—they're a pretty straight bunch. Went through the movements but don't think I ever got the message. It wasn't until I was with the CIA for a while—and been on several assassination teams—that I started to have some doubts. If there is a God I sure have broken my share of the commandments. It was hard to believe in the simple God fearing life when you experienced so many pleasures of the flesh. So I guess the verdict is still out on that one with me. How about you?"

"I've had a lot of time to think about that lately. I put God out of my life a long time ago after what I saw in Nam. Took my share of lives over there. But I'm not sure now about the whole thing. Watching the world disappear so fast this year left me wondering if it was God's work—or did it all happen because there is no God?"

"Pretty philosophical thoughts for a biker—eh?" Tricky commented with a laugh. "When everyone was talking about different Armageddon theories no one ever came up with this one. Maybe that is what this is all about—a new beginning. The world went back to square one in a hurry. Actually—it was even more dramatic than that because those of us living in the modern world had gotten used to the luxuries of things like electric power and transportation. Some of the third world countries are probably better off than us after the Regional Wars because they were still living fairly basic lives without the addiction of technology."

I decided it was time to ask him the million dollar question, "Did you ever become one of the Concern yourself?"

Tricky paused at that. "Not very many ever did. I got as close as one could get but was never invited into the inner circle. But I never said anything. Disloyalty meant death. And I did get to enjoy many of the benefits. Just had to accept my place in the whole thing."

"So—if it was all working so well—what went wrong?"

"The fucking damn Internet! The Concern financed the systems to run the Internet because it seemed like a good method to make their international banking easier. They made billions from the commerce it generated and it made it easier to sell goods from the new Concern countries—like China. But it all backfired in a way no one ever expected."

"What was that?" I asked—not being too familiar with how the Internet worked.

"The Internet went completely out of control. No one was in charge. The Concern didn't realize this until it was too late to stop it. By the time they figured out that anyone could post anything from anywhere—it was too late. In the early part of the new century there were messages leaking about the possibility of the Concern. Everyone thought it was just another conspiracy theory—what they liked to call urban legend on the Internet. The Concern tried to find out where the rumors were coming from but the Internet was too fluid. If anyone sending the messages felt the presence of the Concern they closed down and opened up another site. The Concern had the CIA and eventually the FBI working on it but it was just too complex."

"Never used the Internet myself. Had no use for computers in general. Too impersonal and frustrating for a biker like me. Liked working on things I could touch and listen to. Like motors and boilers. Simple stuff—without all the technology that made it harder to fix and less reliable."

"Then you were really in the minority because almost everyone was using the Internet. It grew like an organism out of control. Developed a mind and will of its own. So when the dialogue about the Concern continued to grow they took a desperate measure." He stopped to let it all sink in.

"Just how desperate?"

"They created the War on Terrorism by recruiting these disparate terror groups around the world—like Al Qaeda—and funded them to conduct terrorist activities against the Concern countries. Those groups would bomb embassies—kidnap tourists for ransom—whatever seemed like easy and visible targets. Do you remember the first bombing attack on the

World Trade Center—the one that exploded in the basement? That was part of their handiwork. But the affluent countries—particularly the US—still didn't believe there was a real threat as they watched the news in the comfort of their homes. So the Internet traffic about the Concern continued to grow."

"So they paid these terrorists to attack their own people?" I was trying to get my mind around that one.

"Remember—life was cheap to the Concern. All that mattered to them was that their secrecy remained intact. But it was hard to keep something that big secret with the Internet. Even after they started all the terrorist activity the rumors about them continued to grow. That was when they decided to up the ante."

"Let me guess—9/11?" It was all starting to come together in my head.

"Bingo! They financed the largest terrorist attacks in the history of the modern world believing they could kill two birds with one stone. Create an act of aggression so great it had to catch the world's attention and get it all blamed on the Islamic militants. It was a cold blooded plan that was executed better than they ever expected."

"But how did the Arabs feel about working with the Concern if they resisted them so much?" This was quite the story to be hearing from a secret agent man.

"They never knew it was the Concern who were sponsoring them. They were so anxious to strike out against the West they didn't question where the monies were coming from. All they could see was the opportunity to spread their Jihad message across the world. So the Concern used the religious fervor of the Islamic militants as part of their plan to draw attention away from themselves."

"Apparently—it didn't work so well," I commented.

"It worked for a while. The world was galvanized by 9/11. They brought down both towers of the World Trade Center and struck the Pentagon—the biggest symbols of American wealth and power. It had the exact effect the Concern was trying to orchestrate. It focused the attention of the world on the new War on Terrorism—and for a while the Internet traffic about the Concern abated. Even those who were trying to expose the

Concern at that time did not appreciate at first that the Concern had anything to do with 9/11. After all that chaos Americans finally believed they were not safe in their own country from the terrorists."

"So—uh—did you have anything to do with the planning of 9/11?"

"Nope—it was kept at the highest levels. When we used it as an excuse to invade Afghanistan was when I got involved."

"I thought the invasion on Afghanistan was to destroy the terrorist training camps?"

"And that was exactly what they wanted the world to believe. But in truth it was an excuse for the Concern to get a foothold in an Islamic country that not too many people cared about. They also wanted to get control of the poppy production because so much of the world drug trade came from there. So it was economics once again. They pretended to wipe out the terrorist training camps but in actuality they let many of them escape into Pakistan. They still had plans for the terrorists. By taking Afghanistan they got themselves a military base and a functioning drug operation in the process. They funneled the money from the drug trade back into their terrorist groups. It all went very well for them."

This was quite the story and it seemed so real the way that Tricky told it. I was starting to believe this incredible tale. "So what happened next?"

"It was the Internet again. It took a while but the traffic about the Concern came back. And this time it was getting closer to the truth. It was even implying that the Concern may have had a connection to 9/11—which was something the Concern could not tolerate getting out to the world. So they started a ruthless campaign to find who was creating these messages and eliminate them. Most people were too busy worrying about terrorism to pay much attention to the conspiracy theory groups on the Internet. If the public had only known how much truth was in those conspiracy videos and blogs."

"So they had people like you taking care of the folks who were trying to get the truth out?" I was testing him now to see how much he would confess to—he took the bait.

"Yep — we created new assassination teams and had them working all over the world. By that time I was training other teams. I occasionally went out on missions to stay fresh at the art."

"Did you ever question why this activity had been stepped up?"

"You didn't ask a lot of questions when you were that far into the system. But I did wonder why some of our targets didn't seem like real terrorist types. Things were moving too fast to wonder about it for long because the Concern took a really bold step against the Arabs when they invaded Iraq. It placed the influence of the Concern right in the heart of the Arab world. The Coalition forces moved so fast into Iraq that the Concern never got the weapons of mass destruction we said were there planted in time. It was a big mess at first but once we were there we kept making excuses why we had to stay. Telling the world we were setting up a free government was the Concern's regular PR campaign." We sat there not talking for a bit as I tried to digest all he had told me about the Concern.

I needed to know one more important thing about Tricky. "So — you killed a lot?" I made it sound like it was just a question from one soldier to another. But I had another reason to ask.

"More than my share. Like I said — that's one commandment I would have a hard time getting around if I ever got to meet God." So now I knew I was dealing with a cold blooded killer if he needed to be. I'd keep that in mind when we made our plans to cross the river. My survival might only be important to him long enough to get him across — then I could be expendable too. Guess I'd learned something from those years on the streets about trust — or when not to trust. But I wanted to hear the end of the story.

"So how did it all come down if the Concern was keeping everyone's attention fixed on terrorism and their own security?"

"No matter what the Concern did they couldn't slow the chatter on the Internet. Someone on the inside must have been talking. The groups trying to expose the Concern were getting their facts straight and they were starting to publish photos of alleged Concern members. The traffic on the Internet picked up in volume and an international audience was starting to listen. Those were crazy times inside the CIA. It felt like it was all coming apart at the seams."

After I thought about that I answered back, "I seem to remember that stories started to appear in some magazines. Even in a veteran's magazine somebody showed me."

Tricky went on, "We knew there was going to be trouble when the non-mainstream media was picking up the conspiracy theories about the invisible government. It even made it onto a couple of well known talk shows. People called it different things but the truth was coming out about the Concern. The final straw was when the link between the Concern and 9/11 started to dominate the traffic on the Internet. That was in 2018. There was no stopping it after that. Some of the anti-government groups that were very powerful in the U.S. and who'd been challenging government authority for years picked up the cause. But in their fervor nobody understood how it was going to come down so catastrophically for everyone."

"It did happen quickly. Seemed like there was this talk about something called the Concern and then the world came apart at the seams."

"In their rage the extremist anti-government groups took it on their own to start taking out the Concern or anyone they thought was Concern. It became a witch hunt. But they didn't stop long enough to think about how they were attacking the core of the world's financial infrastructure. In a final desperate move the Concern shut down the network systems but along with it went all the power grids — communication systems — military command and control — the whole frigin works. Boom! Instant and overnight insanity. The Regional Wars followed. People everywhere tried to survive and set up local governments. It was brutal. Billions of people died. In a strange way — it was the Armageddon every one had been talking about."

I offered, "Maybe it was meant to be a new beginning for the world? A chance to start over. I wonder what it'll look like in another fifty years?" I considered the possibilities — it was mind boggling.

"It sure is a mess now. Very little technology is left that runs.

Maybe that's good. Who knows?"

"So if the stories about the New Society are true then maybe it is the right place to be now?" Again—I was testing Tricky's motives.

"For now it's the only game in town for me," he replied quickly. "I know the Guardians aren't something I want to be involved with. Maybe the New Society has some good ideas about how things should be run? Guess we'll just have to find out—if we can ever get across this river."

"So—where were you when all of this started to come down?"

"I was in Marin County on a vacation with some friends when the shit hit the fan. We survived for a while on their food supplies and then had to scavenge off the land. Rich urban yuppies aren't too good at that you know. The Guardians closed everything off and I lost communication with anybody from the CIA. I had no other way out but to try and walk to the north. The friends I was staying with got caught in a raid into town and I never saw them again. I'm sure they're dead now—or labor slaves. So I packed up my gear as best I could and started north. I've been raiding cabins and living off the land for over a month now. Don't have a map so I've just been heading north and trying to avoid the Guardians. You're one of the first people I've talked to in a while. It's strange how we met but I'm sure glad we did. Between the two of us we can figure out a way through this command post." He seemed pretty confident in the both of us.

"Sounds good to me," I replied. We'd have to see what he was thinking. But it was good for now.

I wasn't going to ask him where he thought a Concern assassin might fit in the New Society. It would give away my hand. So I left that question unanswered—for now…

CHAPTER 16

Planning the Crossing

A fter learning more than I ever wanted to know about the Concern we decided to get back to planning how we could cross the river. Guess it was time to ask a business question.

"So — Tricky — you got any of that good long range hardware with you?"

"You bet! Got a nice setup with me that has a night scope. That's why I didn't want to swim the river. The kit is heavy and I would have to swim across twice to get all of my traveling gear with me. You want to see my girl?"

This was going to be interesting. He went into his tent and brought out a gun case. He opened it slowly like it was an important treasure he was proud of. The tools of his trade I guess you might say.

"It's a Stoner SR25 with both 10 and 20 round clips. Has a night vision riflescope — Gen four," he explained. "Handles a 7.62 NATO round and its gas operated with a rotary bolt. Has a free floating barrel for recoil. Only weighs ten pounds without the scope. Both the Seals and the Green Berets used these." He assembled the rifle with just a few pieces and then checked the chamber to see if it was empty. He turned on the sights and took a sighting up the ridge. "Has a very accurate range over a mile."

He handed me the rifle. It was amazingly light for its size — even with the scope. I aimed the rifle and looked through the scope. It had a sharp view for a long ways off. The night vision scope would make it very deadly after dark. It was definitely a serious weapon. "So why don't you just shoot them from the ridge and then cross?" I was playing with him again.

"As soon as they take cover in their bunkers," he answered, "I'm out of good options. They got that .50 caliber and those mortars pointing in this direction. If they opened up on my position I'd be in big shit real quick!"

He had it figured right. Once they returned fire he'd be out gunned and then looking for a whole new way to cross because the Guardians would be on the alert. "So what you got in mind?"

"Let's go back up to the overlook and study their positions more closely."

"I agree." We packed up some jerky and water and headed to the top of the ridge that overlooked the river. I brought my binocs to help look things over. I also carried the shotgun just in case we saw some unexpected close action but we were pretty far up the hill from the bridge. I was feeling it by the time we made it to the top. Tricky was pretty spry as he was young and in good shape—something else I would have to keep in mind for when we got across.

It was a nice coast day. There were few clouds and the sun was shining. The view from the ridge was incredible. We could see the opening of the bay just a little ways around the bend of the river and the ocean off in the distance. The town was up to the north—past the bend after the intersection of Route 1 and Guerneville Road—we couldn't see much of it. We just lay there for a while—chewing some jerky—checking out the command post and the surrounding landscape.

Tricky rolled over and started talking while he watched the sky. "Sometimes—at night—they get down to around six or so men for a couple of hours when they have patrols out in all directions. Usually right after dusk. I should be able to take out three or four before they find cover. But then somebody would have to come in from the east flank on their side of the river to flush them." He didn't finish—but he didn't have to. I understood who he was suggesting that somebody would be.

I lay there for a while studying the setting. There were bushes and small trees along the river on both sides. It looked like there was a sandbar upstream a ways that could be crossed as a half way point. However—after the trees—it was a ways to the east flank of the command post over fairly open ground. About 150 yards I estimated. Looked like it had been plowed a while back. I didn't see any sign of mines on that side but that didn't mean there weren't any there. It would be rough ground to cover at night without a light.

If I wanted to take them by surprise it could be close quarter fighting. I'd have to kill them with either the pistol or the shotgun — too old for a knife fight. Wasn't happy about killing them but couldn't see any way around it. Not if I wanted to get the bike across. Wasn't an easy decision.

"I want to go down and check on the bike about sunset. Can we do that?" I asked Tricky.

"Yes – we'll want to look along the riverbank and the hillside facing the river. We're going to have to be very careful. We're too close for comfort down there. We can check on your bike while we're there."

"I want to do that. We left in a hurry last night and I need to check on the girl and see if I damaged her any. Besides — you'll get to experience what it's like being close enough to the enemy to smell 'em. You'll want to bring your pistol." I'd seen him put what looked like a 9mm under his coat earlier.

Tricky suggested, "The path down is mostly covered from view of the command post because it winds down the side of the hill. We'll have to come around in the open at the bottom to reach the houses. That's where we have to watch it. Once we cross the old road we're up against the houses and the garage door is on our side of the river."

"Then let's pack up. I wanna catch a nap before we head out. We'll figure out some dinner when we get back." I hadn't directly answered his question about who was going to take the east flank — after swimming the cold river. But I understood what he was planning.

When we got back to camp I shared a can of fruit with Tricky and then crashed in the tent. The tent was warm from the sun and I could smell the ocean. I went out for a while. Life was okay — for now.

When I awoke I organized my gear for the patrol. I was ready for some serious recon. Had my good luck ball cap on. Holstered the sidearm and grabbed the shotgun. Made sure I had my canteen and some jerky. Also packed the binocs and a sweatshirt for later. We didn't say too much as we headed down the hill. The sun was getting close to the mountain. At least most of the trip down would be in the light. It was quite a hike — even downhill.

We finally reached the bottom as the sun was coming down over the bay. We checked around closely before we started over the open ground to the houses. I went first and Tricky followed behind. It didn't take too long to reach the houses. I hadn't seen much movement across the river since we reached the bottom of the hill — so we got lucky.

There were brief openings between the houses where we could see across the river. We finally came to the house where I'd stashed the bike. But I thought it best to check the road while we had some light to see how far we were from the bridge. I wanted Tricky to see the road to the bridge since he might be driving my bike as I would be across the river — hopefully. We crept down to the bridge. We would hear them if they started to move their bikes in the camp but they could come down from the Goathead direction and we might not pick them up until they were close. We were only three houses from the burned out restaurant. Things were still quiet across the river.

At the edge of the restaurant we could see across the bridge. The command post was back off to the right on the other side so we couldn't see it from where we were. We studied the bridge for a while until we heard some shouting across the river. Then a bike started. I didn't think anyone had seen us. We froze in our steps and listened. It might be a patrol getting ready to leave but we didn't know in what direction. We'd seen enough so we retreated back to the house with the bike and waited. After a few minutes another bike fired up. They were noisy even from this distance.

After a short warm up the two bikes headed east up Guerneville Road. We waited a while and nobody else fired up. I opened the garage and we moved inside and shut the door. I was glad to see the old girl. She looked good for a black primered old Super Glide. We didn't have much light left so I worked fast. I checked over the bike and the damage wasn't too bad. Mostly from dropping it after I slapped the dumpster. Looked like it would run without a problem but I had no way to test it.

"Come here and I'll give you a quick lesson in starting this old beast." Tricky didn't say anything but moved over to watch. I showed him the petcock and choke. "You have to talk to her nice. The electric starter should turn it over without problem. It's cold blooded though — what Harley isn't? Might make some smoke at first. Don't give it too much gas — it's easy to flood." We stood there and looked at the bike for a while. Ancient and mostly black — she still looked damn good to me. My freedom wheels...

"I think I got it," Tricky offered. "Rode a lot of dirt bike in Afghanistan but nothing this big. It will be interesting for sure."

"The clutch isn't too bad for an old bike. Once you get it started let it idle for a minute. Runs better on some choke until it's fully warm." I guess I'd agreed to his plan. "Now that it's getting dark let's go check out the river."

We snuck out a side door. It was about fifty yards before we got to the river. There were trees along the bank that gave us some cover. It was almost dark now and we moved quietly along the road down to the river bank. Fortunately — there was a decent moon so we could see a ways. We found a spot where we could get to the water and observe across the river. We saw the lights of the command post but couldn't make out much since we were so low. I checked the water. DAMN it was cold! I really was getting too old for this shit...

I studied the river and the sandbar in the middle as best I could. "Okay — let's head back. I've seen enough," I ordered.

We started the long climb back to camp. It was turning cool and I was getting hungry. After we crossed over the ridge Tricky said we should check his traps on the way back. Damned if he didn't have another rabbit snared. So we knew we would eat good tonight. "You start the fire JC and I'll get the rabbit ready. What else you got in your larder to throw in?" Tricky inquired.

"I still have some canned fruit we can share and maybe a can of beans." We started getting dinner on the fire. I shared a shot of my brandy while we waited for the rabbit to cook and we finished what was left of the joint from earlier.

While we sat around the fire I started talking about our plans to cross the river. "If we time it right around the patrols leaving the camp they might be down to maybe six or so Guardians. I'll swim the river and try to come in from the east flank of the camp across that open field. If you can take out three or four before they know what is happenin' then maybe I can catch the others by surprise. They won't be expecting someone on their side of the river. It'll get dicey once the shooting starts. I'll take both the .45 and shotgun. Need to keep them dry as possible while I cross the river. I have some trash bags to help out with that. What you think?"

"Sounds like a plan my man. You'll need a dry change of clothes to put on as soon as you're across. If you have to wait any time before attacking the camp you might get hypothermic in wet cloths and not be at your Marine best." Now I think he was playing with me. But I had to admit I hadn't thought about the dry clothes—good idea. And he might yet learn what Marines are made of before this dirty job was over.

"I'll setup in a spot on the hillside where I can still see the camp," Tricky continued, "but a lot closer to your bike and the bridge. I have a small flashlight you can use to signal me when you're in position. If I open up too soon it'll make it harder for you to get close."

"When we go down to the house we'll get your gear loaded up somehow on the bike. Then you can take up your position while we wait for the patrols to leave. Let's hope they all leave at once. If there are too many of 'em still there we might be fucked. You'll need to take out as many as you can and then create some havoc when they go under cover. Keep their attention diverted towards you. They won't know at first where the fire is coming from but if they open up with that machine gun or mortars you may have to hunker down. It'll take me a while to cross that open field and I hope like hell there aren't any mines. Once I have control of the camp I'll signal you again to get the bike and come across. If you can't get the bike started you'll just have to start pushing it across the bridge. That won't be easy."

"I can handle it once you signal me. I saw a spot in the trees earlier where I should have a clear field of fire. I'll take out three or four before they realize what's happening and go to ground. Then the rest is up to you. You think you're up to the swim and the attack?" I guess he was referring to my age.

"Once a Marine always a Marine!" That was a pretty ballsy

answer but I couldn't see any other way we were going to make this happen. "I'm not happy about the killing part but don't see any way around it. Thought I was through with that nasty business in my life." I guess that comment took him by surprise.

Tricky was silent for a moment before he commented, "To be honest—I'm not too excited about it myself. I've been pondering about what you asked me whether I still believe in God. Been thinking about my Dad a lot too. I don't think he'd be too proud about what his son became—an assassin and all. You can't change history but it does make me wonder how life might have been different if I'd stayed in Nebraska after law school and just settled down with a family. But too late to cry over spilt milk now."

"Yeah—I often wonder how life might've been if I'd gone back to the hills after the war. Or if I hadn't even gone to the war. A lot of ifs. But you're right—have to face the job at hand and get it done. I wanna make it to the New Society and maybe have a chance to start over." I thought about the tough and dirty work ahead. "Tomorrow will be a long day..."

We finished cooking the rabbit and it was a good meal for what little we had. After that we sat around the fire and talked about the good ole days. Hunting and fishing and not having much to worry about. I told him more of my biker stories which made him laugh. I liked telling stories. Always felt it was my only art form—except maybe v-twin engines. Then we just laid out and watched the stars pass between the clouds for a while. Didn't talk about much of anything important—just chatter before the battle.

We agreed we'd go back to the lookout in the morning and work out the final details of our plan. I took a shot of the shine before retiring but knew I wouldn't sleep too well that night— never did before a big mission. Tried to make peace with God because I knew I might not be alive this time tomorrow. It was going to be a rough piece of business ahead. So many thoughts were racing through my mind. I doubted that Tricky was going to sleep well either. I was about to trust my life to a stranger and he was going to depend on this old Marine to get the job done. Survival can make for strange bedfellows...

CHAPTER 17

Final Plans

The next morning we ate a cold breakfast of beans and headed up the ridge to lay out our final plans. We looked down the ridge near the bridge and thought we saw a spot that might be good for Tricky to set up. We decided to go down to the spot and check the visibility of the outpost. It took us a while to make our way down the front side of the ridge and stay under cover. We found a spot not too far above the houses that was flat and had some tree cover. We checked through the binocs and we had good visibility of the camp. This would be a good sniper location with visibility of the killing zone.

The spot we found wasn't too far from the road. Tricky could make it down to the house where my bike was stashed once I signaled him from across the river. I looked up the river bank with the binocs and there seemed to be a place where I could reach the river that was upstream from the sandbar in the middle. It was only about two hundred yards from where the houses ended. The river was low since there hadn't been much rain recently. My plan was to let the current carry me downstream while I swam to the bar. Then I would cross the bar and head back into the river to reach the other side. I was trying to guess how far downstream the river would carry me before I reached the other side.

The spot I estimated I'd end up when I reached the other bank was on a level beach where I could change back into dry clothes before starting the approach from the east. Tricky was going to give me a small flashlight to signal him when I was there and ready to move closer to the camp. I'd have to move parallel to the camp for a ways before I could turn to make my approach—coming in on their east flank behind where he was keeping them busy. My hope was that once Tricky opened up they'd be focused on where his fire was coming from and not paying attention to my side. They'd guess from the sound of his rifle that he was across the river. If the Guardians hadn't had any military training they might not realize it was a diversion to expose their flank.

They probably hadn't been fired upon before and I expected it would instigate some chaos on their part. Tricky would have to keep them busy while I made my way in the dark over the plowed field. The shotgun would be my primary weapon so I would need to get close. We decided I would signal him once more when I was ready to move in as his sign to open fire. Hoped the flashlight worked after crossing the river because I couldn't cover that distance without being heard if everything was quiet. I figured they'd try to return his fire and that would create the noise I needed to cover up my approach. It was going to be quite the run in the dark and I couldn't move too fast because of the uneven ground. I wasn't too fast of a runner anyways — even in my younger days. Though there'd been a few times when the Cong had really lit a fire under my ass!

We sat there discussing the plan until we agreed we had it down. I don't think he was going to get cold feet because he wanted across this river as bad as me. I wanted to trade him jobs but I didn't know his rifle and he wasn't experienced at close quarter fighting. So I guess that was that.

I figured once I had control of the camp — if I ever did — I was going to have to keep a low profile so Tricky couldn't get me in his sights too. I didn't trust him once the Guardians were eliminated. I was to signal him one more time once I thought the camp was taken so he could climb down and get the bike across. When I saw him coming across the bridge I'd have to be on the lookout for what he was going to do once he reached me. At that point he might be the enemy also. But I wasn't going to let on to him about any of these concerns. I would play stupid on this one. Easy enough for an old fart biker.

We'd been there for over an hour and agreed our plans were in place. So we started the long climb back up the ridge to the camp. Couldn't afford to be spotted at this point or it would really screw the pooch. I was running short on food but between the two of us we scrounged up some lunch and planned on what time we would eat and leave later today. I was going to need a lot of energy to swim the river and press the attack on the camp.

I planned on raiding the Guardian food supplies before heading north to Sea Ranch — which was my destination for the night. There was a place I knew of there where I planned to hide out for the night. Tricky was going to head back into the mountains just east of the guard post. He'd be moving through unknown ground in the dark and would need to get into the woods a ways to find protection. The Guardians would be real pissed if we pulled this off and looking for revenge.

We calculated it would be best to leave in time to climb down the ridge just before dark. We'd go to the bike first and get everything loaded. That was going to be a trick in itself with his added gear. Then he'd climb up to his sniper position and I'd wait down the road for the next patrols to leave. We sure hoped they'd do their usual routine of sending out several bikes at once right after dark so the number left in camp would be small. We agreed that if they didn't follow their usual plan — and only sent out one patrol — that we might have to scratch our plans and try again the next night. But our food was getting slim.

I was pooped from the mountain hiking so I crashed in the tent for a while. I had crazy dreams about the night ahead — all jumbled up with memories from Vietnam.

When I got up it was the middle of the afternoon and Tricky was already getting his gear ready. He was loading the sniper rifle and had a second clip ready for action. I started to get my stuff together and was sorting out what I'd take across the river. Would bungee my leathers to the bike so they'd be ready to put on in a hurry. I knew I'd need them for the ride north to Sea Ranch. The road past Jenner was very windy and slow as it ran along the cliffs for quite a ways. Be a bad place to run into a patrol. I guessed it was about twenty miles to Sea Ranch and my planned hideout. I wanted to get as far away from the outpost as I could after the bloody mess we'd leave.

The next town where they might have a command post or supplies was Gualala — so Sea Ranch would be the place to stop as it was about a mile before there. Back in the day Sea Ranch was a pretty exclusive place to live with some real fancy houses. I knew where there was a tree house to the east of the development in the woods and that was where I was heading. One of my biker friends knew the guy who'd built the tree house before Sea Ranch became a big money place. The place was down a side road back into the woods. Duke and I used to camp out there sometimes when we were heading north. Great little party spot. With any luck the Guardians won't know it exists. Just hoped it was still there.

I got my tent and bag packed up and went over the shotgun and pistol one last time. They were ready. Didn't have too many rounds for the shotgun so I'd keep the extra clip for the .45 handy. I'd strap the Kabar to my leg once across but hoped it wouldn't come down to a knife fight.

I placed Jake the Snake's rubbers over the barrel openings of both weapons to help keep them dry. Knew those Trojans might come in handy somehow. The sheep would have to wait. We put the shotgun and pistol into some of the garbage bags Gladman had given me at the party. Threw in my only change of clothes and my recycled long underwear. Hoped they would stay dry in the crossing. Tricky gave me a small towel to help a little with drying off after I came out of the river. I'd throw the wet clothes back in the bag before I started north to the east side of the command post. I'd carry the bag until I got close to the action and then drop it when things started to heat up.

There was some time to kill before we ate and headed out so we kicked back for a while and talked about life when we were young studs. I told Dick about life in the hills and he talked about times in Nebraska when he was a kid. I remembered how we swapped stories before a patrol in Nam to try and remember better times. Guess we were doing the same thing to take our minds off what lay ahead.

The afternoon was getting chilly but there was no sign of fog yet. Fog could be bad for his sniper mission but good for my approach from the river. There were some clouds moving in so the night would have intermittent moonlight. That would work for both of us.

We decided not to make a fire and had another cold meal. Finished it off with my last can of fruit in the pack and topped it off with some candy bars Tricky had. He gave me the last one to take with me to eat on the other side of the river in case I had to wait any time. We were ready to take on the night's work. If I was going to die tonight I wanted it to be quick—didn't want to be another scalp on Blackie's torture belt.

Found myself saying a prayer. Still not sure about God's place in all of this but figured it didn't hurt to ask. Maybe even Dick was having similar thoughts since we'd talked about God yesterday. He was very quiet. I used to say prayers in Nam before a patrol but it didn't seem like too many were answered. Maybe that was a mystery I'd solve tonight if I didn't make it…

CHAPTER 18

Combat!

We waited until about two hours before sunset to start for the ridge. Tricky wasn't saying much. I'm sure we were both thinking about what was to come. My gear was heavy and I was feeling it when we reached the ridge. Good thing it was downhill from there. Tricky was really loaded down with all his camping shit and the rifle. Must have been quite the job for him carrying it over the hills from where he started in Marin County.

We checked the command post from the ridge to see who was there and what they were up to. Several bikes were parked near the command tent. It appeared they were planning on sending out patrols sometime after dark—or so I hoped. We agreed to head down the side of the mountain where we wouldn't be seen before making our way to the house with the bike. It was still light when we reached the bottom so we were very cautious about crossing the road and working our way to the river. If anyone on the other side was watching closely they might see us but we hadn't seen anyone checking out our side of the river while we were on top. Just a guard in a dugout on the other side of the bridge and he didn't seem too concerned.

We made it to the house and loaded up the bike. I put my gear on first and then tied Tricky's on as best we could. It was going to be a job balancing everything but all he had to do was make it across the bridge. I expected he could do it if he could get the bike started. The old girl was a temperamental beast but she should start okay for him. Couldn't afford the opportunity to give him a practice try or they'd hear us for sure.

It wouldn't be easy holding on to the bag in the current. Thought about Gladman as I double bagged the load. His garbage bags were going to be very important tonight. Left a little air in it when I tied them off in the hope it would float some as I made my way across the river. We agreed he'd signal me by throwing some rocks down to the road when he was in position. I'd then signal back with the light I was ready to go. As soon as the patrols took off he'd signal me again if it looked clear and I'd head for the river. We turned the bike around and got it pointed in the right direction for an easy exit from the garage. I think he was in good enough shape to handle the weight. One last time we went over the starting procedures. We were ready…

Tricky took off with the sniper rifle to his ambush site and I sat back against the garage and waited. I heard him disappear off into the bushes and then it got very quiet. Every once in a while I could hear voices across the river but couldn't make out anything. The waiting before an ambush was sometimes the hardest part. I lit up the one cigarette I had left out of the pack just to kill some time. Guess I'd think more about quitting tomorrow.

It seemed to take a long time but eventually I heard the rocks from Tricky hitting the road. He was finally in place. I signaled back but wasn't sure if he saw me. No matter—I'd just wait for the next signal. The clouds were moving in but not much fog yet. That was good because fog could interfere with his shooting. It was getting chilly and I didn't have much on for clothes. The time was passing slowly and I had to pee again. Damn that old prostate.

In about half an hour he signaled me again. I heard the bikes starting up on the other side. I couldn't tell how many were running but there were at least two. Good news. It was time for action! The bikes started out and I could hear them taking off in different directions. One group was headed south across the bridge and it seemed like another was headed north. I didn't hear one going to the east. Tried looking between the houses but couldn't see much across the river.

The bikes coming south didn't take long to cross the bridge before they made the sharp turn up the hill to Goathead Rock. They were accelerating hard and I heard them disappear off into the distance. Couldn't tell from my position if Blackie was with them. I waited for Tricky to signal it was time to start across the river. It wasn't long before he threw some more rocks down to the road. Signaled him back with the light and then made my way to the river. I was wearing an old pair of sneakers I'd brought along — my boots were in the bag. Figured they'd be easier in the river and I needed to keep the boots dry for the other side.

I found the level spot next to the river and waded in. DAMN and DOUBLE DAMN! It was fuckin' cold and woke me right up. I did a side crawl across the river dragging the bag. Even at low water this was a wide river to swim. It wasn't easy keeping the bag with me as the current kept wanting to pull it away. It seemed like forever but I finally reached the sandbar. I'd guessed my position fairly good the day before as I was in the middle of the bar. The bushes made it hard to get across and I took some scratches but that might be the least of my worries this night. Sure hoped I didn't step in any holes in the dark.

I paused only for a moment on the other side and when I didn't see any activity near the river I went back into the water. I was getting colder but had to keep swimming. The Marines taught me well. Survival was everything. I kept thinking about how it'd feel to be riding north again once this nasty job was done.

When I finally reached the other side I stopped to catch my breath. But the cold caught up with me and I opened the bag to get the towel and dry clothes. Dried off in a hurry and put on the long johns and outfit. My leather jacket would help warm me up as I moved in. It felt a little better but I was still shivering. The Snake's Trojans had done their job and I threw them on the riverbank. After I stuffed the wet clothes back in the bag I strapped on the .45 and made my way up the river bank with the shotgun at the ready.

It wasn't easy getting through the bushes near the river but before long it opened up into the clear. I started to make my way to a position on the east flank of the command post. Tricky was probably shitting his pants waiting for my signal but he'd just have to wait. I trusted he was a patient man because if he opened up too soon it could be disastrous — for both of us.

It took probably twenty minutes to make my way to a spot east of the camp where I could see the tents in the distance. I wanted to get a little closer before I signaled Tricky that I was ready. But then I got a big surprise!

I could hear loud voices coming from the camp so I went into a crouch while I tried to listen. As best I could tell it seemed like the Guardians were having an argument. Something about heading to a cabin toward Guerneville to get laid—without Blackie's permission. So that meant Blackie wasn't in camp— very good news...

After a while the voices stopped and I heard two more bikes start up. I waited while they took off east up the Guerneville Road. For now that meant two less Guardians to deal with. It would be great if they didn't come back any time soon. Hoped whoever they were visiting she'd get them to take their time— no 'wham-bam—thank you mam' kind of a deal. It was a gamble I'd have to take.

When I was about fifty yards from the camp I signaled Tricky with the light. With any luck he already knew where I was through his night vision scope. Sure hoped his batteries were working. I could see some Guardians moving around and as best I could tell there might only be four or five left in camp. I was moving across the field with the shotgun ready—waiting for Tricky to start his dirty work. Kept praying there weren't any mines in this area or it would be a short battle for me.

I was moving toward the main tent when I saw one of the Guardians go down from a head shot. Tricky was on the job. He took out another one a few seconds later. Give him credit—he was a damn good shot with that high tech weapon of his. After the second one was hit the other Guardians were scrambling for cover. It looked like Tricky took out another as he was making for a bunker. I was getting closer to the tent and no one had spotted me yet. The Guardian nearest me took cover in the command tent and started to return fire across the river. Though I'm sure he had no idea what he was shooting at—or where.

Tricky was laying down cover fire on the command tent and keeping that Guardian busy. As I got within yards of the tent I could only hear the closest Guardian returning fire so maybe he was the only one still in action. But he was under cover where Tricky couldn't see him so he'd be my problem. Needed to close in quick so he couldn't get to the radio.

As I came up on the tent I spotted the Guardian hunkered down behind some sandbags firing his M16. He was too busy to hear me coming from his flank. I had the shotgun ready to take him out but as I got closer I couldn't pull the trigger to kill him from behind. So I made the hasty — and not well thought out — decision to take him out without killing him.

I came in running from the back of the mess tent where he was crouched down and he heard me as I was just a few feet away. He was standing up as I hit him from behind with my body. I knocked him down and the weapon flew out of his hand. He was only stunned for a moment as he turned to fight me. Maybe this wasn't such a good idea as he was a really BIG BOY! I had no choice now but to finish it off — if I could. My adrenaline was pumping and that was always good for a few more horsepower.

I gave him a hard kick to the gut that knocked the wind out of him — he went down again. Then I jumped on his back and grabbed him in a choke hold around the neck. Wanted to cut off his air until he passed out but he had a lot of juices flowing too. We wrestled around the tent knocking shit everywhere. He slammed me back into several tables trying to break me loose. It hurt but I didn't let go. Just hung on and squeezed with all my might. Had a bull by the horns and couldn't let go. After what seemed like a lifetime he started to lose consciousness and went down on his knees with me on his back. He finally went out but I was pretty roughed up from the struggle.

Found some rope in the tent and tied him up before he could regain consciousness. I'm not sure why I didn't just kill him when I had the chance but I couldn't do it. My aching body was paying the price for that quick decision. After I tied him up I picked up my shotgun and tried to see if anyone else was moving. Didn't want to leave the tent where Tricky could have a shot at me so I was being careful to stay under cover. I sat down and didn't hear any other movement. Tricky had done his sniper job well.

Since I didn't know when those other Guardians would be returning I signaled Tricky to get the bike and start across. Once he was on the bike and in the open he wouldn't be able to take me out so quickly. I checked out the mess tent while I waited and helped myself to the chili they'd made earlier. It wasn't too bad. I started to collect some canned food to take with me. More beans — good thing I liked those damned beans.

It was some time before I heard the bike coming across the bridge. Tricky had gotten her started and was on his way. The clock was ticking and we wouldn't have much time to hang around when he got here. Once I knew he was on the move I checked out the rest of the camp to see if anyone was still moving. He'd taken out four of the guards with one shot each. They were all dead so the one I tied up must be the only one left. But there was still the two who were down the road getting laid.

I heard the motorcycle coming in the distance — coughing on full choke — then I saw Tricky coming across the bridge out of the light fog. I watched him carefully until he pulled up to the camp. I had the shotgun ready in case he decided to go crazy on me. He parked the bike just a short ways from the tent and I saw he didn't have the rifle with him. "What happened to your rifle?"

"I decided to leave it there. Tired of carrying it." He looked around to see if we were alone. "I took out four. What happened to the one who ducked inside the tent?"

"I took him down — he's still alive inside."

Tricky went into the tent and saw the Guardian tied up in the corner. He was starting to come around. Then Tricky did something that really pissed me off. He pulled his 9mm and went over to the Guardian — without a word — put a bullet through his head. "We don't want any survivors," he said coldly before he turned around.

I'd just fought this guy to the ground so I wouldn't have to kill him. As Tricky was turning around I whacked him across the head with the shotgun. He went down hard. I tied him up while he was out. I was really angry. Killing that Guardian wasn't necessary since we had control of the engagement.

I took Tricky's gear off the bike and threw it on the ground. Loaded my stuff including all the food I could stash in the saddlebags. I was cold and exhausted — it was time to go. Put on the rest of my leathers and made sure everything was secure on the bike for the ride to Sea Ranch. Dug out my leather flying cap as it was going to be a cold ride up the coast with the fog coming in. I figured it'd been over an hour since the patrols had left. Needed to make tracks real soon. I was still trying to decide what to do with Tricky when he started to come to. He was bleeding from where I'd smacked him on the head with the shotgun.

"Man—what's your fucking problem?" he yelled at me. "Why did you hit me?" He was struggling with the ropes. "I thought we were partners. I helped you get across the river. I kept our bargain."

"Yeah—but you didn't need to take him out. It was a hard fight to take him down. Didn't you get enough killing for the night?"

"No matter! If you leave me here you know what Blackie will do to me when he finds me. You owe me JC! We didn't need any survivors left to tell the Guardians how many of us there were. If he told them you were on a bike they'd be looking for you on the road." On that part he was right but I was still pissed off at him for killing that man.

I stood there for a moment thinking it over. He was right—Blackie would be vicious with him and he'd done his job as we agreed. I left him alone for a minute and started the bike to let her warm up. My mind was racing—I couldn't leave him to what lay ahead when Blackie found him. Particularly with all these dead bodies lying around. I had to either kill him or turn him loose. Blackie would get him to talk and he would tell them about me and the motorcycle. Not an easy decision...

I went back into the tent and took his gun and threw it outside. Then I untied the ropes around his hands. "It won't take you long to untie your feet but I have to go. Don't want to run into a patrol coming back from the north." I hadn't told him where I was going at Sea Ranch so if they caught him he wouldn't know my destination. But I'm sure he'd tell them I was out there once they started to torture him. So it might be best if he got away.

"You should pack up and get into the woods before those boys get back. Hope you make it out okay. Maybe I'll see you in the north. Good luck." And with that short goodbye I got on the bike and headed out into the dark. Figured I was leaving tracks in the dirt but couldn't worry about that now. The fog was coming and it was getting damp. I didn't look back but figured Tricky was already out of the ropes and getting his ass out of Dodge also. Wondered if I'd ever see him again. We still had a score to settle...

I opened it up through Jenner before the uphill climb out of town. I knew the road from here would be along the cliffs and slow riding. I wasn't going to make good time along the cliffs and with the fog moving in my visibility was cutting down. Slowly made my way around the turns and tried hard to keep it on the slippery road. I was feeling the soreness in my body from the fight and I couldn't seem to get warm. Still had a ways to go to Sea Ranch.

I watched the odometer to mark off the distance. The instruments were getting wet and hard to read. Good thing I had my chaps and flight cap to stay a little dry. Kept wiping the moisture from my glasses. The fog was getting thicker as I worked my way up from the ocean.

After what seemed like a long time the road opened up from the cliffs but I still couldn't up the speed much. If there was a patrol coming the other way we'd be on each other before we knew it. Had to keep moving to eat up the miles. When I finally reached Fort Ross Park I knew I was making progress. The next place I was looking for was Stewarts Point Store.

I was starting to get sick to my stomach and light headed. I think it was the fatigue or maybe even shock. I thought about stopping for the night at Stewarts Point Store or Timber Cove Inn but it would be hard to hide out at those places. Gonna have to gut it out and keep moving. I tried to focus my mind but it kept wandering to past times. Everything was a blur — like a crazy dream.

Stewarts Point Store finally showed up out of the fog. Left the bike running while I stopped for a quick pee and a smoke. I was feeling really bad inside so I only took a few quick drags before I got back on the bike to keep moving north. It was under ten miles now to Sea Ranch but I was so tired it seemed like a hundred. The sound of the engine kept me awake and gave me some comfort. The fog was getting thicker and slowing me down even more. I was feeling worse and just trying to hold on till I could hide out.

Seemed like forever before I reached the beginning of Sea Ranch. I had to go a few more miles before I'd find the turn to the tree house in the woods. So far no patrols but I was running out of time. Was looking for Ridgeline Road so each time I saw a road sign I had to slow down and try to read it in the fog. My mind was so jumbled I was wondering if I'd missed it—when I saw the sign. Fuck—an—A! It was hanging by just one bolt but there it was. Looked like someone been using it for target practice.

Made a slow turn to the east and rode back towards the woods—past the million dollar homes that were once Sea Ranch. Couldn't see much in the fog but it looked like many were burned down. Didn't look like anyone was living there which wasn't a surprise. Be an easy target for the Guardians. And I doubt any of the rich folk who'd lived here once knew much about living off the land. I started to enter the woods but knew I had to go in a ways to find the tree house hidden in the forest.

I'd heard the tale many years ago about the guy who'd built the tree house. Story was he couldn't afford one of the expensive Sea Ranch homes after a divorce so he found a V-shaped tree and built a small house in the V with a short wing off to each side. It would sleep about four people—if they weren't big. Had a small stove in the middle for heat and cooking. We used to camp out in the woods around the tree house when we stopped here. Drank some good coffee with the little guy who lived in the house.

When I reached the tree house I was relieved to see it wasn't damaged. I was feeling pretty sick now and barely able to hold onto the bike. I pulled up next to the house. It was all I could do to get the kickstand down. I rolled off the bike onto the ground and threw up. Think I had hypothermia. Felt like fuckin' shit…

Slowly propped myself up against a tree and tried to get my head and stomach to settle down. Then I heard a sound coming from the house. I saw what looked like a candle light up inside.

Holy shit—there was somebody here! Didn't see any vehicles around so I don't think it was a Guardian—who'd be living out here in the woods?

I reached for my sidearm as the door opened. A tall man in a robe—with long hair—stood silhouetted in the doorway against the candle. But I couldn't tell if he had a weapon. I was so weak I could barely pull out my .45. Had I made it through this hell tonight just to die now...?

CHAPTER 19

Helping Hand

Lying there exhausted and sick I tried to aim the .45 against the figure in the doorway. As he slowly stepped closer he looked like a monk. Was I getting delusional? Somehow I felt a calm radiate from him. I sensed no threat from this man—whoever he was. I leaned back against the tree and put the weapon down. Wasn't even sure I could stand up I was so nauseated.

"You look like you need some help my son." He stepped forward and knelt before me. "Sure don't look like no Guardian I've ever seen. Particularly on an old motorcycle like that. You been shot?"

"No—but I'm really out of it. Too exhausted to move. And the Guardians are looking for me. Just thought you should know."

"Then that makes you a friend of mine. And by the way— I'm Brother John. Just call me John. Here—let me help you into the cabin. You look like something the cat drug in." He reached down and touched my forehead like my mom did when I was sick as a kid. "You're cold as ice. We need to warm you up."

"Put your arm around me," he offered. "It's only a few steps to the house." He held me around the waist as we walked. He was skinny but strong. His long hair smelled like incense as it brushed over my face. The damp was getting his robe wet as he supported me to the tree house. For some reason I knew I was in good hands—so I followed his directions.

We slowly worked our way into the tree house and he set me down at the table. "Let's get you into some warm clothes and into bed. Here—you won't need this," he said as he helped me take off the .45 and set it on the bed. "Let's get those wet clothes off." He hung my leathers on some hooks next to the door and gave me a pair of sweats to wear. "You crawl into bed and I'll put on some herbal tea. It will help you sleep and heal."

I moved the .45 to the other side of the bed and crawled in

to try and get warm. I was so cold and shivering. The bed was warm and welcoming—it smelled like John. I watched this tall stranger as he started a small fire in the pot belly stove and put on a tea kettle. He mixed something from several small jars and placed it in a metal ball into the kettle.

"This will only take a few minutes," he informed me. "There's a can next to the bed if you get sick and need to toss your cookies. I'm going to move your cycle back into the trees and cover it up while the tea steeps. I'll bring your pack and bag in. It's pretty wet out there. I left your gun with you in case you feel you need it but you won't in my house." Somehow—I knew I wouldn't.

He moved quietly outside and I could hear him pushing the bike back into the woods. Before long he returned to the cabin and poured me a cup of the tea. "Drink this slowly and let it warm your insides. There are some crackers to eat with it if you feel like putting something on your stomach. You could use the salt right now." He sat down at the table and just watched me in the glow of the stove.

After a while he spoke again, "I'm a long lost member of the Emissaries of the Light Jesuit Order of Monks. Maybe the last for all I know. Got out of San Francisco just before the Guardians cut off the escape routes. Made it all the way to here before it got too dangerous to travel farther."

He paused for some time while I drank his warm tea…

After I finished the tea he suggested, "I'm sure you have quite a story to tell but there will be time for that tomorrow after you get some sleep. The Guardians never come back this far but I will keep an ear out for them since they are looking for you. They don't know I'm here or they would have killed me a long time ago. They don't care much for men of the cloth I hear. But I think you'll be safe for now."

The tea warmed me and helped me feel calm. My stomach settled down and I was very tired. I wondered what was in the tea but didn't ask.

"You can go to sleep when you feel like it," John said in a quiet voice. "I'll be on the cot on the other side of the stove so call out if you need anything. The outhouse is a little walk up in the woods—tell me if you need me to help you get there. The tea will help you sleep and have good dreams."

As I was getting drowsy I remembered I hadn't told him my name. "I'm JC—thanks for takin' me in."

"Well then JC—you sleep and I will pray for your recovery." And with that short comment he slipped outside. I wasn't quite sure who this tall stranger was but for now he'd provided me shelter from the storm. It'd been a hell of a night but I was still alive. I rolled over and fell into a deep sleep with long colorful dreams of better times.

I woke up several times during the night and had to think for a while to remember where I was—then I'd go back to sleep. Whatever was in the tea it did the trick. Slept until after sunrise and woke up feeling calmer than I'd been since I started the trip. Could hear Brother John working outside so I lay there for a while and watched the sun work its way through the small windows of the tree house.

The details of the night before kept running through my head. I was still angry with Tricky for killing that last Guardian. But it was a matter of survival and he was right about that. I don't think the Guardian would've given a second thought about taking my life if he'd had the chance—I'd never know.

I wasn't sure what lay ahead but for now I was safe and lucky to have been taken in by Brother John. I'm sure I must have scared the hell out of him when I came in out of the dark last night on a motorcycle. He seemed so calm about it all—almost like he'd been expecting me. I'd learn more when we talked.

Eventually I got out of bed and sat at the table. My body was really sore and bruised from the night before. That big Guardian had taken a toll on me. I think I was ready for the trip to the out-house. John must have heard me stirring as he poked his head in the door. "You need some help to get up the path to the john?"

"I'm pretty beat up but I think I can make it." I moved slow-ly out of the house and headed up the path. John walked along-side. The morning was warming up but it was still chilly. After I finished my duty—he even had TP—I came back down the path and smelled coffee brewing in the house. It sure smelled good. I sat back down at the table as John poured us each a big cup. "This will help get you going. Hope you like it black and strong."

I savored the coffee as we sat there in silence. John seemed very patient to learn about this stranger who'd shown up so abruptly in his world. "I don't know what was in that tea but it sure knocked me out. Thanks again for takin' me in."

"It's okay JC. Been a long time since I got to minister to anyone being so far out here by myself. I miss it. I'm sure you have some story to tell if you came this far from the City. How did you ever get across the bridge?"

"I started in the City. Came out in a garbage truck—that's another story. Been working my way up the coast at night. Trying to stay away from the Guardians. Last night we had to take on a well armed command post at Jenner."

"We?" he inquired quietly.

"It's a long story but I met someone at Jenner who helped me get across the river."

"Did he get killed?"

"Not exactly," I paused, "but you might say we didn't part on good terms. He's walkin' his way north now if he got away. We did some violence Brother John—not proud of it. Hafta' confess to it. Tell you more about it later."

John handed me a bowl of canned fruit and another with hard boiled eggs. "I have a few chickens in the woods I found at one of the abandoned ranches up in the hills. You need to eat and work on getting your strength back." He didn't have to ask me twice. It was a royal treat to have the boiled eggs and fruit. "Eat as many as you like. I'll make more later." He opened one egg himself and ate with me.

I had to ask, "Didn't I shake you up—coming on a motorcycle in the middle of night and all?"

"Well—you sure did surprise me at first. But I believe God sent you to bring some comfort to my solace. I've been here alone since shortly after the wars started. The rich people at Sea Ranch mostly took off right after the Guardians started coming north. Some went north and some went east. No one really knew what was happening. Those who stayed didn't last long once the Guardians came."

He remembered for a moment and then went on, "The Guardians were ruthless. The houses that didn't get burned right away I raided for food supplies and stocked up as best I could. The Guardians still don't know I'm here. I think there might be some people left in Gualala but I haven't gone there to find out. When I've been close to there I hear the patrols stopping and staying for a time. I still go out when I can to look for food in the houses but I have to go farther each time."

I reached across the table and shook his hand. He had a real solid grip. "You may have saved my life."

"I will always help my fellow man. Even if you were a Guardian. It's part of my life's work. I used to minister to the street people in San Francisco and started an AIDS mission for those who couldn't afford help. I think I have the virus myself now — as I'm showing early signs of the disease." He watched my face to see my reaction.

"I lost a number of friends to AIDS over the years," I responded. "You know — from the sex and drugs. So I'm not afraid to be around it. Is there something I can do for you?"

"No — just your company is great. Known lots of bikers in the City. From the looks of your jacket you're an ex-Marine too — maybe Vietnam? You're welcome in my home. I didn't see any outlaw colors on your jacket but it wouldn't matter if I did. You're my brother in the eyes of God."

I didn't quite know what to say to that. This man knew he was dying but he seemed so at peace with the world. AIDS wasn't an easy way to go. He had dark brown eyes that seemed so deep. He just sat there and shared his life with me. After we ate all of the eggs I made an offer, "Perhaps I can cut some wood or something for you. You know — to pay you back for your hospitality."

"You don't owe me anything JC. Besides — you need to rest. We'll take a hike out to the ocean later and let you breath the fresh salt air for a while. It always rejuvenates me. You might be a day or two healing up. I saw some pretty good bruises on your back last night when you were changing. I'll give you some salve that might help and some other tea I can brew. For now — let's just talk. I really miss conversation."

So we sat at the table and I told him my story about how I'd escaped from the City in a garbage truck. Of course being the storyteller I had to embellish it a bit but it made him laugh — his dark eyes shined. We talked about my time in the City all the way back to coming home from Vietnam. The morning went by without notice as we exchanged stories about life in the City. I felt like I was with an old friend I'd known for years.

Then John told me his story about how he'd grown up in Catholic schools in New York City before he went to Penn State. He stayed there until he'd finished his doctors degree in the philosophy of comparative religions—whatever that was. He was too young for the draft in Vietnam but his dad had served in the Army during the Korean War. Said his dad never talked much about the war and he'd encouraged him to never serve in the military. After finishing his schooling he took a teaching position at Stanford.

"I only ever knew one dude who had a big degree in the biker crowd," I recalled. "He was this really strange character from Berkeley who liked to hang out with bikers. We always wondered if he was a narc but found out he really was a professor and he was harmless. He always talked about the thrill of the counter culture—guess that meant us. He used to say that teaching was a plush gig and once you had something called tenure you never had to worry about a job again. How could anyone in those difficult times—when all the work was going overseas—have guaranteed life time employment? Must of had a good union. That the case? You had lifetime work?"

"Yep—that was one of the reasons I left the university. After faculty received tenure they didn't work so hard anymore and became apathetic. We liked to say we were there for the students but we were really there for ourselves and our egos. It was a self centered and isolated environment. After a while I felt like I'd become part of a decadent pseudo intellectual culture that gave little and expected everything in return. I became very disillusioned with the whole profession. I needed to feel like I could make a difference in people's lives. So that was when I decided to go to Jesuit seminary."

"Sounds like a pretty big change," I offered.

"It was. It really was! My family didn't understand at first why I gave up a really good salary and lifestyle at the university. But it was the right choice. After seminary I ministered at a number of missions around the country but somehow wound up back in the City working with AIDS patients. The ones who didn't have the medical coverage or money to get any care. Mostly street people—you know—prostitutes and junkies—bikers at times. Sometimes just plain homeless. It was hard watching people die and knowing you couldn't help them medically. So we tried to help them spiritually. Sometimes it just meant holding their hand while they died."

"That had to be tough. I remember when Big Spike got AIDS from his heroin habit. Used to visit him every once in a while in the hospital. It was sad to see such a big guy just wither away. AIDS is tough—slow and painful." Brother John stared out the window for a while. I'm sure he was remembering the faces of the many people he'd given comfort. Always said I had to respect anyone who could do a job I couldn't. John was definitely one of those people.

"When did you find out you had the disease?" That was a hard question to ask him.

"I found out I was HIV positive about a year ago but the first signs of the disease just started to show up recently." He must have seen the concerned look on my face. "Don't be worried about me JC—I've made peace with God. I go out every day and celebrate the beauty of nature and sit for hours by the ocean. I'm at peace but don't know how long I'll last. I don't have any medicine—not that it helps much anyways. I do have some morphine I brought out with me but only a small amount."

"Have you thought about trying to make it north to the New Society where they could help you?"

"Yes—but only briefly. Then I decided to just stay here and die in the woods. If I ever wanted to end it quick I could just go out to the highway and pretend to threaten the next patrol that came along. You know—death by Guardian!" He looked at me for a moment and started to laugh. "That's supposed to be joke!" I smiled back at how lightly he seemed to take the matter. It made me feel lucky I was still alive and trying to make it north.

"If you feel up to it let's get dressed and hike out to the ocean. I know you're pretty sore but the walk and ocean air will feel good. I'll pack a small lunch. I know a place where we can get down to the water but it's cold—still early in the summer. Might be just the thing for you."

He paused for a moment, "I want to tell you how special it is to have some company. I always liked bikers. Took care of a number of them at the mission. They were real free spirits who just took life as it came. Didn't have much use for the outlaws because I knew killing was part of their routine. But I gave them care when they needed it. A few even repented with me before they died. Strange what looking death in the eye will do to a person."

"Yeah—I been there. There were many times in Nam I thought I was gonna die. Also held onto a lot of guys while they died. It's something you never forget. Tried talking to God on many occasions over there but I was never sure he was listening because the death never stopped. When I was shot the first time I thought I wouldn't make it back. Crazy things go through your mind when you're that close to dying."

"Then I guess we've both had our own horrors," John said. "So let's pack up and head for the beach and talk about how great it is to be alive. In spite of these crazy times."

With that said we made ready for our hike to the beach. John put some more of his salve on my bruises. I hoped it worked as good as his tea. I put on the .45 as I didn't want to get caught flat footed by any Guardians. John gave me a funny look at first. To him it was just another day at the ocean. "I don't have much use for guns but understand why you need to bring it along. I'll carry the shotgun for you if you want." He must have seen it on the bike when he moved it into the trees.

"No—that won't be necessary. We're just gonna hang at the ocean—right?"

I started to get out one of my joints out but gave it a second thought. I needed to keep a clear head while we crossed the road as it was in the open for a ways. Also didn't want to offend Brother John. Maybe later. It would be nice to take a day off from the mission and try to recuperate. I was still tired and just the hike to the ocean would be a challenge. I was looking forward to the company though. John was a peaceful man and I felt his calm as we started down the road to the other side of Sea Ranch. It was going to be a fun day in the sun…

CHAPTER 20

A Day at the Beach

We packed up a lunch and headed for the ocean. I couldn't remember the last time I'd just hung on the beach. I took the .45 but left the shotgun — didn't feel right asking a holy man to carry a gun. Hoping we would avoid any Guardian complications this day. Counted on the fact that Brother John knew his way around after being isolated here for several months.

My body really hurt but the walking helped me stretch things out. John gave me a walking stick and it helped. After a while we emerged from the woods and could see the homes of Sea Ranch. "I've already checked out most of those places for canned goods so we'll just head for the beach," John offered as we walked across the open fields between the homes. "We'll stay off the road just in case some Guardians come checking. Are they searching for you?"

"Well — they're looking for someone. But I don't know yet if they figured out I'm on a bike. They might of picked up my tire tracks in the dirt at the command post. We left several bodies behind so they gotta be real pissed and looking for revenge. If Tricky got away they probably figure it's someone walking north. If they caught him then he probably gave me up and they'll be looking for me on the coast road. So we need to be cautious. The Guardians will no doubt have a bounty out for who ever did the deed."

John didn't seem to care much about the fact that I was a wanted man. "We'll be able to hear a patrol from a ways off if anyone is coming down the road — it's pretty open around here. When we get closer to the road we'll wait for a bit to see what we hear."

John kept a good pace but stopped every so often for me to catch up. We were getting close to Route 1. John slowed down and he signaled me to keep quiet as we came up behind a burned down house.

"We can see the road for a ways in both directions from here so let's hang out for a while," he said in a soft voice. It was quiet except for the birds. The sun felt great and I could smell the ocean. We sat down and had a drink from his water bottle. "I don't mind if you smoke as long as you don't mind if I don't join you." I guess he'd seen the cigarettes in my pack.

"Well—I'm trying to quit," I responded.

"Sure you are and I'm giving up fish on Fridays." We both laughed. John had a great sense of humor. I was starting to get comfortable with this odd man. He had a sense of peace about him I hadn't felt from anyone in a while. Quite an accomplishment for a man who was alone and knew he was dying. I guess he understood something about life I hadn't figured out yet.

I lit up a cigarette while we sat listening. We waited for a while but didn't hear any patrols. "Okay—we're going to cross the road," John said. "It's about two hundred yards across the road until we can find cover. You ready? Let's pick up the pace."

I gave him a nod and we took off in a fast walk for the other side. We crossed the road and were about fifty yards from the closest house when we heard that terrible sound. It was a patrol coming from the north and they were closing on us fast. John grabbed my arm. "We gotta move!" I didn't need to be told twice.

We began to run. I felt it in my legs but didn't want to get caught with only a .45 against their automatics—so I pushed it hard. I could hear the patrol getting closer and it would only be seconds before they'd see us. We were a few yards from the house when John came up beside me in a sprint, "Go Marine!" and he took the lead stretching out those long legs of his. We ducked behind the house as we could hear the Guardians getting closer on the road.

I threw off my pack and pulled the .45. If they'd seen us I wasn't going to give up without a fight. Only had the one extra clip. I wasn't sure what John would do if all hell broke loose. I assumed he really was a pacifist like Duke used to kid me about being. I'd protect him as best I could.

We backed up against the house and listened. The patrol didn't seem to be slowing down. It only sounded like two of them but I couldn't be sure. In just a moment I saw them passing south and off into the distance. They were really moving. This was one of the few places in this part of the coast where you could make time and that's what they were doing. They didn't appear to have seen us. We sat down and took a drink while we tried to catch our breath.

"I haven't had that much excitement in quite a while!" John exclaimed. "I thought they had us there for sure." He looked down at the weapon in my lap. "You ready to use that?"

Somehow he'd read my mind and knew I had no desire to kill again. "I will to defend myself," I explained. "You don't want these guys to take you alive. Understand what I'm saying?"

"Yes — I think I do. I've never taken a life. Not sure if I could even if it meant giving up my own. But you have killed and you know the feeling. Which is why you don't want to kill again I'm guessing."

"Yeah — I didn't want to take a life again after Nam. But once you break a commandment does it matter how many times?" That was pretty deep for me but I was hanging with a philosopher. Maybe he was having an effect on my thinking.

"Perhaps it matters when you asked for forgiveness. And if you do the sin again after you have asked God to accept your repentance. Did you ever ask God to forgive you for what you did in the war?"

"I don't think I ever did. Just tried to bury the guilt in booze and drugs. You should understand I didn't believe in God anymore after what I saw in the war. I mean — how could a merciful God let people do such things to each other?"

"That's a hard question JC. I've seen a lot of sadness and suffering in my ministry and much of it caused by one human to another. It does tug at your beliefs. I kept my faith in the vision of God for the world even though things don't always make sense to us humans. I expect some answers when I die. If the only answer I get is darkness then I've been wrong. But that's not what I believe will happen."

"Then you're a lot stronger than me Brother John. I've spent most of my life just trying to have a good time. Other than my biker brothers I didn't try to help anyone very much. And that sure wasn't the way I was raised. Back in the hills we helped each other out when things got tough. Particularly family. But I guess I lost all sense of that in the City. My biker bros were my family and some of them weren't always trust-worthy. As a matter of fact—a few would slit your throat over a drug deal or a babe."

John slapped my leg. "So much for the serious talk. Let's get to the beach and enjoy the day. We shouldn't have to worry about the Guardians any more for a while. I want to feel the sand and the salt water." So we picked up everything and headed past more houses toward the ocean. Soon we came to a foot path through some trees. I could hear the surf breaking in the distance. "We can reach the beach through here. Just a little ways farther."

When we came out of the trees onto the beach it was beauti-ful. It was a sunny day and you could see a long ways off over the ocean. There was a sandy section where we threw down our stuff. John immediately took off all his clothes and headed for the surf. He was running in and out of the water whooping like a little kid. I stripped down and followed his lead. The water was really cold but it felt great anyways. Never swum in the buff with a monk before. Before I knew it I was running around yelling and having an awesome time. Felt like a kid again with no worries in the world.

We ran in and out of the surf and took turns jumping into the waves. Finally got so cold we couldn't take the water anymore so we dried off and lay out in the sun in our birthday suits. I wanted time to suspend and just let me lay here forever. This was the freedom I'd missed. I closed my eyes and remembered days I'd spent with Dianne on the coast. We loved watching sunsets over the ocean with a cheap bottle of wine and a joint. I really missed her.

"When you see all this beauty it makes you wonder how the world got so crazy—doesn't it?" John asked.

"I have to agree. Don't think I ever understood why people wanted more than just this. It seemed like people thought they could buy their happiness when all they needed to do was get out and enjoy life. What do you think?"

John answered as he stared off into the sky, "I had it made as a professor with a good salary—no serious expectations—and a lot of time off. But I never felt like I really helped anyone but myself. I wanted to do more. That was why I went to seminary and eventually started the Order. It opened my eyes to a new way of living—all I really wanted to do was help others. But it was hard seeing so much misery surrounded by all the affluence. There were times when I couldn't make sense of it all. I prayed real hard for answers."

"Did you get any?"

"At times I thought I did. But it was through small acts of kindness and not some grandiose light and voice in the sky. It was in the eyes of someone who was close to death as I held their hand. It was helping a child after their parent had died. That was really hard. The people dying of the AIDS weren't the only victims. Their families continued to feel the pain for a long time. I guess my biggest frustration was feeling like I could never do enough."

"Sounds to me like you made a difference in a lot of lives. More than I can say about myself." He was making me think about how I'd spent my life being so selfish and only interested in the moment.

I went on, "Sure wasn't the way my dad raised me. He was a generous man who gave to others even when he didn't have things for himself. Around the coal mines there were many who didn't have enough to get by so he was always helping folk. Makes me wonder why I hadn't been more like him. I didn't appreciate him and his values until I came back from the war. And then I was too fucked up in the head to stay in the mountains—couldn't handle the peace of it all. I wanted the fast life of the City where I thought I could forget what I'd done. Maybe that was a wrong decision. Hard to think about after all these years."

"Don't be too hard on yourself JC. Sometimes it takes people a while to wake up to their destiny. Maybe this is your calling now. To make it to the New Society where you can have a chance to start over and make a difference."

"Me? Make a difference?" That was a new concept.

"You never know. God has a plan for you and this may be it.

I sense it in you," John said with conviction.

"Well brother – if he has a plan for me I wish he'd make it clearer. It seems like he talks in whispers."

John chuckled at that. "Sometimes he does my son. You'll have to play it out and see what happens. Maybe you are meant to be one of the leaders of the New Society? It's never too late to find yourself and make a contribution. Maybe that's why you're here with me now – to learn about yourself."

At that comment I closed my eyes and enjoyed the sun some more. Brother John had a lot running around in my head. We lay there for a while before I spoke again.

"Maybe you don't want to talk about it but I saw a grave up the hill from the house." He was silent for some time. Guess I'd touched a nerve in this quiet man.

"We were at a retreat near Santa Rosa when the Regional Wars started. When we realized how bad it had become in the City and the Guardians were coming north three of us decided to try and escape. Brother Dale and Sister Janet came along with me. Brother Dale didn't make it and we had to bury him along the way. Sister Janet made it here with me but she was dieing from the influenza that came after the wars. I buried her there almost two months ago. She was my closest friend at the mission." He started to cry.

"Sorry I brought it up..."

He wiped his eyes before answering, "It's okay. We worked together for a long time and I really loved her. She was so spiritual – an inspiration to the rest of us at the mission. I'm only sorry we didn't make it all the way north. She just wasn't strong enough. We found the tree house by accident and it was a good hideout while I cared for her. I think about her every day."

We lay there a little longer feeling the breeze and listening to the surf. "Let's take one more swim before we head back," I yelled to John as I headed for the water. This is what I missed about life before the Regional Wars – feeling free. I wondered if it would ever be this way again. We swam around until we were half blue from the cold and then headed back for the beach. My sore body was feeling a little better. John was great company – in some ways like a little child the way he enjoyed life.

"You have some serious bruises on your back," John observed, "but you're lucky you didn't crack a rib or worse. You'll feel better in a few days. I'll keep applying the salve and you will heal."

"As much as I appreciate your hospitality John I want to get back on the road in another day or two. I'm trying to use as much of the moon as I can since I'm traveling at night. What can I do to help you while I'm here?"

"Good question. Tomorrow I have a special place to take you and we'll explore some of the houses I haven't checked out yet. I brought some fishing gear with me and I'm going to try catching something while we're here. Let's eat our lunch and go fishing."

We ate the lunch John had prepared and then waded into the surf with John's fishing gear. It took some time but we finally snagged a good sized one. John hollered like a cowboy at rodeo. "This will make quite the meal. We'll eat like kings tonight." It was fun to be with someone who took pleasure in such simple things.

We got dressed and headed up the trail with our catch of the day. I was feeling the soreness in my back as we reached sight of the road. We made our way back to the house where we'd almost been caught before. We listened but everything was quiet. "You ready to try this again?" John asked sounding excited.

"I'll take the lead," I decided, "and we'll head for that first burnt out house on the other side of the road." I looked both ways and started across the open field as fast as I could get my legs to move. John was right behind me — could hear his sandals slapping. We crossed the road and made it all the way to the wrecked house. Sat down behind the building and had a swig of water while we caught our breath. "That sure was better than the first time," I gasped. John nodded with his eyes wide open.

We worked our way from house to house back to the trees. Right after entering the woods we heard a patrol coming from the south but we couldn't see them from where we were. They passed by quickly. "That sure was good timing," John announced.

When we got back to the tree house John told me to go inside and catch a nap while he cleaned our dinner. "I'll put some more of the salve on your back but you need some rest. Let your body and spirit recover. I'll find some herbs to cook the fish with. We'll fix it outside on the fire pit. It's going to be a good dinner. Hope you like fish."

"No problem here. I eat most anything. Too bad we don't have some ketchup to go with it."

"Ketchup?"

"Yeah—back home we used to call it hillbilly tartar sauce. Kind of a family joke. We didn't have much seafood in West Virginia and if we did have fish we always ate it with ketchup."

"Well then—this is your lucky day. I have an unopened bottle I found in one of the houses. So we can pretend we're back in the hills. No problem..."

I went into the cabin and crashed. Slept for quite a while. This was one of the best days I'd experienced since the wars. Being in the ocean had been a total blast. Was looking forward to the seafood dinner with ketchup. All it needed was some French fries or a baked potato to be perfect but we'd make do.

We cooked the fish slowly over the fire at dusk. The clouds had come in and the temperature was dropping. I pulled out the flask of shine Jake had given me and showed it to John. "You allowed to have a drink of some real good home made shine?" I asked.

He looked at me for a moment and replied, "I guess we could say that it's sacramental wine."

"That works for me. Here's to your good hospitality," and I took a swig before handing the flask to John. He took a good pull himself and then started to cough.

"Wow! That's some real top shelf stuff. Where'd you get this?" I told him the story about Jake and Amber as he listened intently.

After I finished the story he commented, "I hope you get the chance to go back and rescue her. That's no life for a young girl." He took one more short sip before handing it back. "That will help to put a glow on the evening," he said with a smile.

John was watching the fish cook and finally declared, "I think we're ready. Let's break open the ketchup." He opened the bottle like a waiter showing off an expensive wine and asked me if I wanted to sniff the cap to make sure the vintage was good. I went along with the fun and commented that 2018 was a good year for ketchup. We took turns cutting off pieces of fish. He'd prepared some canned corn and it was quite the feast. "This protein will help to rebuild your strength," he offered.

The sun disappeared while we were eating. After we were done we stoked up the fire. We sat back in some old lounge chairs John had found around Sea Ranch. We talked about times in the City before the change. I felt like I'd known him for a long time although we'd experienced the City through very different eyes. I shared with him what Tricky had told me about the Concern. He was fascinated. Particularly with the part about how they'd allowed religion to remain a part of the culture to keep the masses sedated.

"Some might think that but I believe otherwise," he responded thoughtfully. "There is a God and I serve Him. It was the Concern who were mistaken. Perhaps the fall of the Concern and this Armageddon was God's way to bring people back to him. A powerful message to us about how far we have strayed from his son's teachings — especially sharing and helping others."

I was thinking about something John had said earlier in the day to me — about having a destiny. "Do you believe everything is already planned out by God like the preachers used to tell us? Does that make any sense to you?"

"That's a good question JC and I have an opinion that is different from what some religions teach about everything being planned by God in advance. I know God exists but he lets us create our own fate by making our own choices. Perhaps our whole society — or even the world — made the collective choices that allowed the Concern to obtain their position of power. You made the very hard choice to risk your life to find freedom with the New Society. That means you created your own destiny. And yes — maybe there is even a bigger role for you to play when you reach the north. God is just providing you the opportunity to take that chance."

"That's a pretty big thought — that an old biker like me could make a difference anywhere. I think I'm just one lone man on a crazy mission."

"Maybe. But maybe you have angels riding with you to protect you along the way. Look at who has been there so far for you on this adventure. Perhaps God and your angels had a hand in that. You've also provided me comfort in this difficult time of mine. I see good in you JC and I believe that I'm here to help you with your journey."

"What do you mean by angels traveling with me?" I was puzzled by that statement.

"Think about who in your life has stood by you in troubled times but is no longer in physical form on this earth. If I asked you who that might be—what would you say?"

I pondered that question as I threw another log on the fire. "I'd have to say my dad and my wife Dianne. They were always there when I needed them. Dianne was a really good woman who asked little but gave a lot of love in return—just like dad now that I think about it. Thought I'd never recover from her unexpected death. I went really crazy when I lost her."

"Then—maybe—they are your angels traveling with you on this journey. They are along to protect you because they loved you so much. Just like Sister Janet is my angel. I hear her talking to me at times when I am lonely."

"Well—I know for sure that I'm always talking to them."

"Perhaps you just answered your own question," he replied in his soft voice.

I sat there staring into the fire and considered all of these deep thoughts. I wasn't used to being with someone who stimulated such intense ideas about myself and the world. I wasn't even high. This was just me using my brain more than usual. What a strange new world...

The fog started to roll in and it got colder. "We'll let the fire die down and call it a day. I'll make up some more of my tea to help you sleep tonight. I want to take you someplace special tomorrow after we raid some houses to the north. We'll take a peak at Gualala across the river to see what's there but I'm not sure how much of the town we can see. It's pretty wooded along the river."

With that John went into the tree house and started a fire in the woodstove. I heard some cans rattling around as he pre-

170

pared the tea. I didn't know what was in that stuff but it really did the job. Didn't know that monks knew anything about magical potions — wasn't going to ask though. He came back out and sat down. "It will be ready in a few minutes. We'll have a cup and then hit the sack. I want to get an early start tomorrow because we need to hike a ways. You feel up to it?"

"I'm sore and tired but it was a great day. That swim and sitting in the sun was top drawer. I'll be ready for the hike tomorrow. Count on it." My confidence and strength were coming back. And for reasons I didn't fully understand I found comfort in John's words. He was a patient teacher — he definitely had me thinking about angels. For sure.

After we drank our tea we put out the fire and headed into the house. The pot belly stove had warmed things up nicely. Between the hooch and the tea I went out like a light. I had wild dreams about reaching the north after a big shootout. It made me wonder if dreams were a reflection of the past — or a glimpse of the future? Only time would tell...

CHAPTER 21

A Visit to the Chapel

We got up with the sun and I made a fire in the stove while John gathered eggs from his stringy looking chickens. He scrambled them up with canned milk. He even had salt and pepper — they were really good. It was a filling breakfast we topped off with some canned fruit.

"You ready for a healthy hike today?" he asked as we cleaned up from breakfast.

"I'm feeling better and the walk will be great. What should I bring along?"

"We'll pack a simple lunch of jerky and beans that we can eat cold. Hope you like cold beans."

I started to laugh and he gave me a strange look. "You're talking to an old hillbilly here who was raised on ham and beans," I explained. "Been on many a thousand miles in forty eight hours runs around California where cold beans was the staple. I'll throw in a can of fruit I stole from the Guardians. We'll be fine."

"Bring your binoculars with you. We'll see if we can get a look at Gualala even though I don't think we can see much. We'll stay on this side of Route 1 all the way."

There was a light fog still hanging on the coast and it was chilly so I put on my leather jacket. John gave me an old pack to carry any goods we found in the houses and I strapped on the .45. I dug out my ball cap and we headed out. Felt like two little boys going on a hike through the woods. I was looking forward to the day with John.

At first we stayed on the edge of the woods while we hiked because John had already scavenged the houses in this area so we didn't need to expose ourselves. After about an hour we heard a patrol coming from the south but we couldn't see the road. So we used it as an excuse to take a break and wait for them to pass by. We drank some water and moved on. The sun was trying to peak through the fog but it was still damp. I could smell the ocean again.

Not long after that John told me we were getting near some homes he hadn't checked out yet. We moved out of the woods to take a look. We broke into the first one that was just a little ways from the trees. It was a nice big ranch style home that had some pretty fancy artwork hanging on the walls. Looked like the owners had packed and left in a hurry. There weren't any signs of violence so maybe they'd gotten out before the Guardians. John immediately went for the kitchen and started through the cupboards. He found a lot of canned goods and was as excited as a school girl on her first date.

"We struck pay dirt," he exclaimed. "What a find. Let's fill up the pack and leave it here to pick up on the way back. Look! There are some crackers in an unopened metal tin. They might still be good. Wahoo...! And over here—jam. Hot diggity damn! This is like gold." I guess that was serious swearing for him. It was fun seeing him get so excited about our booty.

After we filled the pack with as much as we could carry we sat down on the leather sofa in the family room and took it all in. "All this opulence and what good did it do for them?" John commented. "Think about all the poor people we could have helped with the money they spent here. I never understood how people could live with themselves when they knew that people around them were starving. It never did make much sense. We used to spend a lot of time trying to find donors to keep our clinic open. What they spent on the art in this room would have kept the mission running for a year." He got this very sad look on his face and shook his head.

"I wasn't any better," I offered. "I'd give money to the street folk on occasion but I wasn't too concerned about anyone else. Figured if I could hustle for it so could they. Guess I never thought about the fact that maybe there were those who could-n't hustle for it—like your AIDS patients."

"Well JC—you're still alive and you have a chance to make a difference yet. So keep that in mind." That comment had me pondering my fate again.

"Enough of this," John said as he got ready to move on. "We have a ways to go yet. We'll leave your pack here and then fill mine up on the way back. Ready?" And with that we went back outside and checked around for any tools or other stuff he could use. After taking inventory we continued north. It was warming up and with the exercise I was getting warm so I took off my jacket and tied it around my waist. We slowly worked our way closer to the road as we went from house to house.

We passed this strange looking building just off the road and John pointed to it. "That's the chapel. We'll stop there on the way back. For now let's get closer to the river and see if we can get a look at Gualala. We have to be on the watch as we're close to the road with little cover."

It'd been a few hours since we heard the patrol so we had our ears open. Sure enough — we heard another one coming from the north just as we were going to cross an open area to the next house. We hid behind a tool shed and listened as the bikes passed by on their way south. Still couldn't tell if they'd started in Gualala or just passed through. That would be important to know.

John tapped me on the shoulder after they disappeared down the road. "We should be clear for a while. Let's make it to the river." And with that we picked up the pace. We covered some open ground only a little ways from the road before we entered a tree line above the river. Worked our way through the trees until we came to a point where we had a view across the Gualala River. The road dipped down here as it crossed the river and then it was a long uphill to the town. We could see where the river joined the ocean about a half mile to the west.

We couldn't see much of the town from this point. Just the edge of one building. I pointed across the road to a grove of trees on the other side. "I think I can work my way over there for a better look see. It might be dangerous. You should stay here and wait."

"No way JC! I've come this far with you — in for a penny in for a pound." Hadn't heard that expression in a while. "Besides — this is the most exhilaration I've had in a long time. You take command and I'll do as you say." John crouched down close to me and tightened the laces on his tennis shoes. "Me and my PF Keds are ready to hustle."

I checked around with the binocs and didn't see any activity between us and the town. We carefully worked our way along the tree line to the road. I took one last quick look up and down the road before we made the sprint to the grove on the other side. We went a ways into the trees to try and find some good cover before we stopped. My heart was working from the run and we were both breathing hard. "Maybe we both need to stop smoking?" John whispered. We tried to keep the laughter quiet as we sat there catching our breath.

"God must have a sense of humor to have me on recon patrol with a funny monk. You're a trip Brother John."

"I'll take that as a compliment," he replied quietly.

After we cleared our heads we made our way through the grove to a point where we could see the town. My heart was broken—the old Gualala Hotel was burned down! I'd spent many a weekend there in a $10 room partying until I could barely make it up the stairs. We used to sit out on the porch roof and watch the sun set over the ocean. The place was over a hundred years old. It was one of the original stage coach stops in this part of the coast. Boy—the memories I had there.

After my initial shock over the hotel I scanned the town. I saw some activity just past the hotel where there used to be a gas station. There were people moving back and forth between the gas station and the grocery store across the street. But—as best I could tell at this distance—they didn't look like Guardians. And I didn't see any Guardian bikes. It would be nice to observe longer as it might be some time before the next patrol. But we weren't very protected here with our butts hanging out in the wind if anyone showed up.

I studied as much as I could see from this angle but didn't pick up any more activity. Saw a large radio antenna sticking up from the grocery store but maybe it had always been there. Let John take a look also but he didn't see any more than I had. It didn't look like a Guardian command post but there were people living there. I didn't want to find out how friendly they were so I would have to pass through as quickly and quietly as

I could after dark. It was time to get out of here and get John back to safety.

"Let's make some dust John. We've seen about as much as we can. Need to get back across the road where it's safer."

We made our way to the edge of the trees and then sprinted back across the road. We headed for the tree line and worked our way back to the building he'd called the chapel. It was a small strange shaped building with several stained glass windows. As many times as I'd been up this road I'd never noticed this building—even though it was only a short ways from the road. We looked around and then ducked inside.

Sure enough—it was a tiny chapel with a few rows of benches and a small altar. The sun filtered through the stained glass windows and the room smelled a bit like incense. Everything was dusty like the place hadn't seen any visitors for a while. John dropped his pack at the door and went and knelt down in front of the altar. I sat down in the back row and contemplated the scene. It was very peaceful and I understood why he came here. He prayed as I sat there in respectful silence. It was very calming. Maybe he was praying for me. Or maybe he was praying for deliverance from the ordeal he was going to face alone.

When he got up he came and sat down beside me while he put his hand on my leg. "Did you pray for your journey?" he asked.

"Never was too good at prayer. I never felt like anyone was listening. But I did say a prayer for you. Hope that's okay."

"Well—yes. I'm touched. You have a kind and gentle heart JC. I sensed it when we met the other night. That is why I did not see you as a threat. You should open your heart to God and ask him to travel with you on your journey. Who knows what lies ahead for you?"

"The problem is I may have to kill again to stay alive. So far I haven't had to on this trip—but it could happen. Came close at Jenner. Not sure how I'll feel about that. There's bound to be another well fortified command post wherever the Guardian territory ends. But for now it doesn't look like Gualala is one. I should be able to get through there tonight."

John must have been thinking about my comments on

killing when he answered, "The Old Testament is full of violence – like David and Goliath – and Samson. So maybe God is
aware that it's part of the equation."

"Yeah – but the Ten Commandments say 'thou shalt not kill'.
So how do you think God looks upon what I've done in my
past?" It was a question I'd never been able to answer for myself.

"Governments and people like the Concern wanted you to
feel like you were doing your patriotic duty. Every war we've
been in since World War II was promoted as defending democracy. Even in a far off place like Vietnam. Your generation had to
face some tough choices in those times. Either go fight a war
that we now know was wrong or be a draft evader. Which made
you feel like a traitor to your country. I'm glad I was too young
for the draft at that time. It would have been a hard choice."

"You're right. It was a difficult choice but I thought I was
doing the right thing when I joined the Marine Corps. My dad
and most of his brothers had served in the big war and it all
seemed clear cut to them when they served. Think how they
would feel if they knew all their sacrifices went to create the
Concern. I guess that's what a philosopher like you would call
an irony."

"Boy – you're right about that. A sad irony that the greatest
war ever fought for freedom resulted in the creation of the most
powerful dictatorship ever known in history. It does make you
ponder about the greedy ways of man."

"If it makes you ponder – doctor – then how about a guy
like me who doesn't have the brains to think something like
that through?"

"Oh – you're smarter than you give yourself credit for JC.
You have street smarts. The trick is you need to take what
you've learned – what you're learning on this journey – and
put it to use when you reach the New Society."

"You mean IF I reach the New Society?"

John put his arm across my shoulders and counseled me in
his soft voice, "You need to have faith my son that you will per-
severe. You had the courage to start this adventure and you will
have the courage to see it through. Everyone has a calling and
maybe this is yours – to take your message of freedom to the

New Society. You can make a difference."

It amazed me that this man of God believed an old fart biker like me could make a difference in the world. Maybe he understood something I didn't. I wasn't going to argue with him but it was a heady thought. I was just trying to make it through this alive.

"Enough seriousness for now," John announced. "Let's have some lunch. I'm starving after all this excitement. We'll head back to the cover of the woods and then take a break. We still have a long hike back."

We quietly left the chapel and it's serenity for the protection of the woods. I was needing some lunch too. The sun had finally come out and it was a beautiful day. We sat down and leaned next to some trees while we ate our small lunch. Could smell the pines around us. It was invigorating. John asked me to tell him some more biker stories and I never needed much encouragement to tell another tall tale. Enjoyed hearing him laugh.

We relaxed for a bit and then packed up for the journey back to the tree house. We stopped at the house we'd raided earlier and filled up his pack while grabbing mine. It was a good haul of canned food that would carry him for a while. We grabbed a few tools and continued our trek. It was late in the afternoon when we got back.

"I'll make some tea and we'll catch a well deserved nap," John said. "Later I'll open some of those chili cans we found and see if it's any good. Then we can keep ourselves warm by farting up the cabin!" This was definitely the funniest preacher I'd ever come across.

While he made tea I walked up to the grave of Sister Janet and put some wildflowers on it. I read the small marker John had placed on the grave. I knew how hard it was to bury a good friend. When I went back the tea was ready.

"Do you plan on leaving tonight?" John asked me as we sipped our hot drink.

"Don't think I have any choice. I need to make the most of the moon and it's starting to wane. Sure hate to leave your good company."

"How does your body feel?"

"I'm sore but the swim yesterday and the walk today helped a lot. What can I do for you before I leave?"

"Well—after our nap you can help me round up some more firewood. I keep having to go farther back into the woods to find it. I have an old wheelbarrow I found at one of the houses. You can help me cut it and put it in the wheelbarrow. That would be a really big help. The nights get chilly and a few sticks in the stove keep things a little warmer."

We crashed for a while before we headed into the woods. The air was fresh and I could smell the wildflowers that were coming into bloom. It reminded me of home.

We were able to make two trips with the wheelbarrow before dark. That would last him a few weeks. I liked being able to help out this generous man even if it was such a small gift.

"I'll fix us some dinner while you check over your bike and get ready," John suggested. "Where do you think the next command post might be?"

"Been thinking about that. Since we didn't see a lot of Guardians in Gualala—probably Point Arena" I pulled out my map and we studied it. "Possibly in Anchor Bay but that town doesn't have much visibility up and down the road. Point Arena is about twenty miles from here. I'll have to get off the road before then and try to figure out a way to reconnoiter the town. That may not be easy if I remember the terrain around there. Also recall the road after Gualala is twisty and slow going. Particularly if there is fog. Should have enough food to last a few more days in case I have to hang out around Point Arena for long. But it's a big town and won't be easy to get by. Sure wish I knew where the border was between the Guardians and the New Society."

"God will travel with you." John was such an optimist. I was hoping that maybe some of it would rub off on me.

He cooked up the chili and we ate it with the crackers he'd found. A little stale but still edible. We tried to make conversation during dinner but it was all small talk. I wanted to take him along but knew I couldn't. And he knew not to ask.

After dinner I took the derringer out of my pack and put it on the table. "I want to leave this with you. It won't do me much good against what the Guardians are packing."

John gave me a long quiet stare. He knew I was really saying that he could use it on himself when the disease started to immobilize him. But I couldn't say that directly. I seemed to recall that suicide was a sin in the church.

"I will accept your gift but don't expect to need it. Maybe I can shoot me an elephant with it for food?"

In spite of it all he still had his sense of humor. All I could do was reach across the table and shake his hand. He had a faraway look in his eye. This humble man had taught me something about life — and death...

CHAPTER 22

Close Encounters of the Deadly Kind

It was close to dark when I finished preparing my gear and the bike. I was sad to be leaving John. Never thought I could be friends with a man of the cloth but he was something else. I felt like he'd saved my life and I hadn't done a very good job of repaying him. He'd given me a lot to think about as I continued my journey. I was getting close to where I thought I'd reach the New Society but close only counts in horseshoes and hand grenades — especially with the Guardians between me and there.

Since leaving San Francisco I'd confirmed the Guardians ran more patrols in the day than at night. Just like Duke had told me back in the City. Good recon on his part. Another reason why running at night was the best plan. It wasn't very far to Point Arena but that wouldn't make it any easier to get there. The road after Gualala winds around with limited visibility. Also wasn't sure what I would do once I got there because it could be heavily armed. If I knew that the New Society was close to Point Arena I might be able to pack it into the woods and get around the town. But that was only a guess for now.

"I want to help you push the bike down to the road and stay with you while you wait for the next patrol to pass," John offered. That was okay because I'd enjoy the company while I waited. I thought it would be safe enough for him.

"That's a great plan," I replied. "I'll need help pushing the bike to a spot where we can wait. We don't have to get too close to the road because we can hear the patrols so well."

I checked the shotgun and placed it into its holster on the bike. Also double checked I had a round in the chamber of the .45 and put it on. Was about as ready as I could be. As the sun was setting in the distance we each took a side of the bike and started to push. The road was slightly downhill so it was easy work with the two of us.

It was dark and getting chilly when we found a good spot to wait. I could smell moisture in the air like there was fog coming in. We pulled up next to a home where there were some old chairs outside—then we sat down and waited for the Guardians. I lit up a cigarette and without thinking offered John one. He surprised me when he accepted. "I used to be a smoker back when I was a professor," he explained. "Don't miss the habit much. But right now I feel like I could use one. Didn't you say you were trying to quit?"

"Maybe when this is all over—right now they help keep me awake." We sat there in the dark and enjoyed our smoke. We talked for a long time about life in the City and how much we liked San Francisco. John had a number of favorite cultural spots he liked that I'd never been to. Bikers didn't hang out too much around the art studios. Talking helped to pass the time while we waited. John had so many experiences and he wasn't a bad story teller either.

We'd been there almost two hours and I was starting to wonder why there hadn't been a patrol yet. It was getting into the night and the fog was making its way across the road. We sat there in silence for some time as we seemed to have run out of small things to talk about.

I was trying to figure out what to say to John about leaving him alone when he spoke up. "I'm really glad you came my way JC. I hadn't talked to anyone in a long time. You've been good company. I was beginning to think I might lose my mind before my body. But you helped me get grounded again. I want you to think about what I said—I mean—about your destiny and all. Maybe that is why you are on this perilous journey—to make a difference."

"That's a heavy thought Brother John. Pretty heady stuff for an old bro like me. Right now I just want to make it to the north safely and see what they're all about. But maybe you're right. Maybe this is my chance to make a difference and have a new life. I'll sure see if I can make that happen. I've learned a lot about myself on this adventure—never really took charge of my life before. Just kind of let things happen. Maybe it's time for that to change." It was a lot to think about at my age.

We sat there in silence for a while longer and then I heard the awaited sound. It was a patrol coming from the north. They weren't moving too fast in the fog and it sounded like there were two of them. We could barely make out some headlights flickering in and out of the fog as they drove past our hideout. We listened while they disappeared to the south. It was time to go.

I turned to John and put out my hand but he shook his head no. "I want a hug JC. It may be the last time I get to hug someone." And he gave me a big bear hug like Duke used to do. He was really strong for such a wiry guy.

"Thanks for everything John. I'll always be grateful for what you did for me."

"And you provided sunshine into mine. I was here in the wilderness to help you on your journey – to minister to your needs. Thank you for letting me help. God speed JC..."

Reluctantly I got on the bike and opened the choke. I hit the starter and she turned over but wouldn't fire. It acted like it was out of gas which I knew wasn't the case. I checked the petcock and it was open so I hit the starter a few more times. Again it turned over but wouldn't fire. I might have flooded it but that would be unusual for me. "I have to let it sit for a minute," I said out loud more to myself than to John.

I pulled out the small flashlight I still had from Tricky. It turned on but not very bright. I studied the fuel line and the petcock to see if there were any leaks. Everything checked out. Opened the tank and could see plenty of gas. Got back on and tried the starter again. She tried firing but never caught on. Just an occasional misfire. Wasn't sure how long the battery would hold out.

I got off the bike and took off my jacket. I handed it to John to hold. "I've got to try kick starting to save the battery." I gave it quite a number of kicks but the old gal was being stubborn. She just didn't want to turn over. Even John tried kicking it over several times until he got winded. What a site in his long robe and tennis shoes.

"What do you think it is?" he asked out of breath.

"Oh man – it could be a number of things. Hard to do much here in the dark. Need to check out the fuel system." I stood there thinking about my alternatives.

"Let's push her back to your place where I can take off the air cleaner and carb float bowl," I instructed John. Without question he helped me turn her around and we started the long uphill push back to the house. Good thing one of us was patient. Precious time was passing but I needed to get where I'd have better light. If I couldn't figure it out I would just stay another night. Didn't want the setback—wouldn't mind the company.

Finally got her back to the tree house and we had to sit and take a breather. We were both pooped. After we caught our breath John brought a lantern out of the cabin and fired it up. It wasn't great light but better than the flashlight. I dug out my toolkit and removed the air cleaner so I could get to the carburetor. John looked over my shoulder like we were doing surgery on a close friend.

"I guess I could help out more if I made some of that coffee we found the other day," he suggested. "Good and strong—like a Marine is used to." Sounded like a good idea to me. This could take a while in the dark and it was getting damp with the fog moving in.

I got the carb float bowl off and emptied out the gas in it. From what I could tell in the dark there seemed to be a lot of crud in the gas. Could be expected since it was scrounged gas. A little was from the dump I'd raided with Jake—probably rust in it. Could be in the jets. I opened the petcock just briefly and the gas flowed okay. So I was hoping I'd taken care of the problem. John showed up with the coffee and I took a break. "Wow—you were right—good and strong." I exclaimed. "This stuff would remove the hair from a bearded lady." John thought that was funny. Guess he hadn't heard too many biker expressions.

We drank our coffee and stared at the bike—like just staring at it would make her run better. The coffee sure had a kick. I lit up a cigarette and offered John another one. "As long as you're drinking coffee it's hard to quit smoking," I said. "At least that's always been my excuse." I was pulling his leg.

"Well—just for tonight—I'll go along with you. I don't think it will stunt my growth any at this point!" So we both lit up and enjoyed a smoke with his strong coffee. I felt a little bad—like I'd come along and tempted this holy man who was living in the wilderness. But I speculated I could have tempted him with worse. Or perhaps I had with the hooch? Oh no! Maybe God was mad at me for corrupting this spiritual man? And I was going to need to be in his best graces tonight.

I finished the coffee and got back to work. John held the lantern as close as he could. Cleaned it out as best I could and then put the carb back together and opened the petcock to fill it up. Didn't see any leaks in my lines so I decided to try starting her again. The choke was still open and I gave the starter button a punch. She turned over slowly and finally fired. I let out a yell while John danced around. You would have thought we'd just been midwifes at a birth. I let the bike idle to warm her up.

"It seems okay now but this has taken so long that I've got to wait for another patrol. I can go back to the lookout alone if you want to turn in." I was trying to keep him out of harm's way but he wasn't having any of it.

"You kidding me? I plan on seeing this through. Who knows — we might just have to push it back again. There'll be plenty of time to sleep later. I'm ready when you are."

So we suited up again and started the long push back to the lookout. Didn't want to leave her running as we might miss hearing a patrol until they were very close. It'd been several hours since the last patrol so we'd hang out and wait for the next. I could just call it a night and stay with John but I didn't have that far to go to Point Arena and I was anxious to get on with my mission. Guess that was the old Marine in me. This was going to take some patience — not my best trait. Nice to have John along...

"You'd have made a good Marine Brother John," I spoke to him as we were pushing the bike in the dark. Out of the corner of my eye I caught a big smile on his face in the fading moonlight.

We made better time when we hit the down hill part where I could ride while Brother John provided the horsepower. The road was becoming slippery so I took my time. It seemed like forever before we reached the lookout. Luckily John knew where we were even in the fog. He was one cool Brother — and a good lookout. I hoped a patrol hadn't gone by while we were working back at the house. It was far enough back in the woods that we didn't always hear the patrols.

The fog was getting thick and wet. It was turning out to be a rough night with the weather. Had all my leathers on to try and stay a little dry—even the flight cap. John looked around for some shelter and we found a porch where we pushed the bike. At least we were out of some of the moisture. Could be here for a while.

John had brought some old army blankets in a pack so we huddled up under the porch and got ready for the wait. We had some jerky while we killed time. I broke out the brandy flask that Stinky Pete had given me. We took a small hit to warm up our bellies.

"You know we might be hanging out here for a while?" I asked John.

"On the way down I did a probability analysis using Stochastic methods and if we missed the patrol we could have two to four hours to wait. Of course—that's theoretically speaking without fully considering such delta variables as the weather and—or—fog." There was the professor talking.

"Yeah—whatever you said—I think you're right. We may have to set this out for a while." I took the shotgun off the bike to keep it dry. I pulled the blanket around me. The fog was getting thicker.

John reached inside his robe. "I grabbed a deck of cards while we were at the cabin. Do you play poker?"

I was stunned by the question. "Does a bear shit in the woods?" I quickly answered. Now I was really going to be in trouble with God. I was going to play poker with a monk. Back in the Corp I was pretty good with a deck or dice. Not to mention how often I played cards with the old men at the general store back in Mt. Pisquah. Good thing we didn't have any real money—or I would surely go to hell this night!

"We'll play for points. Winner keeps the brandy flask. You in my man?" Brother John challenged me as held out the deck. We made a tent under the blankets and started the game. Clever man this fellow. He knew it would keep our minds off the wait.

We each took another short toke from the flask. It was about three quarters full. We were having fun in spite of the shitty weather.

Now I hate to admit this—but John was quite the poker player.

We tried several different games and he was hard to beat. Must have been that professor mind of his. He could remember every card that'd been played. My old stoner mind had trouble remembering what day it was sometimes. It was starting to look like he was going to win the flask. Good thing I still had a little of Jake's hooch left in the pack. We shared another cigarette—damn I really was going to hell...

Over two hours had passed when we heard the sound we'd been waiting for in the distance. John's calculations were right. It was a patrol from the south. So we hadn't missed one. They were spacing them out—probably because of the bad weather. They were moving slow. The road was probably very wet.

I'd have to give them a half hour head start in case they stopped in Gualala for a break. We played several more hands and John kept winning. I finally gave up the flask. It made that monk very happy to have the brandy.

I needed to give the bike one last check and then try to start her. It was time to get wet. Everything was okay on the pack so I put the shotgun back in the holster. Now for the Kool-Aid Acid test. Got on the bike and went through the familiar routine. Set it upright. Pull the choke. Give it just a small twist of throttle. Push the button. The engine turned but didn't fire. I expected that with the carb being off. I let it sit for a moment and then fired it again. It started to fire but I couldn't keep her running. Close...

I waited a few seconds and gave it another shot. She finally caught and started to run – although rough. I held just the right throttle to keep her running. In about a minute it started to level. Then the girl turned over. She was idling good now. I gave it a few blips and it didn't misfire. Good girl! You have to learn to treat the gals with respect.

It was time to leave. I gave John another big bear hug. He smelled musty in his long wet robe. "Thanks for everything Brother John. Say a prayer for me." Wasn't sure what else to say.

"I already have—I will again. What a treat to have you here

JC. Travel with peace knowing that your angels are with you."

"Having angels with me would be nice on this wet night with who knows what waiting ahead."

Couldn't say much more because I hated leaving him. Just like I hated leaving Amber. It gave me more reason to make it there—so I could come back. But for now I had to find out where the New Society was to the north. Was I close to being there? I sure hoped I was.

I shook his hand one last time from the bike and gave him a salute. It'd been a long time since I'd saluted anyone. He gave me the peace sign in return. Yup—that was Brother John. I pulled onto the road and into the darkness.

When I turned onto Route 1 things were getting wet and there was little visibility in the thick fog. I could run right up the patrols ass and neither one of us would know what had happened until it was too late. I had no choice but to take it slow. Was counting on having time to cover the short distance I needed to go. I was only making about fifteen to twenty miles per hour. The fog was heavy and the road was slippery. It got wetter but the leathers were keeping me a little warm. I figured it was a few miles before the downhill to the Gualala River.

It was some time at this slow speed to reach the edge of Sea Ranch. I had the .45 ready but since everything was wet it would be a tricky draw if I needed to get to it in a hurry. Crossing my fingers that wouldn't be necessary. I would stay on track until a bit south of Point Arena. Wouldn't stop in Gualala because there was someone living there. Just try to sneak quietly through.

Figured I was getting close to the edge of Sea Ranch and about a mile away from the downhill. My heart jumped when the bike shuttered like it was losing gas! That gasping lope was far too familiar. I tried pulling in the clutch and clearing the engine. It shuttered a few more times and then it caught. I let the clutch out easy. The motor stayed steady. Didn't need this...

Finally reached what I thought was the edge of the woods before the downhill. Not much looked familiar in the fog. The road started down. I was at the approach to the river. It was a wide valley where the river flowed through to the ocean. Spent a lot of time getting high on that beach back in the day. Bonfires at night and listening to the big surf. But not tonight.

Going downhill in the wet was even less fun. I was watching my speed carefully. What little I could see of the road appeared to be leveling off so I was reaching the bottom. Then it happened again. The engine started to die—acting like it was out of gas. Might be shit in the carb again. I hadn't had the time or tools to screen the gas at John's.

Tried several tricks but she wouldn't run right. Somewhere on the bottom it stalled out completely. Fuck! This wasn't good. I was in big shit here!

I got off the bike and dug out the flashlight. Wasn't very helpful in all this fog. I didn't have time to take the carb off so I tried draining the line to it. Couldn't tell for sure but thought I saw some more crap in the line. Put the line back on and tried the engine again. Still wouldn't fire. Something must be in the carb again. Damn it! I was in one hell of a pickle. Sitting at the bottom of a long hill—in the fog to boot. Time for serious damage control.

I weighed the odds—just like poker—and decided the best bet was to try and push the bike up the hill to Gualala. Sure could use some of John's muscle about now. It was going to be a long fuckin' night. So I started the long push up the hill. It got real hard to move the bike and I had to take a lot of breaks. The clock was ticking. My body was hurting. The only thing that could be said for this shitty weather was that it was keeping the Guardian patrols a little farther apart. Or so I was gambling…

Every once in a while I got the engine to fire briefly and made it several more yards up the hill. That helped some but I wondered how long the battery was going to last. Little by little I was making it up the hill to town. I was starting to think I should have stayed at John's—but too late for that now. Had to play the shitty cards I had.

It took over an hour but I was almost to town. The road was slowly leveling off. I was pooped and wet. My grouchy side was showing up. I could make out some buildings in the distance. Town was only about a quarter mile away and the pushing was getting a little easier. I needed to find a building to duck behind where I could take a breather and look at the bike again. Wanted to get off the road and out of sight of the Guardians. Didn't know where the locals were staying.

I slowly pushed my way past the burned out Gualala Hotel. What a tragedy. We used to party a lot there back in the day. That was before they added indoor plumbing and the prices went up. Had this great western bar and a good dining room with a view of the ocean. At least until someone built a fancy three story motel across the road back around 2000. Nothing was the same anymore...

I passed the store and reached the gas station where it looked like there might be some buildings behind it. Stopped for a while and didn't hear any sounds or see any lights. I figured the back of the gas station was a good place to hide out so I pushed the bike around the back. There was a small awning over the back door and I tried to fit under it. Really needed a rest. The wind had been taken out of my sails. At least I was out of sight from the road.

As I huddled with my sleeping bag in the doorway trying to get warm and regain my strength I heard a patrol passing through town heading south. That was way too close for comfort! Listened carefully to see if they were going to stop but they kept moving. That was good news for now. It was getting close to dawn and I was in a bad situation here so I needed to figure out what was wrong with the bike in a hurry.

After I finally moved from under the warm sleeping bag the first thing I did was open up the gas line to the carb again to see if it was clogged. It seemed to be draining okay but it was full of crud. Nothing I could do about it now except work around it. Had no choice but to take the carb apart again and drain it. There wasn't much light in the fog so I held the small flashlight in my mouth while I worked. I finally got to it and drained the float bowl. Wiped it out with an old rag from my pack and started to put it back on. I wasn't working too fast with the bad light and the screws were so small. I dropped one and had to search around until I found it.

I finally got the carb back on and let some fuel drain in. The sun was starting to come up and I needed to get the hell out of here in a hurry. I got on board and went through the routine. This was gonna make a racket that would wake up anyone in the neighborhood. I prayed those angels John had talked about were keeping an eye out for me.

Gave the starter button a punch and the battery still had some life so it kicked over. The engine fired and came to an idle. I threw my tools back in the pack and got ready to high tail it out of here. I got on the bike and put it her in gear but as soon as I let the clutch out she died again. Only made it a few feet. Son of a bitch!

I tried starting her again but she was sputtering like she was going to die again. I only made it a few more feet. I was now out in the open on the north side of the gas station. I punched the starter again. The battery was running out of juice and wouldn't turn the engine over. So I tried the kick starter but she just didn't want to start.

In desperation I got off the bike and looked around for a place to push it out of sight. So far I hadn't seen anyone in the town but it was only a matter of time. My only place to go was behind a row of buildings across the parking lot behind the station. I was going to try and push her around the back of those buildings but it wouldn't be a good hiding spot for long. As I was pushing the bike I was startled to hear a voice behind me. "Having some problems with that old hog?"

I quickly put the side stand down and reached for the .45 as I turned around to meet the stranger. He was a large man coming around the corner of the gas station. Had long hair and a beard and looked like some of my biker buddies from the City. He didn't have any weapons I could see so I answered his question but was ready to draw the .45 if I needed. "Yeah—something seems to be clogging my fuel lines." I tried to be casual as I answered him like I was just out for a Sunday ride.

He came over and extended his hand. "Hi—I'm Brew. This is my gas station. My brother and I work on bikes and anythin' else with a motor round these parts." I shook his hand and told him my name. I tried to read his eyes to see if he was a threat. "That looks like an old Super Glide. Haven't seen one of those in quite a while." He knelt down to look at the bike. "You already tried taking off the carb bowl and draining the fuel line?"

"As best I could in the dark. Think I got some bad gas with rust or something. Don't have a fuel filter on it. Wished I did now." I let him look over the fuel system but knew he wouldn't see much. I was being very careful with him—he was living in Guardian territory.

He stood back up. "I thought I was hearin' things when I heard a Harley trying to start. You trying to get to the north?"

I had no choice but to trust this large stranger for now. "That was the plan. But I didn't expect to get stuck out here in the daylight. How far is it to the New Society?"

"Just a little ways to Point Arena but the town is heavily fortified by the Guardians. Where you from JC?"

"I started in the City."

"And you made it this far? You're one hell of a biker bro. Were you part of that shootout at Jenner?" Now I was concerned. How could he know about that if he wasn't working with the Guardians?

He saw the look on my face. "Don't worry bro—the Guardians stop here for gas and I hear all the talk. Blackie's still trying to figure out who took out his men. He's been lookin' for someone goin' overland. They found a sniper rifle. Doesn't look like the kind of weapon you'd be carryin'."

"Did they catch anyone?" I was curious if Tricky had made it out.

"From what I hear—not yet. I don't think he's lookin' for someone on a bike. But from what I hear he's pretty pissed off about the whole thing. Made him look bad to the Guardians back in the City you know." He let out a little laugh. "Let's get your bike in the garage and see what we can do."

We turned the bike around and started to push it toward the garage. Another man stepped out of the garage with a look of surprise on his face. He stood there in quiet amazement for a moment. "I told you I heard a Harley," Brew informed him. "JC—this is my brother Nick. JC is trying to get to the north but his bike died. Let's get her in the garage before anyone is up and about."

Maybe I'd found some friends who might help me but this

was a dangerous place to be stuck. Had no choice but to trust them. It didn't sound like they had much use for the Guardians themselves—I couldn't be sure. There was probably a reward for anyone caught trying to escape from the Guardians. Particularly if they figured I had anything to do with the killings at Jenner.

We were just coming to the open bay door in the gas station when I heard that dreaded sound. It was a patrol coming from the south. You could hear them coming across the river at the bottom of the hill. I looked across the street and saw someone peering from the windows of the old grocery store where I'd seen the antenna the day before. Shit!

This was going to be the shootout I'd been trying to avoid! And I didn't know what my new friends were going to do. They didn't seem to have any weapons. I was in a really tight spot here and my mind was racing.

I turned around to grab the shotgun but Brew had taken it from the bike and was pointing it at me! He would drop me before I could get the .45 out of my holster. "JC—you're just gonna have to trust us. We want to get to the north too but right now we have to look like we're doin' our job for the Guardians. Quick—give me your gun and holster. We want them to think you only have the shotgun." The bikes were getting closer and it seemed like I had no choice but to go along with the boys.

Brew threw the gun and holster to Nick. "Quick—hide this in the station. JC will need it later." I wasn't sure what that meant but for now things weren't looking too good for this old Marine.

"Blackie doesn't kill people right away," Brew explained in a hurry. "He likes to play with them first." Could only imagine what that meant. "You bein' on a bike will be of special interest to him. We gotta play the odds. My brother has an auto in the garage behind the counter but it'll be touch and go with the Guardians if it comes to a shootout. Here they come!" he shouted to his brother.

There were three of them in the patrol and the lead one sure looked like Blackie. It was getting light and I could see his large body and long hair on the all black bike. They pulled up a few yards away and got off. The two with Blackie immediately pulled their weapons and pointed them at me. Brew kept the shotgun trained on me. Blackie was even bigger than I thought. He was the size of Duke and had fire in those black eyes of his.

He came straight toward me without saying a word and before I knew it he threw a punch. I tried to block the shot but it caught me on the side of my face. It was a hard punch and I went down. That made me angry and I wasn't going to take this lying down. He watched me get back up and must have seen the old emblem on the jacket. "You Marine trash think you're so tough!" He spit out at me. "You're the one who killed my men in Jenner aren't you? We found your sniper rifle."

"I didn't kill anyone." I wasn't lying about that but wasn't going to tell the whole story either. Not if I didn't have to. "The only gun I'm carrying is the one pointin' at me right now by this traitor over here." I moved in closer and stood my ground with him. Eye to eye.

Nobody else moved. They were waiting to see what Blackie did next. He only paused for a second before he started a foot kick but thanks to Duke's boot camp I was ready. I deflected his strong kick with my arm and did a leg sweep under him—taking him down hard on his back! Perfect timing—maybe one of my angels helped! Everyone looked stunned but nobody moved or pulled a trigger. Maybe they hadn't ever seen anyone try to stand up to this mountain of a man. Particularly an old guy my size.

I had my arms up and ready for the next round. I wasn't going out without one hell of a fight. Even if it was a short one. Blackie got back on his feet but I could tell the fall had knocked the wind out of him. We circled each other as he glared at me with his eyes full of hate. "I have better plans for you jarhead," he spoke slowly with a menacing voice. "What's your name old man?" He moved in closer as we intently sized each other up. The Marine in me was riled up and ready to take this big man on.

"JC—what do they call white trash like you little man?" I was taunting him—playing with his head. Had to be careful how far I pushed it. Wanted him pissed—but not enough to shoot me on the spot.

He spoke slowly and loudly so everyone could hear him. "I'm Blackie. The meanest mother fucker on this coast and you're in my fuckin' kingdom now. I'm gonna have you for lunch — you old excuse for a biker. You'll wish you'd never come into my territory when I finish with your sorry ass. I'm gonna run you and your fuckin' ride off a cliff. Watch you burn at the bottom!"

"Talks cheap rice grinder boy. You wanna go another round?" I stood my ground in front of him with my arms raised. I was bluffing because I thought he could kick my ass in hand to hand. He had age and size working for him.

He turned to Brew. "What's wrong with this piece of shit old hog?" he demanded to know.

"Don't know yet. Hasn't been here that long. Might be a gas — maybe electrical — problem," Brew lied back to Blackie.

"Think you can fix it?"

"Sure — but it might take some time. Don't know until we get to take a look." Brew was trying to buy us some time.

"Then do it. I'll give you two hours," he ordered Brew.

Blackie stepped so close to me he blocked out the early morning sun. Could see him thinking about trying another punch. I was gambling he didn't want to lose any more face in front of his men — but I was ready for another round.

He spoke to me loud and clear, "I'm gonna teach you a lesson — you fuckin' biker prick. When your bike's runnin' we're gonna take a run up the coast. Just you and me. Then we'll see how tough you are." He stood there glaring at me but I showed no fear. He know he'd met a Marine today — no matter what the outcome…

After a drawn out silence — guess he was a slow thinker — he turned around and told the other two Guardians to keep an eye on me while he went across the street to the general store. They stood there with their weapons fixed on me. I wasn't sure but it seemed like they'd enjoyed seeing him get put on the ground. But when he turned to face them they put on their serious faces. "You bet boss," one replied, "he ain't goin' nowhere."

Blackie was only at the store for a few minutes. When he came back across the street none of us had moved. We waited to hear what he'd planned. He signaled the other two to get on their bikes. "I'll be back in two hours," he yelled at Brew. "Make sure the old grunts ready and running when I get back. If he gets away you'll pay the price. I have plans for his head."

He came over and spit on the ground in front of me and we exchanged stares for a while. Was on the ready if he swung at me again. There was serious anger in his eyes—sometimes that clouds the judgment. What I was counting on if we went one on one. "I'll be back for you—you fuckin' asshole—count on it!" he spoke slowly to me.

"I'll be waiting for you," was my only reply.

He saddled up and the three of them headed north with a scream of noise from their three fast bikes. I watched them disappear over the long hill out of Gualala.

I was going to have my work cut out for me today—but I wanted a shot at his ass. Just one shot...!

CHAPTER 23

A Run Up the Coast

As soon as Blackie and the boys disappeared north out of town Brew handed me back the shotgun. "You're a tough son of a bitch JC—I'll give you that! Blackie's got quite the reputation in these parts. He won't be easy. Time to get to work on your bike. Want you to be ready."

"Yeah—ready for what?" It was an important question of the day.

"Knowin' Blackie like I do—my guess is he plans on takin' a ride with you and makin' sure you never come back. But first he'll play with you for a while. He's a sadist with a twisted mind. It'll take all the Marine you got in you to come out on top," he said looking at my faded patch.

Brew continued, "When I was in the Army I served with Marines during the Persian Gulf—you guys are tough at any age. I took your .45 so he wouldn't know you're carryin' it. Maybe you can put it under your jacket and he'll be in such a hurry to have his revenge he won't check you too close. If they find it we'll all be in hot water—I mean M16 hot water! But that's a chance we'll have to take."

Brew turned to get the bike and push it into the garage. "Nick—let's check the Glide out and see if we can get this old girl in top running condition. JC's gonna need some real go power to take on Blackie if they go for a run on the coast."

Nick started on the carburetor while Brew got ready to drain the tank. "Need to get this bad gas outta here and put some premium in the tank—maybe with a little octane booster. We'll check the plugs and air cleaner. Are those stock pipes?" Brew asked me with an amazed look on his face.

"Yeah—put them on to be quiet," I explained.

"Well bro—we need horsepower and intimidation now—not quiet," Brew barked to Nick, "I'll check out back and see what we have. We're gonna make this old girl hum real nice." Brew was a man on a mission. These boys were okay.

"I'll get you some grub prepared so sit back and relax for a bit. We'll take care of the bike," Nick offered before he left to go across the street to the general store.

Brew reached into a cooler and pulled out a soda bottle. "Here's somethin' I bet you ain't seen in a long time – real Coke in the bottle." He opened it and handed it to me. I looked at it in brief disbelief – like so many things on this trip so far. Man it tasted good. What a treat.

I took off my leathers and sat down on the shop floor to enjoy the Coke. Brew disappeared out back to look for parts. It'd been a long night and the day wasn't even close to over. I laid back against the work bench and dozed off...

After some time Brew came back with a pair of short drag pipes and I woke up. "These should work nicely," he said, "but we have to open up the air cleaner and re-jet the carb to give you some more juice. Sure hope this old girl can take the modification. It'll add about ten horses and give you some kick on the acceleration. But you still won't be faster than Blackie – so you'll have to be smarter."

"Already figured that out..." I answered as I stretched and yawned.

While he worked Brew told me their story. The brothers had both served in the Army back in the nineties where they learned to work on trucks and tanks. When they came home from the Army they left Southern California and came to Gualala to open up their own shop.

"We been workin' on bikes – trucks – cars here ever since," Brew told me as he worked. "Just about anything with a motor – even farm equipment if they twist our arms hard enough. We both ride and thought this looked like the closest thing to heaven we'd ever seen. So we stayed. The Guardians stole our Harleys right after they took over this part of the coast road. We didn't get out to the north soon enough."

Brew went on, "We have a radio hid out we use to keep the New Society posted on what the Guardians are doin'. We want to join 'em but decided to stay a while and provide them intelligence on the Guardians. Get to hear a lot of talk while they're hangin' out here at the station havin' their bikes worked on. We know that Point Arena is their last command post. The New Society is fortified just north of there. The Guardians are pretty well dug in up there. That's where most of them stay when they ain't runnin' patrols. So what's your story JC. How'd you get here?"

Nick came back to the garage and started to give his brother a hand with the bike. They definitely knew what they were doing and didn't waste any time. I entertained them with the story of my escape from the City in a garbage truck. Everyone liked that story—so I was getting good at the telling. We had a laugh while they worked. I told them about staying with Jake but didn't mention Amber. Didn't want anyone sharing that information in case we got caught by the Guardians before this day was through. Also didn't mention John but just that I stayed in one of the old homes in Sea Ranch. That was all they needed to know for now.

"So what's with the old man I saw across the street in the store. He with the Guardians?" I asked with a little anger in my voice.

"Theodor is okay. He probably called the Guardians on you—he had no choice," Brew explained.

"Had no choice? How's that?"

"A few months back the Guardians beat up his wife real bad and told him if he didn't report everything he saw they'd come back and finish the job with the both of 'em. It took her quite a while to heal. They're good people though—trust me on this. They hate the Guardians and want out too."

"So what's your plan?" I inquired with deadly interest.

Brew stopped working and sat down next to me with a Coke of his own. He handed me a cigarette and we both lit up. Maybe tomorrow would be a good day to quit. I felt like he was preparing me for something major. "JC—you're about to experience one of the toughest challenges of your life. You got combat experience?"

"Been a long time—Vietnam in '69. Been shot once and blown up one time—shrapnel. But I stuck it out for eleven months before they shipped me home after the second purple heart. Don't like killing anymore—so I've been trying to stay away from the Guardians. But shift happens."

"Shift?" Brew questioned.

"Yeah—you know—changes." I was thinking about John when I answered.

"I certainly understand but now you gotta play it out. Hope you're ready. I'd go for you if I could but he wants you—real bad! Make his anger your advantage. Blackie is one tough cookie. He won't cut you any slack once you're on the bikes. He lost face today in front of his men and he intends on settin' that right with you. You won't have any choice 'bout the killin'. It'll be you or him. Need to get your head 'round that."

I thought about it and knew it was true. "Don't worry—I'm ready. You know the saying—once a Marine always a Marine. He's better armed and faster but I'll bet I can out ride him for sure. Even on the hog. I'll need to take the .45 if I want to have a decent chance. So what happens when I take him out?"

"Then you hightail it back here. We'll be waitin'. If we hear his bike come back then it'll be business as usual. We can't let them know we're working with the New Society or we'll be next on the hit parade. But if we hear your bike comin' back we'll take out the other two guards. Then we'll all saddle up and head for Point Arena."

"If Point Arena is that well fortified how'll we get through?"

"The New Society has been plannin' an attack on the town for a while. They want to push the Guardians back farther south. Just talked with 'em on the radio and gave 'em the low down on what was happenin' here. They're gettin' their troops ready to launch an assault on the town. When they find out we're comin' they'll hit 'em from the north—and east—to take some of the Guardians away from the southern checkpoint. But we're still gonna have to blaze our way in with weapons firin'. Won't be a piece of cake! It ain't easy shootin' an auto from a movin' bike but they'll think it's a Guardian patrol at first so we have to close in while we can. Surprise will be our advantage."

"So it all depends on me?" I was wondering how I'd suddenly gotten this important role. "I'm supposed to take out a rather large—very pissed off—sadistic—and well armed

Guardian on a much faster bike? Sure—just another day at the office!" I said sarcastically. Maybe this was the destiny John had been talking about—to help these folks reach safety. But why me? My insides were churning at the thought.

"Semper Fi—Bro," Brew said with a short chuckle as he reached over and gave me the biker handshake. "You can always count on a grunt when the chips are down. Time for me to get back to work. Your food will be here in a minute. You could use the boost. You can have a hot shower if you want one. Might help you feel awake. We have a little time. Blackie might take some shit from the troops when he gets to Point Arena and have to kick some ass as a warm up for you." Brew had a strange sense of humor—maybe the Army did it to him?

These brothers were good—worked like a pit crew at a race. Hung on the new mufflers and high flow air cleaner in quick time. Nick filled the tank with new gas. There was a charger running on the battery to give it some life back. They put in new plugs and checked over all the fluids.

Nick commented on the chain drive. "It's a bit worn but we don't have a replacement. It'll have to do. We'll leave the pack on the bike to give you some cover from the rear. Maybe I can rig a steel plate in the back for protection that won't be too obvious. Is the oil fresh?"

"Changed it just before the trip. It's good."

When he finished he wiped off the tank and got on the bike. "You mind if I kick it over?"

"Help yourself," I replied.

"He kicked her through a few times with the kick starter to get some gas in the engine. Then he punched the starter. It came alive after just a few turns of the motor. Man it was loud—sounded great. A real Harley now. We shook hands and patted backs all around. Just hearing the motor gave me renewed confidence. If I was going to go out—at least I'd do it in a blaze of glory. Then I remembered the Marines had taught me the only glory was in winning. So that would be the game today.

Our food arrived from the lady across the street. Nick introduced her as Erma. It was biscuits and gravy with sausage. We all sat down and ate several plates. It was delicious. You could see where they'd scarred her face and she walked with a limp.

While we were eating her husband came across the street. He knelt down to my greasy spot on the floor and put out his hand, "I sure pray you understand I had no choice but to call the Guardians. I'm very sorry about that. I'm Theodor—but I prefer Ted from a friend. You've met my wife Erma. Good cook isn't she?"

I looked over at his wife—wiped off my hand—then accepted his handshake. "I understand. Brew explained it to me. You didn't have any choice—just like you say. I'm cool with that. Maybe this will work out for the better in the long run. Blackie needs to be dealt with—for sure."

Theodor knelt down and looked me straight in the eye. "Brew told me the plan. I saw you take Blackie down from the window. I want you to kill him for me. He's no good. A real bad apple. Take him out—we'll be waiting when you get back. I want some Guardian blood." His eyes were intent with anger.

It was interesting how everyone had so much confidence in an old biker they'd just met. Maybe they saw something I didn't. Maybe it was the same thing John was talking about. But this certainly wasn't going to be easy. After I ate I checked over the Colt and fitted it inside my jacket. I might not get more than one shot—if even that. Sure didn't want to fight it out with Blackie hand to hand. He wouldn't be easy to take down.

"We have some time. You want that hot shower now?" Brew asked.

"Yeah—that's a great idea. Haven't had one in a while. My tired body could sure use it."

Ted took my by the arm and pulled me up. He was strong for an old cuss—well—at least older than me anyways. "You let me take care of that. We have plenty of hot water. You can take as long as you want. I been checking the radio and Blackie won't be back for at least another hour. We want to help you JC."

While I was walking with them to their house in the back of the store I asked what'd happened to the Gualala Hotel. "Those damn Guardians were partying there one night while there was still liquor and they caught the place on fire." Ted sounded pretty pissed off. "We thought it was going to take Brew's gas station also. It was sad to watch. Had many a drink there after a long day at the store. The dining room was pretty good too. You know the hotel?"

"Yep—spent quite a bit of time there myself. One of my favorite places along the coast. Sure was disappointing when they built the hotel across the street and took the view. Lots of memories at the Gualala Hotel..."

Ted and his wife couldn't pay enough attention to me. They reminded me of family back home in West Virginia when I'd go back. Always wanting to do things for you. Guess they were good folk after all. I was getting more used to being a hillbilly during this journey. Maybe that wasn't so bad after all?

The warm shower was a true luxury—hadn't had one since Jake's place. Just let the hot water work my sore body. At least if I was going to be the sacrificial lamb today—I'd go out clean. I chuckled to myself. This wasn't the first time I'd entertained myself with morbid thoughts before a tough battle. But then I thought back to Amber's sweet face and John in his priestly robe. Wanted to go back to rescue them—so I had to take on this mission with all the courage I could muster. I was ready to kick some Guardian ass!

When I finished my shower Ted told me he'd received a radio message that Blackie would be on his way back shortly. Even with that news Erma insisted on drying my hair with a hair dryer. "You have such long soft hair. Just like our son so many years ago. We don't want Blackie to know we helped you while he was gone—so I need to get it dry." Felt like I was having a day at the beauty parlor.

She smelled like my mom after she'd been baking in the kitchen. What a wonderful memory. If mom only knew what her little boy was up to now. But then maybe she was one of my angels that John talked about. "I'll pray for your safe return my son," she offered with a warm hug before I left the store.

I could hear Nick running the bike down the road and back while I was in the store. It sure didn't sound like the bike I'd been riding. More like a dragster with those open pipes.

Nick and Brew had the bike all ready to go. "It runs real good," Brew said with a proud look on his face. "I wanted her all warmed up for you. Sure hope they don't notice we modified the bike. Blackie was probably too busy focusin' on you to check out the machine. Nick put a steel plate in the back of the pack to give you some limited bullet protection. Let's hope they don't ask you to take the pack off. We have our weapons ready in case the shit hits the fan but it'll be touch 'n go. You ready to get some gunny?" I'd never been a gunny but liked being called one anyways. It showed his confidence in me.

I was putting my leathers on when I wondered out loud, "What happens if they frisk me? If they find the .45 the shit will hit the fan right there."

Brew contemplated for a moment. "Been thinkin' 'bout that too. Why don't you give me the gun. I'll figure out a way to give it back before you leave. We'll have to play it by ear but you're gonna need it. Leave the Ka-bar on your leg. If they want to take somethin' they can have that."

I closed the jacket enough to hide the holster. Then we heard the bikes coming from the north and they were moving fast. Blackie must have been anxious to finish his business with me since I humiliated him. Saw Ted and Erma watching from the window across the street. It was show time!

When they came across the ridge to the north of town Brew trained the shotgun back on me. His brother stayed back in the door of the station where his weapon was close by. I'd never tried acting but this was going to be the time to find out if I was any good at it.

We stood there quiet while they pulled up. The two Guardians with Blackie stayed back while he got off his bike. He came right up to me and stood a few feet away. A piece of big logging chain was hanging around his neck. Think I knew where that was going. He didn't smell any better than the last time. Guess he hadn't had a shower and a groom like me.

I considered if he was going to throw another punch to try and soften me up. This time I was ready. "You ready to die scooter trash?" he snarled as he got closer. "You and that Harley piece of junk." Blackie spit on the ground and tried to stare me down. Kind of like old gunfighters. I stood my ground and stared back — right into those dark black eyes.

"It'll be a sorry day when I can't kick the ass of prison trash like you — on or off the bike," I answered trying to piss him off. It worked — his eyes lit up with anger.

"Spider — give him a weapons check," he ordered loudly to one of the guards. "Don't want him carryin' no firepower." The Guardian stepped forward to give me a frisk. I held my breath while he did a quick pat down — not the first time I'd been through this procedure. He didn't feel the holster. That was good news.

"What about the knife boss?"

"Leave it. Doubt he'll get a chance to use it. Maybe it'll give this old Marine some courage on this day of days for him," Blackie taunted me.

Blackie barked to the other Guardian, "Throw his sleeping bag on the ground so I got a good view of him. Toss the pack too." That wasn't good news.

The Guardian went over to the bike and took off the sleeping bag. He was fumbling with the pack when I decided to up the ante with Blackie and get him more pissed — and in a hurry.

Took a step closer to him. "We gonna talk all day mother fucker — or get this done? I can out run you any day on your little toy."

"Fuck you little man!" he said as he glared back. "Let's get it on…" and with that he turned to say something to the closest Guardian. Probably gave him instructions to kill me if I came back. Then he headed toward his bike.

He yelled over to the other one who was still trying to get the pack off, "Leave it go — I can see him well enough without the bag."

Bingo! That was what I'd hoped for. The pack with the steel plate was still on. Close…

Brew quickly stepped over to me. "You're gonna get your ass kicked good today old man," he said loudly as he pretended to shake me by my jacket while he slipped the .45 into my holster. I zipped my jacket up so the Guardians wouldn't see it. "Doubt we'll see you again — good riddance to bad rubbish!" he continued as he gave me a wink. He walked over to the bike with me while I got on. He whispered in my ear, "We'll be waitin' for you when you get back. Good hunting."

I started the bike and revved her up to make a lot of noise. Man — she sounded like a real machine now. The old girl was gonna have to hang in with me today.

Looked over my shoulder and Blackie was just starting his machine. Decided to get him rattled and catch him off guard. So I kicked it in first and took off up the road as fast as I could get the bike to move. Didn't wait for him as this wasn't going to be a gentleman's game. As soon as I had it in third I zipped my jacket down to give me access to the .45. Those boys really knew their stuff because the old girl surprised me. I was one with the machine and flying...!

It was uphill out of town and I knew it wouldn't take Blackie but a few seconds to catch up on his fast machine. I gave it all the juice I could knowing my biggest risk would be in the straights. It was about a half mile before we'd reach the turns. I saw Blackie catching up in my mirrors. He was coming on fast. When he got just a few feet behind me he veered over to my right side and swung the chain at me. He was using his left hand and the pack took most of the blow. Good thing they left it on. Needed to keep him too busy to get another shot with that chain.

Dropped down a gear and gave her full throttle. He'd slowed briefly to take that shot with the chain so I pulled ahead a few yards and moved over to the right side of the road. I knew he'd have a hard time swinging that chain across his body and he couldn't let go of the throttle.

He was back on me in a flash but as he pulled up I swerved to the left just enough to throw his concentration. He jerked to avoid me and left off the gas for a split second. I pulled back out in front and prepared for the first curve I could see coming. I'd done some flat track racing back in the day and I wasn't afraid to lean it into a turn. He was coming back up on me as we reached the turn.

I only backed off the throttle a hair and went into the turn really fast. Had to put her into a serious lean and I felt the pegs scraping on the left side but I hung on. Sure I was kicking some sparks back. I was in full combat mode and ready for this fight. Only had a brief second to look in the mirrors but I saw Blackie leaning it hard to stay up with me. He was too busy now to think about the chain. This was going to be harder than he expected. I could hear Duke's voice in my head saying, "It ain't the machine but the man on the machine." Blackie was about to learn that lesson.

I came out of the turn with Blackie hot on my heels. It was only a short straightaway before the next turn. He used his horsepower to get along my left side but he couldn't get a good swing of the chain from there. He clipped me on the shoulder with the end of the chain and I felt it through the leathers. Kept my focus on the road. In a few seconds we hit the next turn which swept to the right. Once again I went into the turn too hot and had to really lean her over. This time I was scraping metal on the right. Blackie put both of his hands back on the bike to handle the turn. He was only a few feet behind as we both tried to hold the curve.

The road then swept to the left and back to the right. I was holding my own but he wasn't far behind. Figured he wasn't having as much fun as he'd planned. In the next straight he came up beside me but this time he tried to throw the chain into my wheels. Lucky for me he missed and hit my tank. I took the chain across the chest before it bounced off to the side of the road. If he'd caught it in my wheels this battle would be over real quick.

It was time to get aggressive so I let him get back up on my left side and I swerved toward him and kicked his bike. That took him by surprise! He wobbled for a minute and dropped back. He knew now this old Marine was going to give him one hell of a run for his money.

By the time he caught back up we were entering the next turn. In the turns it's gravity and balls – not horsepower – that makes the difference. As best I could tell he still hadn't pulled his weapon on me. I was keeping him too busy to take his hands off the bars to get a shot. But I knew he was going to try the first chance he had.

We came out of the last turn and the road opened up into another straight section. I dropped a gear and gave it all she had – took her to redline. The bike really made a racket as I topped the rpms. Was praying she'd hold together. It was a lot of stress on the ole gal but it was a Harley and she hung in there. Blackie fell back a short ways and I figured he was getting ready to take a shot. Could barely make out in the vibrating mirrors he was trying to get his weapon to bear. Leaned over on the tank and tried to open up the distance.

He let out a few rounds and I felt one of the shots hit the pack! The metal plate took the force and it gave the bike quite a jolt. She shook real hard but I hung on. Saw some of the rounds hitting the ground around me and heard them whistling by. Was like a firefight in Nam with bullets flying everywhere. But as long as he was firing he couldn't work the clutch and had to stay in whatever gear he was in. I swerved back and forth to make it harder for him to take aim. Heard a round go right past my head!

There was another turn coming up and I knew he couldn't keep firing and make the turn so I pressed it as hard as I could into the curve. The firing stopped as he shifted down for the turn. I was going too fast for the curve and gave a quick shot of rear brake before I leaned in real hard. The pegs were dragging on the left and trying to push me back upright—I just let the sparks fly.

He tried coming along side me in the turn but I crowded him out. All he could do was hang on and try to stay with me. It'd been a couple of miles since Gualala and I knew we were getting close to the town of Anchor Bay. The road would go straight through town which would give him another shot at me but I had a surprise in store for him.

The town was only a few buildings long before it went into a hard downhill turn to the right. This would be the best chance to get my shot. As we came roaring out of the last turn before town I gave it all she had and got a brief lead on Blackie. He gassed it to catch up and then reached for his auto again to try and finish me off.

Then I used a trick I'd heard from those Air Force fighter pilot boys. As he was getting ready to take his shot I put on all the brakes I could pull for just a second. He went shooting by me before he realized what'd happened. He was getting close to the downhill turn so he grabbed onto the bars to get control.

I reached inside my jacket and pulled out the .45 with my left hand—instinctively cocking the hammer. I was only going to get one shot at this!

All I had to do was hit him somewhere—anywhere. I took quick aim and pulled off a round. There was an explosion of blood as I caught him in the left shoulder. He went out of control as he approached the turn. He couldn't stop the bike and went flying through the guardrail and off the edge of the road into a lot of air. It was a long drop down into the woods and I saw him take wings off the cliff.

Now I had a serious problem! Didn't want to follow him over the cliff and I was going way too fast for the turn myself. Had no choice but to take her down on the side. I let the gun fly while I grabbed all the brakes I could muster and started to take it over on the right side. This was gonna hurt!

I hit the ground hard and went into a slide. The bike started to turn in a circle—there was scraping of metal and sparks everywhere. Hung on for dear life and tried to ride it out. Knew the cliff was coming up fast. Sure hoped my angels were riding with me.

The bike did a full three sixty on the ground and started off into the dirt before the cliff. It was one hell of a ride! Came to a stop just a few feet from the busted guardrail with dirt flying everywhere. Could smell the burning rubber from the pegs. Just then I heard an explosion at the bottom of the cliff. It was Blackie's bike. The son of a bitch was toast now. Even that bastard couldn't live through that free fall. Couldn't happen to a nicer guy.

I lay under the bike for a few seconds trying to figure out if I had any right leg left. I'd taken a lot of the spill on my right side. Smelled gas running off the bike so I pushed out from under in case she was gonna catch fire. I was scraped up bad but still had my right arm and leg intact. Now that was a miracle…

I tried to stand up. Man was I light headed—probably in shock. But at least I was alive. Tried getting the bike up to stop the gas flow but couldn't move her. Then the adrenaline kicked in because I tried one more strong pull and she came up. I set her on the stand and went to look over the cliff. There was fire where Blackie's bike hit the ground and it was catching the trees on fire. I saw his body several feet from the impact and he wasn't moving. Don't think even Satan himself could have survived that fall. The fire was spreading and that could be a problem.

Then it all came rushing in on me and I had to sit down. Tried to light up a cigarette but my hands were shaking so bad I couldn't get the lighter to hold still. It finally lit and I took a long drag. I leaned back against the guardrail and felt the pain come through my body.

My leathers were torn and I had some serious road rash but nothing was broken. Maybe this prayer thing worked after all. All I could think to say was, "Thank you God." I sat there trying to get my head back on. The smoke from the fire was coming up over the cliff—so I couldn't hang around too long.

When I finished my smoke I got my battered body off the ground and checked out the bike. I'd taken a good bit of machine off the right side. The bars were bent but everything still seemed in place. The front highway peg had taken most of the force and that is what had protected my leg. The peg was half gone. Good old Milwaukee steel. The right saddlebag was mostly missing and my canned goods were spread out down the road. Good thing it was loaded with cans because it'd taken a lot of the impact.

The back pack had a hole blown in it where Blackie had connected with a round. The bullet was flattened out against the metal plate. Nick's idea had saved my life! I remembered feeling that round hit the bike and almost losing control. If it'd caught me in the back the contest would've been over.

There was another bullet hole in the left saddle bag that'd come out down near my leg. Damn—I was one lucky son of a bitch. Maybe my angels were traveling with me? I thanked Dianne and my dad for protecting me. I wondered if the girl was going to start again.

I walked down the road looking for my pistol. I could see the damage I'd left in the road when I ground the bike down. There was also blood from where I'd hit Blackie and skid marks from his tires where he'd tried to brake before flying through the guardrail. Hope his last thoughts were about this old Marine who'd cleaned his clock. Call me scooter trash will ya! Adios—mother fucker...

It took a while but I found the .45. It was pretty scraped up but looked like it'd still work. I checked the action—fired off one round to be sure — and put it back in my holster.

I limped back to the bike. The pain in my right leg was swimming upstream against the adrenaline. I remembered the bottle of hooch in the pack and much to my wonder it hadn't broken. Took a short swig. Thanks Jake — this really was good snake bite medicine.

I sat down on the bike to start her. She coughed for a while but eventually turned over. What a sweet girl — and after all this abuse. I let her idle and wondered if I was in shape to ride. The hooch was working and dulled some of the pain. Took one last look toward the cliff. The fire was burning out as the wind was coming from the east toward the ocean. "This one's for you Blackie," I said as I spit on the ground.

I was shaky as I put the bike in gear and turned around to face south. The front brake lever was broken off — so I'd only have rear brake for the trip back. Not a big problem. I was going to take it slow while I got my strength back.

As I worked my way south I saw the many deep marks where I'd dragged through the turns. It'd been quite the chase. Guess all those years of riding had paid off. Briefly thought about what it'd be like to just take a ride for fun after all this. What a concept. But there were still more battles ahead today. Had to get focused once more.

As I got closer to Gualala I stopped to figure out my plan of action. I let the old girl idle while I moved the .45 to the outside of my jacket for a better draw. It was working and ready for more action. I was ready for the run back into town. Took one long breath and put her in gear.

I'd gain as much speed as I could before cresting the down-hill into Gualala. The sound of the Harley would alert the guards but they'd pause to see if it was Blackie or me. Didn't want to give them much time to think about it. Hoped the brothers were ready as it was going to get hot real quick. I gunned the motor and headed for town.

As I was picking up speed I thought about the childhood game of hide and seek we used to play — the rhyme we chanted came to my head — "Ready or not — here I come…"

CHAPTER 24

The Battle for Pt. Arena

I sped over the ridge and downhill into town at full bore — hell bent for leather. Saw Brew and the Guardians standing next to the gas station. Imagined the Guardians had quite the look of surprise when they figured out I wasn't Blackie!

One Guardian ran for the store and the radio but the other stepped into the middle of the road and brought his automatic to bear on me. Brew and Nick hit the ground. What the hell was that all about? Maybe they weren't my friends after all? I wasn't going to have much of a chance against the auto at this range with my .45. Had I been suckered? I'd need to get closer to take a shot. I asked the bike for all she had.

When the running Guardian was about twenty feet from the store Ted stepped into the doorway with a shotgun and took him out. The blast lifted him backwards about ten feet. The other Guardian turned to his left quickly and sent a spray of bullets toward the store and Ted. He was back inside as the bullets hit the building but it took the Guardian's attention off me for a few precious moments.

I was getting closer and almost enough for a good shot — drew the .45 and took aim. Just then I saw a figure in black step from the garage and cut the Guardian in half with a blast from an automatic. He never knew what hit him. That was why Brew and Nick hit the ground — to give this other person a clear shot. They had it planned.

I quickly put the sidearm back in the holster and tried to slow down remembering that I didn't have a front brake. Went into a controlled skid as I slid past the boys. I kept it under control and made a slow turn around back to the garage. As I got closer I saw the figure in black checking out the bodies. There was blood everywhere and the familiar smell of gunpowder in the air. Brew grabbed the bike and held it while I got off. We stood there with stunned faces all around.

All of a sudden everyone was around me—patting me on the back—shaking my hand. Even Erma. "You did it JC! We knew you could. Is Blackie dead?" Ted wanted to know.

"Yeah—I'd say he's quite dead. Kind of barbecued—you might say. Took him out in Anchor Bay. It was really—and I mean really—close! The bike took a few rounds before I got him." I shook Nick's hand. "Your steel plate saved the day. Take a look." I pointed to the back. Everyone checked out the damage to the bike.

"Man—you took some real hits. You okay?" Brew asked as he saw the damage to my leathers.

"Got some serious road rash when I took the bike down but nothin's broken. I heard rounds going past my head. It was some ride with Blackie on that faster bike. The old girl's wounded though."

Brew stepped back as the stranger in black turned around. It was a girl! I was speechless...

"JC—I want you to meet your protector," Brew said introducing me. "This is our sister Duffy. She was a Marine 'bout ten years ago. In her younger and crazier days. We been hidin' her out all this time from the Guardians."

Duffy took off her hat letting her red hair fall down her back. She was good looking - maybe in her thirties. Pretty buff too. A female Marine who looked good and could handle an automatic. I think I was in love.

I stepped over and looked her straight in the eyes—what pretty green eyes they were. Tall to boot. I gave her a big long hug and then stepped back. She smelled like flowers. Just like Rhonda. "You sure like to cut it close but you did the job," I told her in a loud voice.

She looked back with those bright green eyes. "I had him in my sights the whole time. I wasn't going to let him hurt a fellow Marine. You're quite the hero JC. Blackie was a tough cookie to take out. Can't wait to hear the story but we've got to get ready for the push into Point Arena."

I walked back to the group still inspecting the damage to the bike. Brew was the first to speak, "We've gotta get ready for the ride into Point Arena. The New Society is waitin' for word from me before they start their attack. How long you think it'll take to get the Harley back in shape?" he asked Nick.

"I'll need to get a new brake lever on—see if I have any other bars. We might have to go with 'em bent. Can you ride it this way if you have to?" Nick asked me.

"It's awkward but I can make it work if I have to. Having the front brake back would be a big help though."

"Think I can have it ready in less than an hour," Nick announced to everyone. "How 'bout the rest of you?"

I interrupted, "If you guys have a plan—would you like to include me?"

Brew laughed. "Sorry JC—I forgot. We talked about our plans while you were gone. We're all goin' with you. Erma will ride with me and Ted'll go with Nick. Duffy's ridin' with you. So you'll hafta take off the pack or sling it on the back of the sissy bar. The New Society will start their attack on Point Arena when I give 'em the word we're comin'. But the Guardian's southern outpost might still be intact when we get there. So we'll hafta take it out. With any luck the Guardians will pull a lot of their troops to the north of town to fight off the assault. They're well armed—so it'll be one hell of a battle."

"Don't you think they'll recognize the sound of my Harley when we make our approach?"

"Already thought about that," Brew answered. "We're gonna make a call to 'em on the radio and tell 'em the Guardians are bringin' in a prisoner. They won't know Blackie is dead yet. We'll lead the way down the hill to Point Arena on their crotch rockets and then when we get to the outpost we'll open up. You and Duffy will come through the middle. You'll have to take 'em out. Duffy's a pretty good shot with that Uzi. Better than either of her brothers. Just lean over and give her clear aim. We'll take our bikes into the dirt and take up coverin' fire behind 'em."

It seemed like a crazy plan—but it was a plan. This was turning out to be a real fuckin' long day!

Then Erma spoke up, "You boys get on with the motorcycle. I'm taking JC to the house to tend to his wounds." She took me firmly by the arm and pulled me to the store. What a kind woman. She reminded me of my mom. Ted followed along to help get ready.

Erma helped me take off the leathers and I was pretty black and blue with a lot of road rash. This adventure was taking quite a toll on this worn body. I wondered what the day still had in store? Never thought I'd be in full blown combat again but there was no choice now if I wanted to finish this journey. For the first time in my life I understood what it truly meant to fight for freedom. Maybe freedom wasn't an illusion after all? It was turning out to be a painful lesson...

Erma put some ointment on the road rash. It burned at first but I knew she meant well. She was arguing with Ted about what they could take with them. He kept telling her that they couldn't take anything but the clothes on their backs. Must be hard to leave all of one's memories behind in a moments notice. She said they'd been running the store for almost thirty years. She gave me a bunch of aspirin and I swallowed them down. I was hurting but had a ways to go to complete this mission. I was pulling way down inside myself to find the strength. It was time to see this through. I asked my angels to hang in there a while longer.

Erma and Ted got dressed for the run into Point Arena. This was going to be very dangerous for them but they seemed determined to get out. Ted reloaded his pump shotgun in preparation for the assault on the command post. He had a serious face on. I saw Erma sneak a few family photos into her purse. Certainly understood — didn't say anything. Prayed they had angels traveling with them this day. Had a thought about Brother John and his calming smile. Glad he wasn't in the middle of all this killing.

The burning from the road rash had calmed down so whatever Erma used was working. I picked up my leathers and went outside to check on the bike's progress. Nick was busy working on her while Brew and Duffy were preparing for the mission. I moved the pack to the back of the sissy bar to make room for Duffy.

The .45 was beat up but still worked — good military hardware. I filled the clip and put the shotgun back on the bike. I was expecting the outpost to have a machine gun so Duffy would be the key to taking it out. She seemed pretty sure of herself—just like a Marine.

Duffy came out of the gas station all loaded for action. She was wearing all black and had her face painted for combat. She had the Uzi ready with several extra clips on her body. A couple of hand grenades hung from her web belt. This was my idea of a real woman for sure. She'd of made a fierce Celtic warrior princess with that red hair and green eyes.

She came over to me and handed me a lit cigarette while she lit one for herself. Decided not to mention I was trying to quit. "How you feeling JC?" she asked like one soldier to another.

"Pretty damn sore but Erma fixed me up a bit. So what you think we're in for?"

"Expect they might have something like a fifty millimeter targeted on the road. Don't know how many of them to expect at the post if there's a lot of action around. Even with the attack coming from the north and east I don't think they'll abandon the post completely. But their attention will be elsewhere."

She paused while she took a drag, "We'll be in the open when we make our approach so surprise is our ally. They'll think we're friendlies at first. As soon as we make the break through the middle I'm going to open up. I'll target the machine gun nest first—can't let them open up on us with that kind of firepower. We'll be pretty exposed on the bikes. Just keep your head down and get me in close." She looked at me intently with those green eyes and I saw no fear. This gal knew her business.

"When did you serve?" was all I could think to ask her.

"In the Iraqi War. Got sent over but they didn't like gals on the front line. Went out on a few helicopter rescue missions and saw some action. But not what I'd expected. The whole thing was totally fubar. Damn politicians and their oil!" she spit out.

"It was all about the Concern and money anyways," I said like I was now a Concern expert. I hadn't had the time yet to tell them what I'd learned from Tricky but that could wait until another time. After we'd made it through this insane day.

She went on, "I was young and stupid when I joined the Corps. Nobody could tell me nothin'. It was rough but it straightened me out. Came back to the world with a whole new attitude. I was working in the City as a bodyguard for some rich dude when the shit went down with the Regional Wars. Got out quick before they closed everything off and made my way up here to join the boys. When Blackie heard I was around I had to disappear into hiding. He kept asking about me. I was getting ready to hike to the north but didn't want to leave my brothers behind. So you're showing up changed all our plans. But I know we can do this." Just like a damn jarhead to have a positive attitude even with the odds against us.

Nick stood up and got on the bike. "I've done all I can. You'll just have to live with the bent bars. Did get the front brake working. She should run good. Let's fire her up." And with that he punched the starter. The old gal roared into life and he took off down the road to the river. You could hear those pipes a long ways off. Nick was having fun with the hog. Must have brought back fond memories for him.

Brew came out of the garage with the autos he'd taken from the Guardians. "Had to clean off some of the blood and guts but they both work. It's gonna get hot real quick on the way in. Everyone ready to go?" Erma and Ted joined us and nodded their heads yes. I was worried for this gentle woman but she seemed like tough German stock.

Brew started barking orders at everyone, "Ted—give the Guardians a call on the radio and tell 'em Blackie is on his way with a prisoner. I just talked with the New Society commander and they're kickin' off in five minutes. It'll be a tough battle for the town. The Guardians won't give it up easy but they aren't as well trained as the Society's ex-military troops. They have mortars so they're gonna give them Guardians one hell of a wake up call. We leave in ten—give your gear one last check and hit the john if you need it. It'll take us 'bout thirty minutes to reach town."

We each did a final check and prepared to load up. The brothers had their full leathers on for the mission. Didn't mind having the Army along for the firepower support. As we stood there in a group Brew passed around some cigarettes and we all lit up. When Ted lit one Erma gave him a dirty look. "Dear," she said, "you haven't smoked in years."

"Well love—I think I can make an exception today." He coughed after the first few puffs and we all got a chuckle. Nobody said much after that...

When we were done Erma asked if she could say a prayer. We joined hands while she spoke. "God—please be with us all today on this difficult and perilous journey. Forgive us our sins and give us the courage of David as we face a ruthless enemy. We thank you Lord for your protection." After a moment of silence we all said "Amen!" Just like prayer services back home. I was moved.

I shook hands with everyone while Duffy gave each of the brothers a hug. Erma and Ted shared a long hug and a final kiss. It might be their last time. I'd try to prevent that from happening but in war everyone is in harm's way. We started the bikes and got on.

What a strange looking attack force we were! Two hippie bikers with grandparents on the back and me with a painted red headed Marine who was loaded for action. I don't know if we were heroes—or just crazies. But we only had one direction to go and it was north—into the firestorm. Wondered if God was laughing at our assembled group?

We took off with Brew in the lead and me in the middle. Took it slow to give the New Society some time to press their attack. As we went through the turns we could see where Blackie and I'd ground down our bikes. I saw Brew pointing to the road and talking to Erma. When we got to Anchor Bay Brew slowed down as he worked his way through the debris from where I'd gone down. He pulled up at the end of town where Blackie had flown off the cliff and we all got off. Everyone stood there in amazement checking it out. They looked over the cliff at the burned out woods and what was left of Blackie's charred body.

All Brew could say was, "Wow! You really did the job on him JC. Didn't know what you meant when you said 'barbecued' but now I understand. Well done for sure."

Duffy came up and put her arm around my shoulder. "Good job Marine."

We only stayed for a minute and then got back on the bikes. Even I was having trouble comprehending I'd taken Blackie out with his superior speed and firepower. It was like the wicked witch was dead. We headed north with grim determination to finish this business with the Guardians.

In about fifteen minutes we reached the last spot where we could stop before the downhill approach to Point Arena. We could hear a fierce battle going on just over the hill. There was lots of gunfire and mortars going off.

Brew shouted out last minute instructions, "We'll take the lead and you stay tucked in behind us JC. If they got the message they'll be expectin' Blackie and figure we're reinforcements. But when they see who we are they'll open up. We'll get as close as we can and separate as soon as we see 'em bringin' their weapons to bear. You two gotta take out the machine gun. Hope there's only one heavy weapon pointed our way. We'll get off to the side and take up fire. Good luck everyone. Godspeed..."

Duffy had one short reply to Brew's instructions. She leaned over my shoulder and hollered, "Let's get some!" She was primed and ready...

On the downhill approach Brew and Nick opened their throttles. I stayed close behind 'em. Once we were in the open we could really hear the battle. It was an old — but familiar — sound I'd never expected to hear again. My heart was racing and my mouth was dry. Duffy was tucked in tight behind me as we braced for the assault.

Brew was pushing it hard to close the distance to town before the Guardians figured out what was happening. He and Nick moved to the side to give me and Duffy a view of the outpost. I could see a gun emplacement with several Guardians looking north toward the battle. We were about a hundred yards out when one of them turned around and saw us approaching. Took him a moment to figure it out but he soon realized we weren't Blackie and the patrol. He yelled at the others and raced for the machine gun.

Just as he was bringing it to bear on us I leaned over as far as I could to give Duffy a clear shot. Felt her raise up on the rear pegs. I raced ahead of the other bikes at full throttle. Duffy opened up on the Guardians. She took out the gunner in the first burst. This babe could really shoot!

The other Guardians scrambled for cover. Ted fired his shotgun on my right as they got closer. I lost track of the others as I aimed the bike directly at the outpost. Duffy was laying on deadly suppression fire and several more went down. Their return fire was hitting the ground around us and I heard them whizzing by.

I came to a sliding stop just a few yards from the sandbags outside the outpost and Duffy jumped off with her Uzi blazing. Pulled out the shotgun and let the bike drop to the ground. Sorry girl.

I could hear one auto firing from behind us but didn't know which of the brothers it was. Duffy and I had our hands full. She lobbed one of her grenades over the sandbags and we went flat as it went off. After the explosion we jumped up and took aim at anything that moved. Saw several more men go down. My shotgun went empty and I reached for the .45.

Then I took a round in the left thigh. FUCK! I went down next to the sandbags. It really hurt and was bleeding but it'd missed the bone. What else could happen?

Duffy gave me a quick glance but knew she had to continue the firefight until we had control. I looked up the road and saw Brew coming down the hill firing. Nick and Ted had gone down and weren't moving. Erma was kneeling over them. I was trying to get a tourniquet on my leg to slow the bleeding. I was swearing a lot trying to stop the flood of pain—"Shit! Fuck! Damn! Son of a bitch!" Whatever came to mind...

In a few minutes the firing slowed down. Duffy had taken most of them out and we had the outpost temporarily under control. But we knew they'd be coming back our way when the attack from the north got closer. We prepared for the coming counterassault.

Brew finally reached the bunker and was all winded from the run. He looked up the hill and saw Nick on the ground. "Damn—I hope they're okay." He looked over at me and saw the bloody hole in my leathers. "Can you hang in there?"

"Don't have no fuckin' choice! They're gonna be back this way real soon."

Just then Duffy jumped back over the sandbags to my position and loaded a new clip into the Uzi. "They're gone for now but we need to see if the machine gun is operational." She poked her head over the top of the bags and went back over to check it out. I heard her working the mechanism and shoot off a burst. "It works," she exclaimed. "Let's move it to the north side of the bunker and get ready for their assault."

Her and Brew grabbed the machine gun and moved it next to the sandbags on the other side of the bunker. Then Brew helped me up and we took positions on both sides of Duffy against the sandbags. He threw me one of the autos from a dead Guardian. The battle was coming back our way...

"Here they come!" Duffy yelled out. I pulled myself up to a firing position as best I could. Could see several Guardians working their way back to us. Duffy opened up and mowed several down. She was one deadly Marine.

They returned fire and rounds were hitting everywhere. We wouldn't be able to hold out long if the New Society didn't get here soon. Brew and I opened up. It was a hell of a firefight and getting more intense. We hunkered down when Duffy tossed her last grenade which slowed them down a bit. We were fighting for our lives and it was getting danger close.

I had the firing position to the east and when I looked over the sandbags there were more Guardians moving in from my side. Propped myself up on the bags and opened up with the M16. Hit several of them but the return fire was everywhere. The auto went dry. Ducked back below the bags as I listened to rounds hitting all over my position. I tried to move down a few feet to the east side. My leg really hurt and was bleeding again—I didn't get far.

Duffy and Brew were laying down heavy fire on their end. "Incoming!" Duffy yelled and we took cover. The grenade went over the post and hit on the south side where it threw up a cloud of debris that covered us. That was fuckin' close!

I pulled out the .45 and crawled back to the top of the bags and resumed fire. I could see them moving in several positions. It was like Con Thien all over again—with enemy in the wire! The air was filled with the smell of gunfire and explosions— shit flying everywhere.

Out of the corner of my eye I saw Duffy turn the machine gun in my direction and open fire on more Guardians coming from the east. Got off a few more shots but wasn't sure if I hit anything — couldn't see much. She took out a few more but they were getting close. Was hoping they'd taken their mortars to the north. The return fire was vicious and I had to take cover behind the bags again. Wanted to call for a Medic but there weren't any around. A little helicopter gunship air support wouldn't hurt about right now either. Wishful thinking...Heard Brew yell and fall back behind the barrier. He was bleeding from his left arm and was trying to stop the blood. He was out for now. Duffy must of taken out a Guardian who was tossing a grenade as I heard an explosion fall short of the post. She ducked down briefly to check on me. "How you doing? It's up to us Marines now to hold the day!"

"I hurt like hell but I can try one more time. Let's do it!" I shouted as I struggled again to the top of the bags. There were rounds hitting all over and dust was getting in my eyes.

Duffy was back on the machine gun and we both opened up. I swept east and she tried to cover the middle and west. Gave 'em hell until my clip ran out. Several more rounds hit the bags under me and I went back down to reload. Only had one clip left and my Ka-bar. But they'd know who they tangled with this day...!

Duffy kept up her fire but took cover when they really laid it on her position. They were tearing the shit out of our sandbags and our cover was disappearing. Brew was still out of action. Duffy helped him tie his bandana as a bandage. She crawled back to check on me. "They're getting close and I'm running out of ammo. Going to try another burst," and she moved back to her position. That gal had big Marine balls.

Just then I heard an old familiar sound. I couldn't believe it! It was AK-47 fire. Came to dread that sound in Vietnam but now it was music to my ears. The Guardians weren't using AK-47s. Had to be the New Society. I listened to see if I could figure out what direction it was coming from in all the noise. It was from the northeast. Signaled Duffy to hold on.

"It's got to be the New Society," I yelled over the sound of the battle. "Brew said they'd be wearing orange armbands." I readied the .45 with the last clip and gave Duffy a hand signal. We went back to our firing positions and watched. We both whooped when we saw the orange armbands on the troops moving in from east of town. We had the Guardians in a cross-fire but were running out of ammo. Most of the Guardians broke to the west but a few came our direction. I took out one with the .45 and she caught another with the machine gun. Then I heard it go empty.

There was a Guardian heading right for our position and he was moving fast. He was on the barrier before I could get him in my sights but he made the mistake of trying to take on Duffy. She threw him into the bags on the other side as he came across her position. He started to get up but she took him down with a kick to the chest. Before he could catch his breath she let him have it with another kick to the head. He was out cold.

She took his weapon and sat down next to me. "Thought I'd take me a prisoner — just for fun." We laughed in the middle of this wild firefight. I had the .45 ready for whoever came over the bags next but I was too weak to get back up again.

We sat there next to each other — ready for whatever came next. There was an intense fight going on just on the other side of the outpost but we couldn't see what was happening. Heard the sounds of the AK-47s moving to the west after the Guardians. That was a good sign...

Sounded like there was still plenty of action going on in town as the New Society moved south. I could hear their mortars all over. Somebody was catching hell. The Guardians had only one choice and that was to fall back to the west. The ocean was not far away so they'd run out of options pretty soon. If it was the Cong they'd fight to the death but I bet the Guardians weren't so willing to die.

I looked up the road as the dust cleared a bit. I could see Erma still kneeling over someone trying to protect them. What a gutsy lady. Didn't see either Ted or Nick moving. That wasn't good. But I was too out of it to go check on 'em.

We heard some voices coming closer and braced our weapons. Someone yelled out, "You there in the command post."

I yelled back, "Yeah...!

"We're the NS. You guys need a medic?"

"You might say that—and now!"

Duffy stood up slowly with her weapon at the ready. She didn't fire so I took that to be good news. A couple of soldiers came around the barrier. Well—they didn't really look like soldiers—but they had on orange armbands. Had we finally made it? Damn—what a long fuckin' day!

I heard some people running in the distance and two of them came around the corner with medical bags. The medics were here and none too soon. I signaled one of them to head up to Erma and the boys. The other one knelt down to check on my leg.

"Hi—I'm Magdaline. I'm a doctor," she introduced herself. She put on a pressure bandage as best she could over the leathers and said it would hold until she could look at Brew. Gave me a shot of morphine and told one of the guys to help me light the cigarette I was pulling out of my pocket. Duffy grabbed it away from me and told me to, "Find your own soldier boy—ladies first." Yes—I was definitely in love.

The morphine slowed down the pain a bit. I moved over closer to Duffy and Brew. I handed him a smoke once he was sitting up and the morphine was working. The shot in his arm had probably shattered the bone. He was really hurting. We sat there in post combat numbness. It was hard to believe I'd made it to the end of this journey. And to think what I'd learned along the way…

We were silent as the medic came back down the road. She had her head down. Duffy was the first to speak. "What's the story?"

The medic knelt down to talk with us. "The younger guy is gone. He took a shot to the lung. He was done pretty quick. I'm really sorry."

"What about the old man?" I asked.

"Looks like he broke his collar bone in the bike crash but I think he'll be okay. His wife wasn't hurt but she's pretty shaken. Probably in shock. She wouldn't leave him. If you guys are stable for now I want to get him on a stretcher. We have a field hospital set up north of the town where we can take care of you when everything is secure. The Guardians are leaving town and heading west. We're going to leave some of them alive to tell the others what happened here today. We don't want this to be a massacre."

Duffy leaned over and took Brew in her arms and they both started to cry. I understood.

The doc came back to me to put on a better bandage. She pulled out a scalpel to cut off my leathers. "Man—don't cut the leathers," I pleaded.

She looked at the hole blown in the leathers and just shook her head. "You bikers and your leathers." She chuckled to herself as she unzipped them and took them off me. She cleaned the wound and put on another bandage. The bleeding had slowed down. She was a good medic—better looking than any I'd ever seen in Nam. One of the leaders knelt down to talk to us. "I'm sorry you lost your brother," he offered as he looked at Brew and Duffy. "It took a lot of guts to do what you people did today. He reached over to me and put out his hand. I shook it back. "You must be JC. You really kicked some ass today. I hear you were a Marine?"

"A long time ago..."

"Well—you sure did the Corps proud today. The New Society is glad to have you here. You're all heroes to us. Welcome to the north." With that he got up and moved off to take command of the action.

I moved over closer to Duffy and held both of them as we cried together. Hadn't cried since my dad died. They'd taken a gamble and lost their brother in the play. I remembered the faces of several I'd left behind in Nam. It was a great sadness.

In my morphine haze I watched them bring Ted down the hill with Erma holding his hand. They covered up Nick's body and put him on a stretcher to take back to their territory.

After a while an old van showed up to move the three of us to their field hospital. These New Society people seemed like good folk. Sure hoped it'd been worth the journey. I was thinking about Jake and Amber—and Brother John. Wanted to keep my promise to them and go back but I was pretty stove up for now. I'd have to see how long it took to heal.

It'd been the adventure of a lifetime—one I never wanted to

do again! The old girl was down for the count and I had to leave her. What a ride she'd been. Gotta love a Harley! One of the troops grabbed my pack and shotgun and I put my sidearm back in the holster—hopefully for good.

I wondered when Duke would show up and if Tricky would ever make it. Not sure how he'd fit in with the New Society if they ever found out what he'd done for the Concern. Not sure how Duke would fit in either but I sure missed that smelly old bear. He'd be proud of how I'd used what he'd taught me on this journey. Maybe the fight for freedom was worth it?

As they moved me into the ambulance I thought about John and my angels. Someone had been looking out for me today. Maybe he was right after all...?

My last thought to myself as I drifted off into the morphine was, "You done a good job Marine—Semper Fi..."

Freedom & Recovery

It'd been almost two weeks since the Battle for Point Arena. It was the first major confrontation between the New Society and the Guardians. I'm sure it was a wake up call for the Guardians. The New Society took over the town and fortified it as their southern command post on the coast road. Their intelligence said the Guardians were using Gualala as their new northern outpost on Route 1. Many of the Guardians had surrendered and asked to join the New Society. Their High Council was debating if they could be trusted.

My leg was slowly healing and I was doing rehab to get my strength back to start walking again. Brew had lost the use of his arm and was still pretty down from losing his brother Nick. Ted was up and around and the NS—as they called themselves— had given them a cabin where he and Erma could be together.

The NS had a field hospital setup in Albion and were taking good care of us. Duffy came to see me every day and brought me something. What a babe! My room was starting to look like a mafia funeral with all the flowers everyone was bringing by.

The NS was calling me a hero. Didn't feel like a hero - just an old Marine who'd done what he had to so those good people could make it to safety. They said my journey was a symbol of their fight for freedom and a new way of life built around family and community—rather than materialism. I sure didn't feel good about killing again—but couldn't see any way around it at the time if we were going to make it to freedom. Wished we hadn't lost Nick. He'd made the ultimate sacrifice for the rest of us. Seemed like someone I'd have enjoyed getting to know.

It was a new experience for an old fart biker like me to be treated like somebody important. That never happened after Vietnam. They'd taken my bike and put it on display in their headquarters along with my torn up—and shot up—leathers.

The long johns had bit the dust. Heard they were talking about me around their campfires all across their territory. Pretty heady stuff…

Duffy told me she'd been offered command of the troops at Point Arena. She thought it was cool that a former grunt was being offered a commanders position. In my opinion she was the real hero in the fight at Point Arena. She kept control of the situation and showed no fear even when it looked like we weren't gonna make it. A real tribute to her training in the Corps.

Duffy said she might accept the offer because they needed the help. I really think she liked the idea of being in charge of a lot of men. Yep—I'd definitely fallen for that gal but didn't know how to tell her. Probably never would. Heard a lot of the young bucks were trying to make time with her but she just pushed them away. She could afford to be picky and wait for the right one. I was happy she came to see me everyday. Every time she stopped by I got lost in those green eyes. Like a love sick puppy—and at my age.

The leaders of the NS came by often and had long friendly talks with me. They told me about their society and the values they believed in. It was about community and helping each other. The same things that Jake and Isaac and Brother John had talked about. They welcomed new members to their territory as long as they shared the same ideals. They introduced single people to each other and encouraged folk of any age to start up homesteads in their territory. People were being taught how to live off the land again and to practice bartering for their needs. Freedom and peace were very important to them even though there were hostiles on all their borders.

The NS wouldn't allow individuals to collect wealth but focused instead on brotherhood and love. Everyone working together for their mutual survival and well being. They'd created a defensive perimeter around their territory to try and protect their citizens from marauders. They only used limited technology for things like medicine and defense. Parts of the power grid had been restored but their generation capabilities were limited. There wasn't a television system—just radio. They were trying hard not to repeat the mistakes of the past.

They didn't promote any specific religion but were very spiritual and talked a lot about God. They felt the details of belief were up to the individual. Many of them liked weed because it encouraged folk to be mellow. They strongly discouraged the use of tobacco as being harmful to the body. Someone would bring me a small joint every day and sit around while we smoked and talked together. I'd finally quit smoking cigarettes! Hard to believe...

The more I learned about their new order the more I liked what I heard. It was built upon many of the values I'd left behind in the hills. John was right—this was a new beginning for me. Didn't plan on letting this opportunity to be a better person slide by. I'd received a message on this difficult and painful journey.

Told the NS my story and asked them to keep a look out for Duke at their outposts in the hills. I said they'd recognize him because he was big and smelly—a real grouch. They'd be tempted to shoot him on first sight but I asked them to be tolerant. I wanted to see that old bear again if he made it this far.

Also told them about Tricky and the fight at the river. Informed them he was an experienced sniper but didn't say anything about his being a Concern assassin. If he ever showed up I'd see what he told them about himself. I'd give him the benefit of the doubt at first but would keep an eye on him. I'd be the only one who knew his story. Maybe he was looking for a new way also—always possible.

I informed them as soon as I could walk I wanted to figure out a way to get back south to rescue Jake and Amber. I'd made a promise to Jake and planned to keep it if there was any way possible. We agreed it would be a difficult mission but they'd work with me on a plan. They had topographical maps to help out as I couldn't use the coast road again and would have to find a way overland.

I'm sure the Guardians had a major bounty out on my head. The NS military commander said he'd find some experienced volunteers who'd be willing to take the risk to go into Guardian territory with me. They wanted more intelligence on the Guardian locations and their troop strength. I was hoping

Duke would show up before then because I knew I could count on him. No matter how insane the mission. Maybe Duffy would go with us?

I thanked God for his protection through this perilous journey and asked his forgiveness for the men I'd killed at Point Arena - and back in Nam. It wasn't like I wanted to. I think he understood why I had to kill—like David and Goliath—sometimes you don't get a choice.

Some of John's lessons were sinking into my dense skull. I definitely had angels looking over my shoulder during this dangerous adventure. Sure felt that way. I asked them to travel with me again when I went back south.

I'd probably never get used to being called a hero. For now I was just glad to be alive—and FREE! I'd never take my freedom for granted again.

Maybe freedom wasn't an illusion after all...?

About the Author

Gene Lewis has been riding—and writing—for over forty years. He attended his first Rider Rights Rally in San Francisco in 1975 and remained an activist with ABATE for over two decades promoting motorcyclist rights and rider education. In '75 he also experienced the unforgettable exhilaration of traveling solo around the country on a Triumph Trident witnessing America and freedom at its best. Over the years he has belonged to numerous motorcycle organizations and clubs including the American Motorcycle Association, HOG, the Platte River Valley Riders Club, the 40+ Motorcycle Club, the Motorcycle Touring Association, and the Mountain and Plains Riders Club.

Gene is a proud veteran (Air Force—'68 to '73) who holds in esteem all those who have served in peacetime or war. He wrote this story as a recognition for fellow veterans who often don't receive the gratitude they deserve in our country.

Currently a retired university professor he previously taught technology in a business school—an interesting irony in light of the story's discerning messages about materialism and technology. His publishing record includes over 30 articles and several technology textbooks—although he enjoys writing motorcycle stories the best. He is a musician who likes playing drums with his surf band—Vintage Winds—whenever possible.

"A Run Up The Coast" is a story about courage to find a new way of life. It's about a struggle against overwhelming odds to find freedom—and the self discovery that occurs along the journey. Gene offers this story to promote his belief that *Freedom Is Not An Illusion!*

About the Senior Editor

Denise Lewis was born in Doylestown, Pennsylvania and grew up in Colorado. She now lives in Johnstown, Colorado. Denise greatly enjoys teaching and has been working with young children since the age of twelve. She is currently a 2nd Grade Teacher in the Loveland school district.

Her hobbies include hiking, yoga, snorkeling, reading, riding ATVs, and traveling. She has been across the United States including San Francisco, the Northern Coast of California, Washington D.C., Key Largo, and Maui. Denise has been riding motorcycles with her dad since she could reach the pegs and has seen a lot of Colorado with him.

After reading a draft of **"A Run Up The Coast"** she believed in the messages about freedom and values so she decided to work with her father to finish the novel. She is the Senior Editor for Colorado Winds Publishing where she contributes important editorial and writing input and helps to develop the interesting characters. One day she hopes to apply these skills to creating children's books—maybe about motorcycles or "Sam Spade the Cat".

Acknowledgements:

Denise Lewis
Senior Editor
Colorado Winds Publishing
Loveland, Colorado

Becky Asmussen
Cover Design & Desktop Publishing
Image Graphics, Inc.
Loveland, Colorado

Kris W. Charles
Cover Motorcycle Illustration - Charcoal
Soul's Image Tattoos
Sterling, Colorado

Julie Kramer Cole
Coast Image on Cover - Charcoal and Ink
Cole Fine Art
Loveland, Colorado

Technical Consultants:

Theodor L. Lampe
Lance Corporal - USMC
1941 - 1944
Guadalcanal - Tarawa - Anewetok

Robert D. Lewis
Gunnery Sergeant - USMC
1966 - 1977
Con Thien - Ashau Valley

James "JC" Holcomb
Master Sergeant - USAF
1967 - 1991
4315th Combat Crew Training Squadron

Larry Bibri
Lance Corporal - USMC
1968 - 1970
Quang Tri

Dale T. Lewis
Staff Sergeant - USAF
1960 - 1968
Dew Line - King Salmon, Alaska

Lloyd "Brew" Brewer
2nd Class Petty Officer - USN
1959 - 1963
Carriers - Vietnam - Gulf of Tonkin

Edgar U. Peyronnin
Captain - USA
1979 - 1992
Artillery Battery Commander - Germany

Our Angels...

Harry W. "Jake" Lewis
1907 – 1991
Mt. Pisgah, West Virginia
My wonderful dad who introduced me to motorcycles

Ethel P. Lewis
1914 – 1993
West Newton, Pennsylvania
My gentle mom who taught me the joy of reading

Dianne Marie Lewis
1953 – 1995
Salt Lake City, Utah
Friend - Wife - Mother
We miss you...

Jessica Standridge
1982 - 1999
Loveland, Colorado
Loved beyond words

Magdaline "Sis" Kelly
1931 - 2012
Bradenton, Florida
An exceptional woman who made the most of life

Please send your comments to:
freedom@arunupthecoast.com

For additional copies visit us at:

www.arunupthecoast.com